Praise for Susan McBride's Books

"I'll read anything by Susan McBride."
—Charlaine Harris, *New York Times* Bestseller

"Exciting, sassy, and filled with deliciously wicked wit."
—Katie MacAlister, *New York Times* Bestseller

"As alluring as an Escada evening dress and as tempting as a slice of death-by-chocolate cake."
—*Publishers Weekly*

"Smooth, sassy, silly, slick, and sexy."
—*Sauce Magazine* (St. Louis)

"McBride knows her territory. She has put together a funny, eccentric bunch of characters who bound around town with perfect manicures, big hair, and lots of social savvy. . . . [A] hilarious romp."
—*Dallas Morning News*

"Entertaining."
—*Sun Sentinel* (Ft. Lauderdale)

"Smart."
—*St. Louis Post-Dispatch*

"McBride's writing is fresh, funny, and entertaining."
—*Wichita Eagle*

"I enjoy McBride's humorous writing style and quirky characters."
—*Pilot* (North Carolina)

Two-time Finalist, Anthony Award for Best Paperback Original

Finalist, William Rockhill Nelson Award for

Kansas and Missouri Authors

Also by Susan McBride

The Cougar Club

SUSAN McBRIDE

AVON

An Imprint of HarperCollins*Publishers*

THE COUGAR CLUB. Copyright © 2010 by Susan McBride. All rights reserved. Printed in the United States of America. No part of this book may be used or reproduced in any manner whatsoever without written permission except in the case of brief quotations embodied in critical articles and reviews. For information address Harper-Collins Publishers, 10 East 53rd Street, New York, NY 10022.

HarperCollins books may be purchased for educational, business, or sales promotional use. For information please write: Special Markets Department, HarperCollins Publishers, 10 East 53rd Street, New York, NY 10022.

FIRST AVON PAPERBACK EDITION PUBLISHED 2010.

Designed by Rhea Braunstein

Library of Congress Cataloging-in-Publication Data
McBride, Susan, 1964-
  The cougar club : a novel / by Susan McBride. — 1st ed.
    p. cm.
  ISBN 978-0-06-177126-2 (pbk.)
 1. Female friendship—Fiction. 2. Middle-aged women—Sexual behavior—Fiction.
3. Young men—Sexual behavior—Fiction. I. Title.
  PS3563.C33363C68 2010
  813'.54—dc22   2009036503

10 11 12 13 14 OV/RRD 10 9 8 7 6 5 4 3 2

This book is for all the women who've achieved their greatest success and found their truest love after forty. Rock on, y'all!

The
Cougar Club

Prologue

L ET'S have a toast then, shall we?" Carla picked up her martini and waited until Kat and Elise both had their drinks in hand before she offered, "To the three of us and to our friendship, which has survived men and careers and God knows how much other crap. Here's to our enduring sisterhood. May it bind us together more tightly than the Lycra in my Spanx underpants."

"I'll drink to that!" Kat laughed.

"Cheers!" Elise chimed in, the spark returned to her gaze.

They touched the rims of their glasses, eyes meeting eyes as they each took a sip, and Carla wished she didn't have to go back into work that night to face Burton again. She wished she could stay here with her two best friends, catching up and leaving the rest of the world behind for a while. It had been so long since she'd felt like anyone was there to watch her back.

<u>KAT</u>

Kat Maguire on getting older:

Aging gracefully isn't about aging gratefully. *It's about living life with your engine on overdrive, making love with all the lights on, trashing your diet books, and diving into the chocolate cake.*

Chapter One

W*HEN it rains, it pours.*
The sky opened up just as Kat Maguire exited Grand Central Station after taking the express train from Chambers Street in Tribeca. She'd left Roger's loft without an umbrella as the chirpy meteorologist had promised "cloudy skies with a slim chance of afternoon showers." *Right!* Maybe she should have peered out the window instead of sparring over whose turn it was to pick up the dry cleaning and running around like a chicken with her head cut off before dashing out the door. She had a client meeting scheduled for eight-fifteen, and it was nearly that now.

The late February drizzle turned the air gray around her, and Kat shivered in her trench coat. Mist settled on her face and falling drops pelted her hair. With a resigned sigh, she did the only thing she could, much as it pained her: she set her black leather Coach briefcase atop her head and merged into the mass of shuffling humanity. She noticed plenty of *them* had umbrellas.

She ignored her stomach, which loudly complained about skipping her daily fix of coffee and bagel from Hot 'n' Crusty. She was running late and couldn't afford to slow down, much less stop. The BuzzShots account was too important to the advertising agency's bottom line, since profits weren't what they used to be. With an unsettling shake-up in the employee ranks of late—"thinning out faster than Donald Trump's hair," as one nervous staffer had put it—Kat felt like her career was on the line as well.

Just a block to go and she'd be standing in front of the building that housed Dooney & Marling, set smack across the street from the stone lions guarding the New York Public Library. Good thing she could walk it blindfolded after fifteen years, because she could hardly see two feet ahead of her.

She didn't slow her brisk pace until she pushed through the glass doors. With a "woo" of relief, she lowered her briefcase and her aching arm, then brushed damp strands of hair from her brow.

"Raining cats and dogs out there, eh, Kat?" the white-haired security guard quipped as she passed his desk with a cursory wave. "Bet it's the dogs part you hate."

Ha ha. He was lucky she didn't have a moment to waste, or she might have tasered him with the lonely weapon dangling from his utility belt. Her mood was as foul as the weather.

"Hold it, please!" Kat called out as she made a beeline for the bank of elevators just as a pair of doors slapped shut.

Dammit.

Sneezing, she sent soggy brown bangs into her eyes again as she pressed the Up button. While she waited, she stamped her drenched leather boots, leaving tiny puddles on the marble floor.

She watched the long hand on the clock above the elevators tick ahead a notch, to thirteen minutes past eight, and panic set in.

Mindful of the slick tiles, she hurried toward the stairs. High heels tapping, she climbed rapidly at first but had to slow down around the fourth floor. When she arrived on nine, she was panting, heart skidding against her rib cage. With no time to catch her breath, she pushed open frosted glass doors and trudged through the lobby of D&M, homing in on the glorified cubicle that served as her office. She'd scarcely gotten off her coat to hang it up when someone cleared their throat behind her.

"Ms. Maguire? Mr. Garvey wants to see you."

"Now?" Kat blinked at the ponytailed stranger standing at the cubby's threshold. Gertrude, her secretary for a decade, had departed just last week in another round of brutal layoffs, and every day there were fewer familiar faces and more per diem fill-ins floating around the place. "I'm sure it can wait."

"He said ASAP," the girl insisted, her unrouged skin positively bloodless. She gnawed on her lower lip, most of her plum-hued lipstick already chewed away.

Kat laughed. "Like that's gonna happen." She quickly wiped off her boots and briefcase with a handful of Kleenex and tried not to drip on the paperwork she'd dumped atop her desk. "I've got a meeting in the conference room that started already. I'll duck into Chace's office after I'm done."

The temp cleared her throat again. "He said it's urgent."

"Urgent?" As in her client meeting had been canceled? Kat couldn't imagine any other reason for being summoned pronto. Had she missed an important text?

She snatched her BlackBerry from her bag, but it didn't show anything but a fresh message from Roger—the only way they communicated lately besides arguing—getting in the last word on the Great Dry Cleaning Debate:

Its UR turn! And wld U plz get Chinese 2 nite while UR at it?

Wow, placing his dinner order already? Well, at least he'd said "plz."

"Mr. Garvey's waiting, Ms. Maguire," the girl prodded, obviously not going away. "You want me to walk you down there?"

"No, thanks, I can manage," Kat said brusquely, and left her BuzzShots files on her desk. She couldn't very well blow off her boss, even if it meant having to apologize profusely to the energy drink execs. She just hoped her two juniors on the account had arrived early enough to ply the clients with Krispy Kremes and coffee. "You can let Mr. Garvey know I'm on my way."

The temp scuttled back to her desk as Kat marched toward the office of Chace Haywood Garvey, Jr., the very young senior vice president who lorded over the New Accounts division. She passed the conference room en route and glanced through the glass panels to see Steph and Marsh on their feet, well into the PowerPoint presentation she'd been working on for weeks.

Kat jerked to a standstill, so startled they'd begun the pitch without her that her head spun. She nearly barged into the room, forgetting Chace altogether; but a weird feeling in her gut made her reconsider. Something bad was brewing, and it wasn't the Sam's Club Kona.

One foot in front of the other, as her daddy liked to say; so she moved on.

"Morning, Maryanne," she greeted her boss's secretary on the way into his office; but the frizzy-haired woman didn't even peer over her monitor. In fact, she seemed intent on looking down at her keyboard, avoiding Kat's eyes.

Uh-oh.

Kat drew in a deep breath before briskly knocking on her boss's door. She didn't wait for an invitation to step inside.

"Do you realize Steph and Marshall are mid-pitch with Buzz-Shots, and I've been slaving over that account for months?" she complained as he rose from his desk and motioned for her to take a seat. "Whatever you have to say, please make it quick."

Chace frowned, puckering his baby face. "Uh, yeah, sorry about that."

He seemed to have as much trouble looking up at her as Mary-anne. Usually, he was all smiles and backslapping, like he was still in the frat house at Penn State and not a decade removed. He didn't even mention that she looked like a semidrowned rat.

Run, Kat's intuition was telling her. *Run straight back to the loft and call in sick.* Only it was too late for that. She sat down opposite him, and the anxious knot tightened in her belly.

"I don't know an easy way to put this." Chace leaned forward and blinked pale-lashed eyes in her direction. "The economy's not doing us any favors. We've had to make some tough choices here at D&M, and sadly that means letting go of valuable employees on every level."

"I've already lost Gertrude, so what else do you want from me?" Kat asked, and rubbed her hands over her knees, wondering who was next. "Are you breaking up my team? Steph's a little green, but she's a fast learner and ambitious as hell—"

"We're not letting Stephanie go," Chace interrupted.

"You're laying off Marshall?"

As soon as Kat said it, she knew it wasn't possible, considering her boss had been the one to hire him, a fellow Penn State grad and brother in Sigma Chi. The two of them hit bars together after work. Which could only mean one thing, couldn't it?

Oh, shit, it's me, she realized just before Chace puffed his cheeks and exhaled. "I'm sorry, Kat. We hate to lose another seasoned player, but things are tough all over. We either have to trim the budget or take down the whole ship."

A neon Exit sign started flashing in Kat's head, though the rational part of her thought, No, no, no, this can't be real.

"*I'm* being pink-slipped?" She grinned like a goof, praying it was some kind of bad joke. She'd been with the agency since well before Chace's family connections had gotten him his cushy veep gig. Hell, since before Chace had taken his first legal drink. "You're kidding, right?"

For a third of her life, she'd devoted herself to this place, sacrificing holidays, her family, and her social life, all so she could ravage her manicure climbing the ladder from lowly copywriter to New Accounts team leader. If the BuzzShots campaign scored a hit, she'd be due a more senior position with plenty of perks and more job security.

"It's a scary world," she heard Chace saying as he slid a dreaded red folder from beneath his pudgy hands. "Nothing's certain these days."

Like loyalty of any size or shape?

"I think you'll appreciate the package we put together for you. A year's severance, a year of COBRA health coverage, glowing references," her boss intoned as he rose from his ergonomic leather chair and skirted his desk to drop the red folder in Kat's lap, snapping her out of her momentary haze. "It's painful, I know, and I guarantee it hurts us as much as you."

"So *you* feel like a million Ginzu knives just impaled you?" she asked, bitterness flooding her voice as she flattened her palms on the file, unwilling to open it up and look inside. That would make it all too real. "How can you do this to me?"

They were keeping Marsh and Steph, who were barely out of school, but letting a veteran like her go? She suddenly wondered how many of the recently shed D&M staff were old-timers like her, deemed too expensive to keep?

"Please, don't take it personally," Chace murmured, giving her a wounded look, but Kat wasn't having it. "We certainly appreciate all the contributions you've made to this company. If only things were different."

But Kat heard instead: *If only you were younger.* She felt like she'd been kicked in the gut.

"You can cut the crap," she said, fighting mad. "It's not like I don't hear talk around the cappuccino machine. You're pushing me out because the new D&M vibe is all about being hot and hip. Your accounts want rap-loving fresh-faced execs, not old-timers like me who grew up without iPods and Wii."

"Not true," he denied, turning red-cheeked and blustery. "It's fiscal viability, Kat, that's all. Image has nothing to do with it, and age isn't an issue. Staying out of the red is. We've had to cut back in every department. There won't even be a company Christmas party this year."

"Wow, that makes me feel so much better," she replied, thinking this "age isn't an issue" crap sounded like the party line shoveled out by corporate hacks. "What if I decline this delightful exit package of yours?" she asked, tapping a finger against the red file in her lap.

Chace frowned, turning his wide brow into accordion pleats.

"I don't think you'd want to do that, Kat. We're eliminating your position in our restructuring, and you're really overqualified for the only other job we've got open right now in copywriting. You'd be bored as hell."

"You bastards," she uttered, shaking her head and smoothing damp palms over her thighs. She fought tears, staring down at the flecks of brown in her skirt. She'd found the suit on sale at Bergdorf and it fit like a glove. She'd put it on this morning, sure it would increase her karma. Well, it had. Only her karma sucked. "I need to think about this—"

"Okay," Chace said, his thick neck turning a vivid pink, "but we'll need your answer in twenty-four hours."

She nearly picked up his crystal globe-shaped paperweight and hit him upside the head. "You know what, I don't even need that," she shot back. After this kind of treatment, she wouldn't have stayed with the company if it meant living on the streets in a cardboard tent, sharing scraps with cat-sized rats. "Where do I sign?"

While Chace pointed to Post-it tagged spots on several sheets of paper, Kat scribbled her name.

"Please, don't be angry," her boss said to her back as she got up and started to leave. "You've had such a great ride here. I'd hate for you to go on a sour note."

You have got to be kidding me.

Kat paused and turned, cocking her head. "I'll say one thing for you, Junior. You're very good at what you do."

"Advertising?" he asked, his furry eyebrows bunching like feuding caterpillars.

"Lying through your teeth," she corrected him. Fighting tears, she clutched the dreaded red folder and walked away.

This time she didn't even look as she passed the conference room. She went directly to her office and tossed the file into her briefcase. Atop it, she shoved in other items more precious to her: a years-old framed photo of her family, one of her and Roger at a restaurant opening, a fancy Cartier pen set Roger had bought her for her last birthday, and a pack of paper clips, just because.

"Mr. Garvey said to please leave any papers relating to accounts at D&M," the girl instructed from the doorway.

Kat snapped her briefcase closed and glanced up. "Please tell Mr. Garvey he can kiss my middle-aged ass."

"Um, okay," the temp said, utterly serious, as Kat brushed past, biting her cheek to keep from crying as she walked out of her office.

She raced down the stairs and through the lobby, emerging outside to find somber clouds still dripping with rain; and all she could think was that a hunk of her life had just been flushed down the drain. Gone, just like that. It felt worse than any breakup, and she couldn't stop her chin from quivering.

Despite her best effort, tears slipped down her cheeks as she retraced her steps from fifteen minutes earlier. She made her way back to the subway, jostled by the umbrella-wielding army that still swallowed up the sidewalks. She rode home with her head in her hands, smothering her hiccups lest they turn into full-blown sobs.

When she reached her stop, she staggered out of the train like a wounded beast, emerging onto the street and trudging toward the converted neo-Renaissance warehouse situated at the conflux of Chambers and Hudson. She left tiny puddles of rain on the pristine tiled lobby before slipping through the waiting doors of the caged elevator. Her new wool suit smelled like wet dog, and she cried softly as she rode up four floors and got out.

By the time she let herself into the loft, her nose was running and she desperately needed a hot bath and a slug of whiskey. If she allowed herself to grieve alone for a while, she could face Roger when he returned from work and describe how she'd gotten the ax from baby-faced Chace without bursting into tears.

As she shut the door behind her and securely bolted it, she noticed the lights were on. Roger must've forgotten to flip a few switches when he'd left, which was typical. She was the one who cared about wasting electricity and burning a hole in the ozone layer. "It's my place, and I pay the utilities, so stop griping," he argued. At twenty-eight—and armed with an MBA from Wharton and a healthy trust fund courtesy of deceased grandparents—Roger acted like everything was disposable.

Disposable like my fifteen years at D&M, Kat thought glumly. With a sigh, she dropped her briefcase and leaned against the console to unzip her boots before peeling them off. Then she noticed the set of keys still in the silver tray.

He was home? That made no sense. If Wall Street had the day off, he hadn't mentioned it. Maybe he'd forgotten something, like a file or an umbrella, or he'd had a sudden attack of ESP and rushed home to console her.

"Rog?" she called out as she crossed the open living area divided by tall bookshelves from office space. Drizzle slid down the floor to ceiling windows, punctuating her gloom. The kitchen and living areas were empty, save for Roger's jacket tossed over the back of a dining room chair.

Something prickled the hair on the back of Kat's neck as she walked toward the closed door to their walled-off bedroom, and her hand hesitated before she pushed back the velvet drape and stepped inside.

She heard moans before she spotted him sitting at his desk, his back to her. He looked like he was madly scratching an itch as he watched something on the large flat panel monitor, and she didn't realize until she'd come up behind him that he was scratching an itch all right, the kind men got when they viewed a naked woman with her hand between her legs.

"Aaaagh!" she cried out, and squished her eyes closed. Call her old-fashioned, but watching her boyfriend jerk off to live porn wasn't a turn-on for her; in fact, just the opposite. "Christ, shut it down, would you!"

What happened to the good old days of taking a Playboy *into the bathroom and locking the door?*

"Kat!" Roger yelped, and slapped his laptop closed with his free hand. He jumped up from the chair and hopped around, stuffing himself back in his boxers and pulling up his pants. "You're not supposed to be here!"

"Obviously," she said, wanting to throw up as she watched him tuck in his banker-blue button-down and tug up his zipper.

He swallowed hard. "It's not what you think."

"So you weren't having cyber sex?" she said, her legs turned wobbly. "I guess phone sex is passé these days, huh?" She let out a hysterical laugh. "Can you Twitter an orgasm yet? It's like you don't even need me anymore."

"Calm down, okay? It's no big deal."

He'd caught his shirt in his fly, which would've been funny in any other light considering how careful Roger was about how he dressed. He ran a hand over his expensively cut hair, and Kat could practically see the gears churning as he contemplated how to get himself out of this latest mess.

"It's not like I cheated. Jesus, but your generation is so uptight," he remarked, as if that helped his cause. He rubbed his jaw, then ran his hand around the back of his neck. His tie hung loose from his collar. "Besides, I've hardly seen you lately, and I've been so fucking lonely. It's been forever since we've, uh, done it. What the hell did you expect?"

Forever since we've done it? Try a week ago, she thought, after a disastrous attempt at celebrating Valentine's Day, when he'd gotten so drunk he hadn't exactly risen to the occasion.

She waited for him to dig himself in deeper, whining something like, *I'm a twenty-eight-year-old guy with needs!* But then, she'd heard it all before.

"So," she said when he remained quiet, "it's my fault you're getting your rocks off on a porn site, because I've been working my butt off, trying to keep my job?"

Which didn't pan out too well, did it? she realized, and her chest ached so much it felt like something was about to break.

"It's the safest kind of sex there is," he declared, the hint of a smirk on his lips as he tightened the knot on his tie.

"You're joking, right?" She stared at him, suddenly wondering how often he'd done it before she'd walked in on him. "You think masturbating with Viral Ho isn't the same as hooking up with that college girl from the cleaning service?" She brought up his last indiscretion, the one that had prompted her to give him an ultimatum.

"So now you're throwing that back in my face?" The smirk vanished and he looked at her with big puppy-dog eyes, shuffling on his Bruno Maglis. "I apologized for that a hundred times already. What else do you want from me?"

Oh, yeah, he'd sworn up and down that he'd made a horrible mistake in a moment of weakness. He was deeply ashamed and vowed he'd never stray again. Foolishly, she had forgiven him after he sent her several dozen roses and a Cartier charm bracelet, and *she'd* sent his sorry ass to her internist to get tested for STDs.

But what she'd just witnessed gave her the same icky feeling. How'd that saying go? *Fool me once, shame on me. Fool me twice, and I'm a freakin' imbecile?*

Maybe she'd woken up on the wrong side of the bed this morning—correction, the wrong side of the universe—but she wasn't about to take anyone's shit anymore. She opened her mouth to tell Roger exactly that, only he spoke first.

"Damn, it's late," he said, looking at the mother-of-pearl face on the Rolex strapped to his wrist. "I've got to get going." He moved in front of the bureau mirror to finger-comb his hair. "Hey, shouldn't you be pitching to those energy drink execs?"

"I'm no longer employed by D&M," she told him as another rush of tears threatened, despite her attempt to stand strong. "My life sucks," she whimpered.

"You were canned?" Roger arched his dark eyebrows. "The fucktards," he said, and came over to put his arms around her, drawing her against his chest. "I'm sorry you're having such a bad day." He wiped her cheeks with the pad of his thumb. "We should go to Nobu for dinner. That'll cheer you up."

"Go to Nobu?" Had she missed some essential segue? Did she actually seem in the mood to celebrate anything? What was wrong with him? She shook her head and pushed him away. "I don't want to go out."

"C'mon, babe, we need to have a little fun. You've been so wrapped up with your job. I'm kind of glad they cut you loose."

He was *glad* they cut her loose?

Kat stood stock-still, feeling like one of those giant glaciers in

Alaska that breaks apart, sending a huge chunk falling into the ocean.

"Hell, you've been like a robot for months, kissing ass at D&M, working nights and weekends," he complained when she said nothing. "And look how they've repaid you! I'd say, grab your parachute—they did offer you something, didn't they?—and pour yourself a glass of champagne."

Is that how trust fund babies dealt with disaster? They made a toast and said, "Screw the world!" How lovely that must be, never having to face failure.

Kat found herself staring at Roger, wondering if he even really knew her at all, or if he truly cared. It was clear he had no idea what was important to her and how hurt she felt. They came from two different planets; no, *worse*, they were from two totally different generations, as he'd already pointed out.

What in God's name had made her think this relationship would ever work? His washboard abs? His cocky grin? His bottomless wallet? The way he'd persistently wooed her with flowers and trinkets from Cartier and Tiffany, with carriage rides and expensive dinners until he'd won her over, convincing her of his commitment and maturity? Ha!

"I'll be home by six," he told her, taking her silence as acquiescence. "I'll feed you and then we'll come back here for dessert."

He kissed her hard on the lips and then strode out of the bedroom, whistling, like nothing eventful had just happened between them; like her whole world hadn't just turned upside down.

A minute later the door banged shut and she was alone.

Something beeped across the bedroom, and Kat looked over at Roger's desk. It took her a second to figure out where the noise was coming from. He'd left his computer on. She walked toward the laptop, pushed it open, and lightly touched the mouse pad. The sleek machine whirred back to life, and she nearly powered it off. Only something stopped her, and she glanced over her shoulder once before settling into his chair. She clicked on his browser cache and began scrolling down it, finding site after site with names like HotnSticky.com, DownandDirty.com, and others that left less than nothing to the imagination. She went to his e-mail box next, and the subject headers told her plenty without her reading a single message.

For several long minutes Kat couldn't move, could scarcely breathe. Then her chest wrenched and she started coughing, getting dry heaves. She stumbled up from the chair, knocking papers from the desk as she grabbed onto the edge to steady herself. Inside her head a tiny voice began screaming, *Leave, leave, leave!*

Kat fled the room, gathering keys, pulling on boots and coat, and dashing out of the loft, escaping the building.

She walked several blocks up Hudson through the cold and steady drizzle, stopping beneath a familiar teal blue awning. Nose to the glass, she peered through the window of the Moore-Green Gallery, looking for movement and seeing nothing but dim track lighting showing off the mixed-media collages of a local artist.

Even though the schedule painted in small script announced hours starting at 10:00 A.M. or BY APPOINTMENT ONLY, Kat pressed the bell by the door.

Please, Rosalie, let me in, let me in.

Rosalie Moore had given Kat her first job when she'd moved to the city, and Kat had loved the few years she spent there, working with Rose and her partner Annabelle, until she finally scored the advertising gig at D&M. Rosalie was like a second mother and one of the few constants in her shrinking social circle. Most of the women Kat had befriended years ago had married and moved to Scarsdale or Greenwich, and Roger's party-minded twenty-something pals were hardly her own.

Wet hair plastered to her cheeks, she shifted on her feet and waited until she saw the slim figure in flowing purple silk emerge from the back. Dead bolts clicked free, the door opened, and a firm voice scolded, "Darling Kat, is that you? What're you doing standing in the rain and it's not even nine o'clock? Are you crying?"

Damn straight, she was crying!

"I'm forty-five years old, and my life is over," Kat wailed, and a fresh crop of tears sprang anew. "I don't know what to do, Rose. I just don't know what to do."

Her elegant friend swept her inside, past sculptures and softly lit oils and watercolors, into a back room with table and chairs, and a Krups machine spewing coffee into a shiny stainless steel pot. Rosalie sat her down and pressed a napkin in her hands. Kat dabbed at her tears while her friend poured them each a mug, then Rose settled in the seat beside her.

"Having a lousy day, are we?" she asked very matter-of-factly.

"Let me count the ways," Kat replied, and proceeded to reel off the injustices she'd suffered in the past hour alone. "I'm un-employed, my boyfriend's apparently been getting it on with a cyber whore, my Nina Ricci suit reeks like a drenched collie, and I think I've caught a cold." That said, she noisily blew her nose into the napkin.

"Well, if those aren't sure signs of the Apocalypse, I don't know what is," Rosalie said, and set her chin on a fist. "I've missed you coming by. It's been months."

"I know," Kat said. "I'm sorry."

Stark white hair framed an expressive sixty-year-old face unmarred by ridge fillers or Botox. Polished stones on silver wires dangled from her ears as she gazed squarely at Kat, her dark eyes outlined as always in kohl. Rosalie was the closest thing she had to a best friend in New York, and she needed someone to tell her what to do.

"I feel like I've lost control," she tried to explain, "like I've been spinning and spinning so fast I can't remember who I am or what I'm supposed to be doing."

"Maybe you have." Rosalie nodded, her earrings swaying. "It's easy to lose sight of what it was we began searching for in the first place."

"I'm not sure what that means."

"I think you know."

"C'mon, Obi Wan, throw me a bone, please." Kat's chin trembled as she waited for detailed instructions on how to gracefully step over the pile of doo-doo she'd found herself mired in. If only she could snap her fingers and disappear, or maybe start the day over again and do it all differently.

"Darling girl," Rosalie sighed, thin white brows knitting. "What is it that your heart wants? Because you haven't seemed happy in a while, not from the little of you I've seen."

Happy? What did happy have to do with anything? Lately, her main concerns had involved impressing her boss so she didn't end up unemployed like the rest of Manhattan, and keeping Roger satisfied despite how tired she was, neither of which had proved successful.

"When I first met you," Rosalie said, when Kat didn't respond, "you were so eager to expand your world. You were so wonderfully curious about people and art and trying new things. Somewhere along the way, you felt the need to prove your worth, to make more money. But who was it all for?" she asked, her sweet, caring face genuinely concerned. "Not for you, I don't think. That Kat cared about people, not social climbing and corporate politics."

Tears slopped over Kat's lashes, splashing down her cheeks. She heard what Rose was saying, and thought maybe it was true; but fear outweighed everything else at the moment. "So what am I supposed to do?"

"Sweet girl," Rose said, and took Kat's hands in hers. "It sounds to me like these closing doors have opened a window for you. You just have to decide if you'd rather climb out onto a mossy limb and escape to something new, or shut the damned thing and ignore what your soul craves."

Climb out onto a mossy limb? Find out what my soul craves?

At any other time, she might've laughed at Rosalie's earthy pearls of wisdom. Only today she realized every word her friend had said so far was dead-on, and it scared her that she had no quick answers.

"What do I want," she repeated, because that wasn't something she'd asked herself in a long, long while; not since she started in the cellar at D&M and changed her focus from feeding her soul to feeding her ego. She'd never stopped to wonder if she was truly happy, so she wasn't sure anymore what was in her heart of hearts, if she even had such desires at all.

What did she want? What did she honestly and truly want?

Something more than this, something meaningful, she decided with perfect clarity; one of those après forty epiphanies usually reserved for aging males craving hair plugs, Corvettes, and Viagra. She didn't want to be written off just because she wasn't twenty-five years old. She didn't want to live with a man who had pursued her for sport, who didn't respect her, and who obviously never intended to marry her. What she wanted oh-so-desperately was to grab life by the balls again, to feel like she was important and loved in a way she'd hadn't since she was a kid.

"I want—" she started, only to stop for fear of how foolish she'd sound if she put into words what she was feeling.

"Go on, let it out," Rosalie encouraged.

"I want to go home," she said breathlessly, and the tears fell faster than she could wipe them away. "I need my family. I miss my old friends. I want to be me again, whoever that is."

So much had changed, and not all of it for the good.

Rosalie slapped a palm on the table. "Then that, my dear, is exactly what you should do."

A tiny figure appeared from the stairwell that led to the upstairs apartment.

She was as curvy as Rosalie was thin and as dark as Rosalie was light. "Is everything all right down here? I thought I heard voices," she said, and her mouth broke into a girlish smile. "Oh, hey, Kat, what's up? Long time no see."

"Everything's fine, Anna," Rosie told her partner as Kat blew her nose again. "I was just telling our Kat bon voyage."

Chapter Two

K AT went directly back to Roger's place and packed her suitcase. She didn't have a lot of things. Most of what filled the closet and drawers belonged to Roger, and any of the books and CDs she left behind she could replace. She remembered her jewelry and a few important files, but that was all she took. She called a cab on her way down to the lobby. Ten minutes later, once she was en route to JFK and certain she wouldn't change her mind, she sent a text to Roger from the Yellow Cab's backseat.

Going home 2 STL. Plz forward mail 2 my mom's. Goodbye, K

She couldn't even text *Love, K* and mean it. Something had shifted inside her, shuffling all the pieces of who she'd been.

Her BlackBerry pinged with a reply text from Roger almost instantly:

U R crazy!!! Running away never works. U will B back but don't
expect me 2 B waiting.

Kat read it once before she deleted it. Then she turned off her
PDA.

Once on board the first flight out—to Chicago, changing
planes at O'Hare—she stared out the oval window, fingering the
barf bag in the seat pocket in front of her, hoping she wouldn't
have to use it. Even without turbulence, her stomach flip-flopped.
How could it not? She was forty-five, newly single, and unemployed. Did she truly imagine she could move back to St. Louis
and start all over again without causing a ripple?

Kat sighed and leaned her head back against the seat cushion.
*Well, hell. I've got five hours and two legs of the trip to figure things
out.*

As if she could solve all her problems that quickly.

Hours later, when she safely landed at Lambert Field in St.
Louis, she turned her BlackBerry on again, scrolling past a second
angry rant from Roger and finding a note from Rosalie asking if
she'd arrived in one piece. Kat texted back three simple words: *I
am home.* She could almost breathe.

The day had dissolved to dusk by the time her red cab pulled
into the shoveled drive in front of the rambling 1930s English-
style cottage on Godwin Lane not far off Interstate 64/40. A soft
blanket of white covered the lawn, roof, and trees, and Kat didn't
protest when the driver offered to carry her bags along a slick-
looking path to the front stoop.

Once she'd picked her way there behind him and pressed cash
into his gloved palm, she pushed the doorbell and waited, not
even sure that anyone was there. She should have called first. The

last time she had been back, she brought Roger home two years ago for Christmas. Did her mom still hide a key under the flower pot on the ledge that now held something very dead and very frozen?

Before she had the chance to look, the door swung inward and a slender woman in a fisherman's sweater and blue jeans materialized.

"Am I dreaming?" Eileen Maguire said, dark eyes lighting up a face eerily similar to Kat's save for the depth of the laugh lines and the cap of gray hair that stuck out in every conceivable direction. "Mary Katherine, is it you?"

Kat nodded and her eyes filled with tears. "Got a room for the prodigal daughter?"

"So long as I live and breathe, you're always welcome here," her mother said, grabbing for her bag while Kat brought in her purse and attaché. "Now come inside before you freeze."

Once ensconced in the warmth of the foyer, Eileen enfolded her in a bear hug that didn't last near long enough. When she drew apart, she gently wiped the damp streaks from Kat's cheeks.

"I got pushed out of D&M this morning, Ma. They said they were eliminating my job, and I'd basically have to start over unless I agreed to exit quietly," she blubbered, a mess of tears and snot and stammer. "Then I went back to the loft and caught Roger having sex with a cyber slut—"

"Stop, Mary Katherine, please." Her mother put a finger to her lips. "We'll talk later when you've calmed down. How about you go upstairs and lie down for a bit in your old room? Your sister and Bill are coming for dinner. Take a little nap, then you can wash up before you join us."

"Okay," Kat said, and wiped her nose on her sleeve.

She left her bag in the foyer and obediently headed upstairs to the room she'd grown up in, one whose walls were still filled with Def Leppard and AC/DC posters, random drawings she'd done in her "I am an artiste" period, and corkboards covered with brittle corsages and nosegays. She ran a finger over her whitewashed keyhole desk, which still had an IBM Selectric perched atop it, and pulled open a drawer on her mirrored dresser to find a dozen pair of cotton underwear neatly folded alongside "sock capsules," as she used to call them.

Sometimes nothing changes and everything changes.

Sitting on the bed's rainbow spread, she pulled off her boots and let them fall to the carpet. Then she laid her head on the pillows and clutched her one-eared Snoopy. Though Kat squished her eyes closed, tears still seeped between the lashes, sliding sideways down her face.

Chace . . . pink slip . . . Roger . . . cyber slut . . . Chace . . . pink slip . . . Roger . . . cyber slut . . .

She willed herself to quit reliving the events of the day, and her ragged breaths became slow and more even. Exhaustion wrapped itself around her like a heavy blanket, and it wasn't long until she fell deeply asleep.

When she opened her eyes, the room was dark and still. She rubbed a hand over her face and sat up, confused for a moment until she got her bearings.

"So you're awake, huh?" a voice said, and the desk lamp was switched on. "I figured you'd sleep through dinner at this rate."

Kat saw stars and blinked. "Meg?"

Her younger sister sat on a chair facing the bed. Her arms were crossed and one leg dangled over the other, her foot jiggling. The last time Kat saw Megan, her hair had been long; now it barely covered her ears, cropped into an almost mannish cut parted on the side. The 'do highlighted the square Maguire jaw and made Meg appear older than thirty-eight.

"Can I tell them you're up?" Meg asked before she had a chance to comment on the hair, which was probably a good thing. "Mom's been holding supper forever, so I volunteered to give you a poke if you didn't wake up. FYI, you still snore like a freight train." Megan tipped her head and studied Kat. "So what's the deal? Ma's been strangely tight-lipped, and she usually broadcasts news faster than CNN. Did you rob a bank?"

"I wish," Kat said, and tucked hair behind her ears. "I could've used the cash."

"Did you lose your life savings in a pyramid scheme?"

"No." Kat worked crusty sleep from the corners of her eyes. "I just lost everything else."

"What the hell happened?" Megan scooted to the edge of her seat.

Kat frowned at the eager look on her sister's face. "Could you try not to look so pleased that my life's in the crapper?"

"Ah, sorry," Meg said, and did her best impression of glum, her thin eyebrows knitting sternly. "Is that better?"

"Much." Kat exhaled loudly, deciding to keep things short and sweet. "D&M handed me a year's salary and shoved me out the door, and I realized I'll never trust Roger again. So I'm here with my tail between my legs, picking up the pieces." She reached for Snoopy and played with the remaining ear that their long-ago spaniel Baxter hadn't ripped off.

"No way." Her sister's mouth fell open. "D&M canned you? I can't believe it. They must be crazy. You worked like a slave for them."

"It's turning into *Logan's Run* there, you know with everyone over forty having to either bolt or suffer the consequences, although I got the spiel about the terrible economy and cutting costs," Kat said, feeling somewhat vindicated by Meg's reaction.

"God, that's just wrong." Megan made a face. "I'm sorry they treated you so badly, I really am." She reached over and patted Kat's knee, which was about as touchie-feelie as Meg got. Then she pulled back, the softness in her face gone as she said, "Though I can't say I'm sorry about Roger. The guy was wrong for you in so many ways, besides the fact that he was barely legal."

Roger was twenty-five when a then forty-two-year-old Kat had met him. Now they were both three years older, although how much wiser, she wasn't sure.

"When you're in love—or think you are," Kat tried to explain, "seventeen years doesn't seem like a lot."

"That's like 119 in dog years."

Kat winced. "Way to cheer me up."

Unfortunately, Meg wasn't through. "Until they hit thirty, men simply aren't wired to commit. Didn't I warn you when you dragged him here for Christmas, and he was wearing a T-shirt that said 'I'm with Cougar'?" She let out a noise of disgust. "He thought it was hysterical."

Kat squirmed, not in the mood for a long "I told you so" lecture from Saint Megan the Eternally Right, of all people. "Can we just drop it?"

Perhaps her sister wasn't totally unsympathetic, as she actually stopped yapping for a solid minute.

Kat glanced down at her crumpled wool suit. It still smelled vaguely like Fido.

"I need to get my things and change—"

"Over there." Meg pointed toward the closet. Kat's suitcase sat right beside the closed door. "Bill brought it up while you slept."

"Tell him thanks."

"No problem." Megan uncrossed her legs and got up. "I'll let everyone know you're alive. See you downstairs."

In five minutes flat Kat had on jeans and a T-shirt, plus a pair of fuzzy socks from her top dresser drawer. Her face looked hopeless: blotchy and puffy around the eyes. Maybe everyone would assume it was a cold, or at least pretend she didn't look like a woman suffering a nervous breakdown.

When she entered the dining room, the rest of the family was already crowded around the table—her mom and dad, Megan and her husband, Bill. Kat kissed her father on his bald crown, saying, "Hey, Pop."

"Good to have you home, Kitten," he replied, his hands already gripping his knife and fork. He wore a red and green plaid shirt that he'd owned since Kat was in junior high, although the colors had faded from so many washings and it now strained across his belly. "We saved you a seat."

"Thanks. Hey, Bill." She nodded at her brother-in-law, who peered at her curiously through wire-rimmed specs as Kat settled into the vacant chair.

"Would you like to say grace, sweetheart?" her mother asked, and Kat shrugged.

"Sure." She clasped her hands together and bowed her head. "Rub a dub dub, thanks for the grub."

"Mary Katherine!" Eileen admonished, as if Kat were a rambunctious thirteen again. "Once more, please, and properly this time."

Kat heard Megan giggle, and she smiled, her head still bowed. She cleared her throat and tried again: "Come, Lord Jesus, be our guest and let this food by thee be blessed. Amen."

A chorus of amens preceded the passing of platters piled with meat loaf, potatoes, corn bread, and green beans. Not exactly the braised short ribs with truffles at Dovetail, was it? But she took a little bit of everything. If she didn't, her mother would forgo the plate and force-feed her.

"So how long do you plan to visit?" her brother-in-law asked point-blank.

From his badly cut hair to his gold-rims, he looked every inch the CPA, which he was in actuality. He was so perfect for Megan it was uncanny. They both teetered on the edge of having full-blown OCD and got orgasmic counting money.

"Yes, exactly how long will you be in town, Kat?" her sister echoed, and all eyes fell upon her.

"I'm thinking, maybe, for good," she said, not sounding completely certain—hell, she could change her mind tomorrow—but strangely enough, it felt right.

Suddenly, utensils stopped clinking and dishes ceased to be passed as the table went silent around her.

Kat waited for some comment from her father about finally coming to her senses. He'd never liked the fact that she lived in New York, "The Big Stinky," as he called it. She even expected a snide remark from Megan about the grass on the other side of the fence not being greener after all. Surprisingly, no one took a potshot.

Only Eileen Maguire smiled at her and said, "That's lovely news, sweetheart," before she turned toward her son-in-law and began politely inquiring about the Blues' shot for the Stanley Cup playoffs, like Kat had just gotten a no-cavity report from the dentist instead of making a life-changing pronouncement.

Welcome home, Kat Maguire, she thought as she chewed on a green bean while Bill droned on about hockey and penalties and icing, and Eileen said things like, "I don't understand why they have to fight so much" and "What exactly is the crease?"

She gazed at the floral pattern on the edge of her plate, only half listening as her dad grumbled about local politics and Megan whined about the real estate market. So far no one had started in on her about how she was doomed to old-fashioned Victorian spinsterhood if she couldn't find a worthy man to marry in her creaky old age. That was a definite plus.

When the meal was finally over, Kat's mom got up and squeezed her shoulder.

"Mary Katherine, why don't you help clear the table?"

She inwardly sighed with relief and jumped up, never so grateful to escape to the kitchen in her life.

"I'll rinse, you dispense," her mother said, and Kat stood at the sink beside her, neither of them saying a word as Eileen scraped plates with a knife beneath a steady stream of water. Then she handed the dishes to Kat, who loaded them into the dishwasher. Finally, Kat's mom shut off the tap, put a hand on her shoulder and leaned nearer to say, "I'm glad you left the jerk. He was too handsome for his own good and always so full of crap. You're better off this way."

Tell it like it is, Ma, she wanted to say; but instead a sob rose in her throat, and she found her eyes filling with tears for the tenth time that day. "I thought I loved him once," she confessed shakily, "and I believed he loved me, too. I thought he'd grow up, you know, become mature and faithful, but he wasn't any more loyal to me than D&M." A tremor rattled her voice. "It's like I stopped looking where I was going, and I fell into a manhole."

"Listen to me." Her mom squeezed her arm and pulled her closer, and Kat caught their reflections in the window over the sink, two women pressed together like Siamese twins. "You'll get through this bad patch because you're tough and you're not a quitter. Remember that time on the roller coaster at Six Flags when you were ten? You wanted to ride it so bad, but once you were on it, you were terrified. You cried the whole way through, then you threw up once you got off, but five minutes later you were saying, 'Mom, let's do it again!' "

Kat smiled through her tears. "And that proves what, that I shouldn't have eaten lunch first? Or that sometimes because you're actually tall enough to ride, it doesn't mean you should?"

Her mom drew away and gave her a solid pat on the rump. "It means you'll be okay and you'll hop back in the saddle again when you're ready."

Kat dried off her cheeks and whispered, "This too shall pass, eh?"

"Yes," Eileen promised and tucked a finger beneath Kat's chin, "it will pass. You always were a quick healer." Then she rubbed Kat's arm, nodding, before she let her go to poke her head back into the dining room and ask, "Anyone for dessert?"

Kat dabbed at her eyes with the dish towel, figuring it was some unwritten Midwestern code that said you couldn't refuse dessert, not even in the middle of a nuclear attack. So she sucked it up, hoping no one would remark on her freshly red eyes, and she took her seat back at the dining table while Eileen served coffee and slices of German chocolate cake left over from a recent bridge party. Not ten minutes after, Meg and Bill suggested it was time to go and bundled up in gloves, scarves, and coats.

"Nice to have you back in the fold," Megan said, and gave Kat a stiff hug. "When you've had enough of your old room, give me a call, okay? I've got a place you could stay until you find something permanent."

Kat warily eyed her sister. "Not with you and Bill?"

"God, no!" Megan chortled. "It's a property in Clayton I can't seem to unload, and the owner's long gone. He couldn't stand winter so he bought a house in the Florida Keys with his boyfriend. It's just temporary until you know what you're looking for."

"So I'd be like a glorified condo sitter?"

"It's a three-million-dollar high-rise unit practically next door to the Ritz. Staying there for a while won't involve much suffering." Megan gave her arm a pat. "You'll just have to keep it clean and ready for spur of the moment showings."

Kat bit her lip, not sure how to take this. Her sister was actually being nice. She so wasn't used to that. "Just give me a chance to catch up on sleep and get my head screwed on straight."

"Fair enough," Megan said.

Bill stepped up between them, looking like the Abominable Snow CPA all bundled up for the cold. "Take care, Kat," he said, and she tipped her cheek for a perfunctory kiss before the two headed out the door.

As soon as they were gone, Kat's dad looked at his watch and grunted. "Hell, Eileen, we're late for that Charlie Sheen show," he declared, and made a beeline for his La-Z-Boy in the den, like it was any other average night and his elder daughter hadn't just shown up on his doorstep, hauling the baggage she'd accumulated throughout most of her adult life.

"I'm right behind you!" Eileen called from the kitchen.

Kat heard the noise of the dishwasher being turned on before her mom reappeared and scurried toward the TV room.

Kat followed them and leaned in the doorway for a few minutes as some god-awful comedy played out on the enormous flat-screen television. It had a laugh track that ran after each line of dialogue, funny or not, which gave her a headache. Soon after, she excused herself and disappeared upstairs. Slipping beneath her rainbow bedspread, she curled into a ball, too tired to shut off the desk lamp. She dreamed her mom came around to tuck her in, pulling the covers to her chin and kissing her forehead. When she awakened at noon the next day, the light had been switched off and her battered Snoopy lay on the pillow beside her.

For three days and three nights she didn't leave the bed unless it was to get more Kleenex to blow her nose, drink when she was thirsty, eat when she felt hungry, and pee when she needed to pee.

"Leave her alone for now, Meg," she heard her mom outside the door, warning her sister away. "She'll be fine. She just needs to recharge her batteries."

On her fourth day home, Kat got out of bed and didn't get back in.

She gathered up her old yearbooks and settled on the floor with them. Her flannel-covered legs splayed, she went through each one, page by page, looking back at herself and her "best friends 4-ever" Carla and Elise during their four years at Ladue High School. They'd been joined at the hip for so many years, and Kat had felt like nothing in the world would ever come between them. Tucked in the back of their senior yearbook, she unearthed a drawing she'd done, of hundreds of hearts filling a page, three interlocked in the middle. She'd colored one with red pencil, the second with yellow, and the third with brown for the three of them: Carla the redhead, Elise the blonde, and Kat the brunette.

Suddenly, a million questions filled her head. What if she'd stayed in town like they had, would she be different now? Would she be married with a college-age child like Elise? Or would she be a local girl-made-good like Carla? Maybe if she'd never gone to New York or stayed away for as long as she had, they'd be as close as they once were, doing a grown-up version of burger lunches at Carl's in Brentwood and kvetching about their jobs, sex, and men. God, how she missed them!

"It's not too late," her mother said, standing above her. Kat hadn't even heard her come in. "I ran into Carla at Straub's yesterday. She doesn't know you've come back. You should call her, Mary Katherine."

"I will," Kat promised, and she would, too; after she'd taken care of a few things that required her to shower and put on some clothes that weren't flannel. She even dared to turn on her Black-Berry and confront all the messages, few of which she deemed worth answering. She did text Rosalie briefly to say, *Don't worry about me. I'm at my folks' house for now, and I'm fine,* and she sent the HR manager at D&M her parents' address for any follow-up paperwork. But anything from Roger, she erased.

Afterward, she felt ready to face the world again.

She borrowed her mother's four-wheel-drive Honda and went to the post office in Clayton, using her parents' residence as her change of address. Next she took the handful of trinkets from Tiffany and Cartier that Roger had given her the past three years and pawned them at a jewelry store with a sign out front that declared WE BUY GOLD AND PLATINUM! That cash in hand, she hit the Heartland Bank on Old Bonhomme to deposit it and her severance check—"it'll take five business days to clear, ma'am"—and begin the process of transferring her other balances from Chase Manhattan.

It was mid-afternoon by the time she finished her errands and picked up her father for car shopping. At the third dealership on Manchester, she fell in love at first sight with a 1986 hunter green Jaguar XJ6 with a new paint job and only ninety thousand miles for less than five grand. Joe Maguire even approved of it after kicking the tires and lifting the hood to get a look at the engine. "Clean as a whistle," he'd pronounced it, and Kat used a Visa check to buy it (zero percent interest for six months!), reassuring herself that she'd pay off the balance once her severance check cleared.

On the way back to Godwin Lane in her new (old) car, she dialed Megan on her BlackBerry.

"Still want a condo sitter?" she asked.

If she was going to start on Act Two of her grown-up life, she certainly couldn't do it in her childhood bedroom, sleeping with one-eared Snoopy.

Chapter Three

A WEEK later, as February crept toward March, Kat awakened in a king-sized bed in the high-rise condo Meg had set her up in, thinking, Okay, what next?

She pulled on her fleece robe and tried to shrug off any self-doubt. "Time to pick yourself up by your bootstraps, Kitten," as her dad used to say. She'd surely surpassed her wallowing quota anyway.

Stretching her arms above her head, Kat yawned and surveyed her new, albeit temporary, surroundings. She loved the sleek but spare furnishings, although they weren't hers any more than most of the stuff in Roger's loft. According to Meg, it was all rentals from a staging company, so Kat was scared to use most of it for fear she'd stain something. Still, it was such a pretty place, far more upscale than the Brooklyn studio apartment she'd lived in before she met Roger.

She yawned again and headed toward the kitchen for what

had become her morning ritual: heating water in the microwave to make a cup of green tea.

When she had the warm mug in hand, she padded in bare feet toward the terrace doors of the fifteenth-floor condo in Clayton, Missouri, an almost giddy sensation awakening within her as she crossed the bamboo floors. There, she stood in front of the glass sliders, sipping and gazing out at the horizon, watching the sun rise behind the shiny-steel curve of the Gateway Arch.

The breaking dawn glinted silver off the bowed structure and blinked through the rooftops of the modest St. Louis skyline. Even now with a fresh inch of late winter snow, the view was beautiful, like a fog of gray and white blanketing the world. Kat hadn't been in the Arch since she was ten years old, but the sight always buoyed her. It got her picturing all the families in covered wagons who'd managed to cross the Mighty Mississippi, thinking, *Eureka, we've done it!* What a difference a couple hundred years made, she mused with a smile, thinking of how many New Yorkers she'd known who'd considered this "fly-over country," not worthy of parking a Conestoga wagon here much less putting down stakes.

She squinted past the frozen terrace, trying to pick out the familiar landmarks sprawled across the near horizon, despite the snow that cloaked the city. She could make out the giant red and blue Amoco sign at the corner of Big Bend and Clayton (though the station was now a BP) and the copse of trees and buildings of Forest Park, home to the zoo and the Art Museum.

Running away never works. U will B back.

Kat pushed Roger's text message out of her head, because he was wrong. She hadn't run away from anything. She'd run *toward,* and she knew she'd made the right choice, even if starting over again took some time.

No worries, she told herself. She had her savings, the 401(k) she needed to roll over into an IRA, a year's salary and COBRA insurance, and a pack of Maguires in town, which would tide her over until she figured out what to do with her life.

Precisely what that was, Kat wasn't sure. She did know that she was finished with the advertising game. Her new career would have to be creative and fulfilling in a more spiritual way. She didn't care about the money so long as it paid the rent (whenever she found a place to rent). Until she figured out what path she'd take, she spent a good part of her day perusing the job classifieds, checking out apartment listings, and doing nightly dinners with her family. Of all the pieces of her new life, the latter felt the most surreal. It was like being twelve and forty-five at once, eating her mother's meat loaf and enduring Meg's occasional jabs about her unmarried state like it was a cardinal sin (even though the Maguires weren't Catholic). Kat retaliated by reminding Meg that she was overdue in producing Eileen and Joe's first grandbaby, to which Meg would report that getting pregnant wasn't on the agenda for at least another year.

That was so Megan. Everything in her life had always happened on cue. Meg had known precisely who she would be and what kind of man she would marry—*tall, dark, and boring!*—by the time she was fourteen. Kat had never had that kind of tunnel vision.

Well, at least Megan Maguire Barnes, star realtor for chi-chi Laura McCarthy, had put aside her pious lectures long enough to get her settled into the condo smack in the heart of Clayton, just steps from the Ritz-Carlton Hotel and Forest Park Parkway.

Kat realized this particular roof would only remain overhead while the expensive property sat on the market. She had to keep it spick-and-span in case Megan needed to show it, but that hadn't happened in the past few days so she wasn't worried about being evicted today. Tomorrow was another story.

As if the mere thought of Megan had jinxed her, Kat's cell rang, and she jumped, nearly spilling tea on the pristine floors.

Who else but Meg would bug me before eight?

Kat dashed into the bedroom and snatched her phone off the nightstand before the voice mail picked up.

"Yo," she cracked as she plopped down on the edge of the mattress.

"Tell me you're not in St. Louis, and I won't be pissed at you," said a perfectly modulated voice that could just as well have been reeling off a story about a meth lab explosion in Jefferson County or signing off with, *This is Carla Moss, Channel 3, good night and good news.* "I saw Eileen at the grocery store, and she seemed surprised I didn't know you'd moved back to our little slice of heaven."

St. Louis was less a big city than a network of tiny interconnected suburbs where everyone knew everyone else's business and the leading question when you met someone new was, *Where'd you go to high school?*

"Carla Jean?" Kat nearly fell off the edge of the bed. "What the hay? It's barely eight. I thought the big cheese nighttime anchors got to sleep until noon."

"I'm happy to hear your sense of humor's intact," Carla said dryly. "I've actually got a breakfast engagement this morning. I'm about to head out the door. More importantly, are you back for real? Your mom wasn't sure."

"Yeah, I am," Kat said, and sat down on the bed.

"Seriously?"

"Seriously," Kat confirmed, and gnawed on a thumbnail. "I should've called you sooner, I know, but coming home was pretty spur of the moment."

"Hey, once I heard you were hanging around, I figured I'd give you a few more days to lay low before I pounced. Your mom said you'd been resting."

"Speaking of mothers, how's the Queen Mum?" Kat asked, picturing the ultradignified Genevieve Moss in St. John's suits, panty hose, and pearls, never a hair out of place. Carla had always said it was like living with Emily Post and Queen Victoria smashed into one.

"She's at the Gatesworth with the professor and as glacial as ever," Carla replied quickly and quietly, but didn't dish any details.

"Nice place," Kat offered benignly. The Gatesworth was a genteel retirement community, and Genevieve had to be close to eighty. She had been in her thirties when Carla was born, older than the other moms, and less involved in her daughter's life. Still, Kat was surprised Genevieve had given up the mansion off Litzsinger in Ladue. She'd always surmised that, no matter how many spouses Genny Moss went through, she'd stay there until she went Chanel pumps up.

"So what happened to the house?"

"It was sold about a year and a half ago," Carla told her, adding crisply, "which you would've known if you hadn't been such a stranger."

"Mea culpa," she said, and let it slide off her back, partially because it was the truth and because she meant to make amends now that she was home.

"Okay, no more brow-beating. What I want to know is how you are. I hear you dumped Junior."

"God, did my mom blab about that, too?" Kat rubbed her forehead, which had begun to throb the more she thought about all the things she wanted to tell Carla. "Am I too old to ask for a do-over?"

"A do-over?" Carla repeated before her laughter filled Kat's ear. The sound was bright and lighter than air, like bubbling champagne. "Aw, sweet cakes, I haven't heard that one in ages."

"Well, I'm not sure what else to call it."

They'd used the phrase endlessly as schoolgirls, either after something awful had gone on—like if she, Carla, and Elise had a fight, or if one of them had broken up with a boy. A simple request for a "do-over" worked like magic dust, and it was as if that bad thing had never happened at all.

"Oh, Kit-Kat, it'll be wonderful having everyone together again, won't it?" Carla remarked in a softer voice. "Elise and I haven't had much chance to play, so I have to catch up when I'm at her office for a little, um, rejuvenating. She's still out in West County near Wild Horse Creek, though she may as well be on another planet."

"Chesterfield *is* another planet. All those neat little subdivisions and everyone's a soccer mom," Kat agreed, then apologized, "Hey, I'm sorry for being such a horrible friend." She felt guilty if only because of how they'd all drifted apart without doing much about it. But things would be different now that she was home. She'd make certain of it. "I should've called you and Lisie right away. I should've kept in better touch all along. I'm just"—*how to put it?*—"sorting things out. I don't even have a real place to live."

"You could've bunked with me in a pinch," Carla said. "I have more bedrooms in this place than I know what to do with."

Kat pulled her knees up to her chest and set her chin on them, smiling to herself. "That's so sweet, it really is, but I'd hate to mess with your love life."

"'Mess' is not a bad word to describe it. I absolutely adore Randy, but I'm not sure if either of us is madly in love," Carla confessed, blunt as always. "Still, he's gorgeous to look at and sweet as pie, not to mention that he keeps my motor running."

"I can't believe you're sleeping with a jock," Kat said, shaking her head. "You were the only girl at Ladue who seemed to have her period year-round and never suited up for gym."

"Oh, never fear. Randy's made me appreciate athletics."

"I have no doubt," Kat replied, hardly able to keep from busting out laughing. Then she grew quiet, lamenting the fact that she'd missed so much of her friends' lives while she was gone. "I always hated women who got so wrapped up in their boyfriends and their jobs that they shut out the world, and somehow I became one."

"Please, stop with the self-flagellation," Carla shushed her. "Friendship's a two-way street, and I've been driving one way for a long time, too. I'd say it's high time for some good old-fashioned bonding." She paused. "Does Lisie have a clue you're around?"

Dr. Elise Randolph was the soft-spoken third wheel in Ye Olde High School Clique, the pretty girl with an oversized brain who spent as much time studying as Carla had spent chasing boys.

"I haven't called Lisie yet, no," Kat admitted, and her heartbeat picked up a notch, "but I'm dying to see you both." She hugged her knees and added nervously, "I'm not exactly sure what to do from this point forward. Maybe you guys can help give me some direction."

"Ah, so New York City didn't change you that much," Carla said with a laugh. "You always did beg us for advice you didn't listen to."

Kat cracked up. "Touché."

"Well, we are cheaper than those Manhattan psychiatrists."

"I've missed you guys," Kat blurted out, because she had, maybe more than she'd ever realized. "Are you free anytime soon?"

"Is tonight soon enough?" Carla proposed. "How does Brio in Frontenac sound? I can meet you and Lisie after I do the news at six. So around sevenish? I've got plenty of time before I have to be back for the ten o'clock spot."

"You're on."

"Oh, and Kitty-Kat?"

"Yeah?"

"Welcome home. I missed you something awful."

Kat smiled as she ended the call.

Hanging onto the phone, she lowered her feet to the fuzzy rug upon which the bed seemed to float like an island, someone's upscale version of an Ikea ad. Then she leaned forearms on flannel-covered thighs, found Elise's stored number, and dialed.

CARLA

**Carla Moss in an interview
with the *St. Louis Post-Dispatch*:**

*Aging anchormen are like Santa Claus. The more potbel-
lied and bald they get, the more revered. Anchorwomen,
on the other hand, are pretty much like Kleenex: disposable
and always replaceable with a newer, prettier box.*

Chapter Four

THE beautifully appointed ballroom at the Ritz-Carlton looked elegant as always, with its patterned carpet, molded ceilings, and dripping chandeliers; though this morning it had been embellished in shades of pink, from the balloon centerpieces and soft lighting, the table linens, right down to the napkins. A fair number of the guests wore pink as well, and all now gathered around the eighty tables that stretched from wall to wall. Uniformed wait staff maneuvered about, serving breakfast and pouring orange juice and coffee. The buzz of voices swelled eight hundred strong.

"Great turnout, yes?" the hat-wearing woman to Carla's right—one of the fund-raiser's co-chairs—remarked.

"Fabulous," Carla said, and smoothed a hand down the pale pink wool of her suit jacket before fingering the matching pale pink pearls around her throat. She'd dressed with particular care this morning, knowing she'd be seated front and center at a table filled with committee chairwomen, the mayor's wife, and cancer specialists from St. John's Hospital.

"We're ecstatic that you're here, Ms. Moss." The mocha-skinned woman to Carla's left beamed at her. "Last year we had Fran Drescher, but we sold out so much faster with you on the bill."

"It's my pleasure, Gina," Carla replied with a gracious smile before she speared a fat strawberry from her fruit bowl and delicately chewed. She prayed she wouldn't get seeds stuck between her teeth. Two giant screens sat on either side of the great room to showcase the morning's speakers. So strawberry seeds or, worse, a bit of chives from the scrambled eggs would look about the size of a palmetto leaf.

"We're actually hoping maybe one of these days you can take a larger role with our organization," the woman to her right declared. Her pink straw hat sprouted silk daisies from the band. "We'd love for you to join the board someday."

Dede Rothman, Carla remembered as she replied, "Well, Dede, I'd certainly like to give you more of my time when I have more time to spare."

"That's what we're hoping, too."

"We're so sorry your mother couldn't come with you, especially since she's the daughter of a survivor," Gina remarked from her other side, and Carla again turned to the woman on her left.

"Yes, it's too bad," she politely agreed. "Mother would've loved to be here with so many women who've gone through what my grandmother did. She's sorry her schedule conflicted."

Well, it was only a little white lie, and one that she didn't have a problem telling since it was a whole lot easier than explaining that Genevieve Moss was a few gray cells shy of having to move out of her apartment at the Gatesworth and into an extended-care facility. When Carla had stopped by the past week, Genevieve hadn't even recognized her own daughter. So while Carla wore pink Chanel and nibbled fruit before taking the stage to address the eight hundred breast cancer survivors and their co-survivors, her mother was drinking Metamucil-spiked juice and swallowing pills that only seemed to make her crabbier and more paranoid. Afterward, Genny and hubby Herbert would take an exercise class or do crafts to improve her dexterity. Later, Herbert would settle her down with a cup of tea and read to her.

"Some days, she's perfectly lucid," he'd confided to Carla, "and others, she wakes up and doesn't know where the hell she is or, worse, who she is or who I am."

Carla found it a cruel irony that the mother who'd spent so much time ignoring her when she was growing up suddenly had trouble recalling her name.

"I don't have time for your recital, Carla Jean, I have a Junior League luncheon this afternoon," Genevieve would say, or else it was a cocktail party, a garden club meeting, or whatever else her mother deemed more important. "For goodness' sake, the whole world doesn't revolve around you, Carla, just because you think it should." Maybe it was because Carla's birth was a late life shock, or maybe Genevieve just hadn't been cut out to be a mother. It hadn't helped that Donald Moss died of a heart attack when Carla was in college. Her father had done his best to be there for her even when Genevieve wouldn't.

It was no wonder she had sought attention elsewhere: from high school jocks, to frat boys, and then the older men she'd met starting out in broadcasting, like her first—and last—husband, Burton Echols at KMOK. When her career had taken off, it comforted her somewhat thinking that hundreds of thousands of people turned to Channel 3 every night just to watch her, like she was part of their families, even if her own mother had forgotten she existed.

"Perhaps she'll be able to come next year," Dede remarked.

"Perhaps she will," Carla said politely, lying again, because it sounded far better than the cold, hard truth.

If Genevieve had actually come with her—if she'd been lucid, feeling like her old self—her mother would have watched her with cool green eyes, searching for something to criticize. And she was nervous as it was, with tiny butterflies darting about her stomach as the fund-raiser's chairwoman took the podium to get the program rolling. After a brief introduction, it was Carla's turn at bat.

"Welcome, everyone, to our annual Survivors Breakfast," Allison Hoffman greeted the crowd. She theatrically fluffed the fuchsia feather boa draped over her shoulders, flinging its tail end around her neck. "I do hope you're all feeling as in the pink as I am this morning. Diva pink, I like to call it, though I believe our guest of honor has put on Chanel pink, isn't that right, Carla?" the director teased, looking in Carla's direction.

Carla called back, "It beats Pepto-Bismol pink," which sent a wave of laughter rippling through the enormous room.

"You all know and love her as the face of Channel 3 news. She's been one of our biggest supporters for over a decade, headlining fund-raisers and leading the pack at our annual Save the Ta-Tas walk. In fact, I can't think of enough good things to say about her, so why don't I just let her speak for herself. Without further ado"—she made a grand sweep of her arm, shedding feathers from her boa—"Ms. Carla Moss."

Carla rose to her feet amidst a thunder of applause and hoots. With a graceful wave to all, she ascended the steps to the stage, accepted a hug from Allison, and settled behind the podium. She adjusted the mike before saying, "Thank you so much for the warm welcome," as the noise slowly died down.

The lights glinted off her auburn hair and the gold buttons of her suit, and shone so brightly in her eyes that she could see no farther than the first row of tables. Beyond that, heads appeared faceless, no more than blurred shadows. But Carla smiled and let her gaze roam the room, as if she could see them all.

As she leaned toward the microphone, she lightly clutched the sides of the lectern. "Wow, what a gorgeous group of women— oh, and you don't look too shabby either, sir," she said, winking at a lonely gentleman surrounded by ladies at a first-tier table. The crowd chuckled heartily, and Carla paused before going on. "I'm here today in celebration of all of you, survivors and co-survivors alike. Honestly, after meeting so many of you before breakfast and hearing your stories, I think this amazing tribe of pink could run the world if it wanted to."

The audience cheered, and Carla hesitated until the ballroom grew quiet again. "As you know if you've heard me speak before, I come from a long line of tough broads. My grandmother had breast cancer when I was in grade school, and I was too young to realize what was going on. All I remember about her diagnosis was my mother crying on the phone and then packing her suitcase to head to Texas. She left my dad and me alone to fend for ourselves for a month while she cared for my grandma. But Granny was a fighter, and she made it through just fine."

Carla's finger curled around the lectern's edges and her voice wavered ever so slightly. "When I envision a survivor, I think of my grandmother living another twenty years after her breast cancer, before she died at eighty-five of something else entirely. No, the breast cancer didn't get her. She'd never have let it best her. She'd made it through the Great Depression and two world wars to see men walk on the moon. A pesky thing like Stage 2a invasive ductal carcinoma wasn't going to bring her down, and it didn't."

More hoots and "Here heres" erupted from the depths of the ballroom, and Carla paused until things quieted down again.

"After she was cancer-free, I stayed with her one summer. Every morning, she got up, stuck on her bra, tucked in her prosthesis, and she soldiered on. It was like nothing had ever happened, and it was like everything had happened. She'd become even more of what she was: more loving, more giving, and more fun. Granny took life by the balls, and she held on," Carla declared, and wet her lips, keeping her composure though the memories touched her still. "She lived her life to the fullest, as we all should, every day, no matter what our circumstances. And I challenge each and every one of you to do the same."

A disjointed chorus of "amens" rang out, and others clapped, and Carla felt her nerves finally easing. Her grip relaxed and she exhaled softly through her glossed lips, holding her emotions in check.

"Even though my mother never had to deal with breast cancer, I still worry about her health, and I worry about my own. I try not to dwell on what I can't control, but I can't help wondering sometimes what's in store for me and my boobs"—she lifted her hands to theatrically cup her breasts, glancing southward as she did so—"besides the tug of gravity, pulling them down more every year, of course."

She smiled at the ensuing laughter, pleased she kept hitting the right notes. Her voice stronger now, she carried on. "What I do know for sure is that I'm not leaving much to chance. I've been having mammograms annually since I turned thirty-five and now with digital mammography—and the occasional ultrasound when my doctor sees something she doesn't like—I feel like my knockers are being monitored more closely than any *Playboy* playmate's."

A broad grin slipped across Carla's mouth at the raucous sound of hooting and hollering that followed that remark, which was when even the most lingering of butterflies fled her stomach altogether and she realized her audience wasn't eating their thirty dollar per plate breakfast so much as eating out of the palm of her hand.

You like me, you really like me, she mused happily, and finished up her talk in twenty minutes flat, right on schedule, and left the podium to a standing ovation.

AN HOUR LATER Carla strode through the lobby of KMOK in her full-length black mink, her face hidden behind oversized Escada sunglasses. It was just ten-thirty on a frigid winter morning, long before she would take her seat on the set for the six o'clock news. Even after quickly moving up the ranks from the early morning show to midday and finally to the penthouse suite—co-anchoring the nightly news at six and ten—she still couldn't shake the urge to show up well before lunch. It gave her time to catch up on e-mails, prepare for interviews, or sit in on production meetings. And today, following her presentation at the Ritz-Carlton, she had some on-air promos to tape, and wanted to get them out of the way before her lunchtime manipedi at Wellbridge.

"Good morning, Ms. Moss!" the receptionist chirped like a

trained parakeet as soon as she spotted Carla coming through the revolving doors.

Carla smiled. "Good morning, LaTonya. Hello, Charles," she added with a nod to the security guard who held open the glass door leading to the maze of cluttered cubicles and desks that served as the heart and soul of Channel 3.

Mindful of cables stretching this way and that beneath the Uggs she'd slipped on in the car, Carla strode purposefully toward her office. Heads turned as she passed and raised voices suddenly hushed, but she didn't let any of it faze her. She doled out chipper "Hellos" without missing a beat.

Twenty years on the air—and the last dozen as St. Louis's number-one anchor—had cemented Carla's transformation from mere mortal to local icon. Having the city embrace her made her feel beloved and isolated at once. It had taken a while to get used to hearing strangers call her name or being asked for an autograph on a restaurant napkin. She still wasn't altogether comfortable with seeing her face pop up regularly in photos alongside the *Post-Dispatch*'s society column, detailing what she wore and what she ate, or, even more titillating, the age of every man who dared take her out on a date.

Like this morning's tidbit, which had appeared after she had popped out for a business dinner with an attractive cardiologist she'd met at an American Heart Association gala, although he'd been wooing her to speak at their convention, nothing more:

Celeb Cougar Sighting! "The Face of St. Louis" was spotted at Harry's canoodling with a hot younger man. Meow! Our very own Carla Moss was on the prowl last Saturday evening, caught with her elegant paws on the arm of an unnamed beau. Dare we ask if cub (sports) reporter Randall Mossbacher is already out as catnip of the month? Say it ain't so!

It ain't so, Carla thought, prickling even now at how she'd been anointed the Lou's resident Cougar-in-Chief, but then she reminded herself that, at forty-five—pretty much over-the-hill for a female in TV news—her love life still rated several inches in a daily column. She'd start worrying when they stopped caring and not a moment before.

"Hey, Carla, you know they're shooting your on-air promos in half an hour," her overeager assistant said, popping out of nowhere to block her way to her office door. "Jesse wants to see you in Makeup whenever you're ready."

"Thanks, Deidre," Carla said, and plucked off her designer shades. She blinked as the fluorescent lighting turned everything around her vaguely orange. "Any other messages worth noting?"

"Nothing earth-shattering." Deidre shrugged and pushed her black-framed glasses higher up her long nose. "Mostly requests for appearances or people wanting you to interview them and tell their life stories. Everyone wants to be on TV these days."

"Tell me about it." Carla rolled her eyes. "Thanks for being the gatekeeper, darling. Now if you'll excuse me, I need a few minutes alone before I head over to Makeup."

She tugged off her gloves as Deidre stepped out of her way. Then she twisted the knob and pushed into her office, which was pretty much a glorified shoe box that barely contained all her shelves filled with the dozens of plaques, statuettes, and crystal awards she'd racked up the past two decades.

As she turned to close the door and reach for the light switch, hands grabbed her from behind, one settling on her right breast and the other around her waist. Carla squealed and dropped her bag. Her Escada shades clattered to the carpet and a husky voice whispered, "Shhh, babe, it's just me."

"Randy!" she hissed as he locked the door securely and faced her, a wolfish grin on his chiseled face. "I almost had a heart attack!"

"Sorry, Car, but I missed you." Randy Mossbacher, onetime quarterback for the University of Missouri, and Channel 3's hunkiest new sportscaster, put his muscled arms around her and pulled her tight to his chest. "Are you up for a morning playdate?" His hot breath stirred her hair. "Because I sure am."

"Yes, I got that impression." Carla felt his erection hard against her hip as he slipped broad hands beneath her coat and slid the fur from her shoulders until it slumped in a fuzzy puddle around her feet. One thing about seeing a younger man, you never had to wait for the Viagra to kick in.

"Yum, you smell good," he told her as he nibbled on an earlobe while his fingers edged her skirt up her stockinged thighs. "Babe, you've got your garters on! God, you know how that turns me on."

"Indeed I do," Carla said with a smile, and let him think she'd done it for him instead of for herself. Wasn't that the point of having someone fun to play with?

As his hands snaked up her skirt, she got busy unbuckling his belt.

Did Barbara Walters ever have an office quickie with a twenty-six-year-old when she anchored the news for ABC? she fleetingly wondered.

She gasped as Randy caught her around the waist and hoisted her atop the edge of her desk, toppling her goose-necked lamp.

When his fingers dipped inside the lace of her panties, she let out a yelp before Randy's mouth silenced further cries.

A timid fist knocked on the door then jangled the doorknob. "Ms. Moss, everything okay? I heard something banging."

Carla turned a cheek to Randy's kisses, trying not to laugh as she called out, "I knocked my desk lamp over, that's all!"

"As long as you're okay."

"I'm fine."

"You *are* fine," Randy whispered between impatient kisses and groping.

Carla forgot about Deidre, making quick work of Randy's zipper.

"Hurry," he moaned as she slipped on the lubricated condom he'd unpackaged with his teeth.

Her skirt hiked over her hips, Carla wrapped her thighs around him and gripped his shoulders so he could enter her easily. As his hands cupped her ass, he buried his head against her shoulder and Carla braced herself against the desk, her fallen lamp rattling as he firmly moved against her. Her breathing quickened and she bit her lip to keep quiet until she felt him shudder suddenly; heard his sigh as he slumped against her.

"Oh, God, babe," he murmured, as if their morning delight had anything to do with religion. "God, that was sweet."

Sweeter for him than for her, but Carla didn't complain. She stroked his hair, and they held each other even as she felt the stapler poking into her tush. Then, with a sigh, Randy withdrew from her and stepped back to take care of the condom and tuck himself inside his pants.

Carla reached for a tissue, thinking that younger guys could do it anytime, anywhere, and have it over in a minute. When she was twenty-three, having sex, say, in the stall of a ladies' restroom might've been exciting and edgy; now, not so much. Not that she was complaining, but she much preferred a spot softer than her desk, and she generally liked a little more, ah, attention paid to her beforehand.

"You feeling as good as I am?" he asked.

"Better," she replied with a smile, another little white lie. She didn't utter *I love you,* nor did she expect to hear it. Their relationship was what it was, and she was okay with that. She didn't have the energy for a real commitment. She'd already tried marriage once, and it had wrung her dry. It would take an awful lot for any man to convince her to try it again.

"You rock," Randy said, and kissed her as she methodically put herself back together, tugging her panties and adjusting her gartered stockings, buttoning her blouse, and smoothing her pencil skirt down to her knees again.

As she finger-combed her auburn hair, she remarked, "It's a good thing Jesse hasn't worked his magic on me for the promos. You would've made a mess of things."

"I like you better without so much goop on anyhow." Randy grinned, flashing dimples, and finished pushing his shirttail into his pants and buckling his belt. "Well, damn." He frowned, catching sight of the face on the Tag Heuer strapped around his wrist.

"What's wrong?"

"I've gotta go, babe," he said, and leaned forward to plant a wet one on her forehead. "I've got an interview with the Rams head coach." He ran a hand through his close-cropped brown hair after yanking down the cuffs of his jacket. "And I'm hitching a ride with that new morning anchor Amber Sue. She's doing a fluff piece on the coach's wife for five o'clock."

Carla stiffened. *The new morning anchor Amber Sue?* What the hell was he babbling about? She felt like her head would explode. *Amber Sue, Amber Sue.* Was that the "Sunrise Show" reporter who had breasts the size of summer melons and a smoky-smooth voice like she'd eaten Demi Moore? Surely *she* wasn't doing features for the early evening broadcasts?

"I thought that girl did morning traffic?"

"She did until a few weeks back." Randy shrugged broad shoulders. "Guess the boss decided to move her up from 5:00 A.M. What a surprise," he said, and chuckled, only to stop abruptly when she wasn't laughing, too. "So you don't know about her and Burton?" He winced. "Awkward."

"What about them?" Carla pressed, unnerved by the look on his face.

Beneath his neat brown hair, his brow furrowed as he leaned over to whisper, "Uh, apparently there's something going on between the Big Guy and Amber. Word around the station is he's priming her for a five o'clock co-anchor spot."

Carla blinked. Surely Randy was mistaken about Amber Sue jumping up from sunrise to sunset. The last time Burton had slept with a young reporter and bounced her up the ladder that fast was when he'd taken her under his wing—and into his bed—which could only mean one thing.

No, no, no. It isn't possible. Or is it?

She clutched the edge of her desk, suddenly nauseous.

"You okay, babe?"

"Uh-huh," she lied.

"All right, I'll see you later, then," Randy said, and kissed her soundly on the lips before ducking out of her office.

Five seconds later Deidre poked her head in, the blank look on her face giving no indication that she'd just caught Randy leaving. "Jesse's waiting," she said, and her nasal twang acted like a starter's gun, setting Carla into motion.

"I'm on my way. I just have a stop to make first," Carla told her, and stepped over her black mink, still lying on the floor.

She strode up the corridor, past Makeup, and barged past Burton's secretary and into his office before anyone could stop her.

His bald head angled up as she entered, and Carla slammed the door behind her for good measure, taking pleasure in the way it rattled the framed photographs that smothered his walls.

"Just what the holy hell are you up to, Burton?" She marched straight up to his desk and planted her palms on the polished surface. "Are you screwing that blond reporter with the cleavage who's moving up the ranks faster than Danica Patrick drives at Indy? Or are you just giving me another reason to be thankful I've divorced you?"

She glared at her one and only ex, comfortably ensconced in his overstuffed leather chair. Just because he was the station's general manager didn't mean she couldn't rip him another hole whenever he tried to pull a fast one on her. And this latest was a doozy. Or, perhaps she should say, it was a *floozy*.

"And a very good morning to you, too, Carla," he said smugly.

"I've gotten wind of your secret agenda," she informed him, leaning across the paper-littered blotter and getting right in his face. "You're promoting what's-her-name, Paris or Britney or Brandy—"

"It's Amber Sue."

"Of course it is," Carla snapped. "How on earth can you justify giving her a feature for the evening news? You didn't even let

Karen Findley cover the school board elections until she'd been here five years! She must give great blowjobs." Carla sniffed and stood up straight. "Is she even out of college, for Christ's sake?"

"For your information," Burton roared, "Amber Sue graduated from the top of her class at Indiana University, and she interned for two years before she did any on-air reporting."

"Give me a break." Carla snorted. "You're not promoting her because of her degree. You're swayed by a pair of breasts that could easily score her a spot on the Girls of Hooters calendar."

Burton fingered his comb-over. "So I'm giving her a hand?" He shrugged. "I gave you a chance once, or have you forgotten?" he remarked in his slow Bootheel drawl. "If not for me, you would've been covering supermarket openings and county fairs, still waiting for a break in a bigger market."

"So my success has everything to do with you and nothing to do with me?" She wished she had something to throw at him.

"I made you a star, didn't I?" The entrenched grooves between his wayward eyebrows deepened as he continued his pitch for his newest pet. "Now it's time for me to do it again. Amber's got your gut instincts, and she's as smooth at reading the news as anyone I've ever seen, including you."

"Smooth between the sheets, too, I'll wager," Carla flung at him.

Burton's lips pulled back like a snarling pit bull. "My personal relationships are none of your business. Just as it's not my business if our new jock reporter is your latest boy-toy." He bent over his desk, sniffing the air between them. "Do you realize you reek of his cologne right now?" He smirked.

Carla thought about slipping off an Ugg and smacking him over the head with it.

"I can't believe you just said that."

Even if it was the truth, who *she* was banging at the moment didn't affect either of their careers.

"If you want me to play nice, then don't give Amber a hard time," he said, and stabbed a stubby finger in the air. "C'mon, sweetheart, I'm only asking that you be reasonable."

Be reasonable? Who was he kidding?

"I'm the goddamned voice of reason," Carla growled.

He settled back in his plump leather chair. "You need to calm down."

She felt anything but serene. "If you're figuring the next step is to have her take my anchor seat, you've got another thing coming."

"No one's making any changes that affect you directly."

Not yet hung on the air unsaid between them.

Carla wished like hell she could believe him, but it was safer not to. Besides, the hair on the back of her neck prickled in warning. The last time it did that, there had been a 5.2 earthquake in St. Louis, shaky enough to knock a few of her Emmys off the shelves. She sensed another disaster looming, and she prayed this one wouldn't knock her off her feet as well.

"Just don't forget who has the most recognizable face in St. Louis news," she brought up, in case Burton had become oblivious to all the posters at the bus stops and on the billboards surrounding downtown. She snugly crossed her arms and narrowed her eyes on him. "Do you know how many e-mails I get every day? Or how many babies have been named Carla since the mid-nineties? I've got the highest Q rating of any anchor in town, male *or* female. So if you're plotting with your new bed buddy to nudge me out—"

"Sweetheart, stop, you're wasting your breath," he cut her off, and shifted in his seat. His bespectacled eyes darted every which way but hers. "No one's plotting to shanghai your anchor spot. So would you pull on your big girl panties and stop reacting to station gossip. You're here as long as you want to be."

What a lying sack of shit, she realized then, clear as day. If she hadn't been convinced of it before, she was certain of it now.

Despite a smile meant to reassure, beads of sweat congregated on Burton's thin upper lip. He reached out his hand. "Can we call a truce?"

Carla noticed his palm looked slick with sweat, too. As tempted as she was to turn up her nose, she couldn't afford to, not now. "Truce," she said, even though she didn't mean it any more than he. She shook his hand briefly, then surreptitiously wiped Burton's transferred sweat onto her pink wool skirt.

"I'm glad that's settled."

"Right," she said, though her mind stuck on something else. *You're here as long as you want to be.* That was a phrase she'd never forget. The last time she'd heard him utter those words was twenty years ago when he'd promised then number-one anchor Sandy Chase that her place with KMOK was rock-solid. Only Carla had known different. After three years at the station, reporting from new rides at Six Flags in Eureka to the giant catsup bottle in Collinsville, Burton had noticed her big-time, and within weeks they were sleeping together on the sly. Not long after, she'd been promoted to weekend co-anchor, and he promised her during pillow-talk that the weeknight desk was hers if she wanted it. Oh, hell, you bet she did, and by the time she celebrated her twenty-eighth birthday—and her engagement to Burton—Sandy Chase was on her way out to make way for Carla Jean.

Which could only mean one thing: the universe was having a big laugh on her.

Why did karma always have to come back and bite her in the ass?

"Is there something else?" Burton asked when she'd stayed silent for too long. "Oh, yeah, how'd your little chat go at that breakfast this morning?" he asked, though he kept his gaze downcast as he thumbed through the papers in front of him.

"The breast cancer survivors' breakfast went beautifully," Carla replied, doing her damnedest to keep her cool. If she showed Burton even an iota of fear or weakness, he'd pounce on it, like a starving lion on a limping zebra. "My speech was very well-received. Actually, they'd like me to sit on the board one of these days, although it's nothing I can do actively while still working five days a week at the station."

"Great," he replied, too distracted to hear her.

He'd already moved on, she could read it in his face. He used to pretend he still respected her, even after they'd split, because he knew she was the station's moneymaker. But nowadays when he dared to look her in the eye, he stared right through her.

"Oh, I nearly forgot," she added, speaking to his nearly hairless pate, "Once the breakfast was over, I stripped off my suit and ran naked through the streets of Clayton. It was cold enough to freeze my nipples."

"Great," he repeated, still focused on his files. "That's just great."

Carla sighed, wondering how she'd ever found him handsome, with his ill-fitting suits—the shoulders always bunched up—his sweaty palms, and that expanded forehead, more a five-head these days with that receding hairline. But her standards had been different then, back when she'd been a hungry J-School grad from the University of Kansas with big ambitions. She'd canoodled with (and married, in Burton's case) older men—*any* man—who could give her a leg up, or sometimes a pair of them.

Only just as she reached as high as a woman could get in the local TV market, and in the midst of her marriage to Burton, two devastating things happened to her: she miscarried before she'd even had the chance to tell him she was expecting—hell, before she'd had the chance to tell *anyone*—and she found out that her husband was having an affair with a college intern. She had been firmly convinced that she was not meant to be either a mother or a wife.

Unable to cope with her real life, Carla had thrown herself into her job. She spearheaded a five-part series on women in poverty, even going undercover on the streets, documenting cases of single moms who'd fallen on hard times and how they'd scratched to survive. She appeared at every function and fund-raiser that invited her to speak, and never missed a single newscast, soldiering on from her anchor seat and smiling for the cameras like everything was hunky-dory.

Oh, yes, and she had filed for divorce, something Burton had fought tooth and nail, garnering plenty of nasty headlines in the local paper. The only thing that had kept her from killing him back then was the fact she still had to work at Channel 3. The idea that he still controlled her fate made her crazy.

Carla cleared her throat, and Burton glanced up, startled to see her still there.

"We'll talk more later, all right? I've got work to do, if you don't mind."

"Of course," she told him, wondering if Amber Sue knew about his foot fetish and that weird toe-sucking thing he liked.

Instead, she swallowed down her frustrations and exited his office gracefully. It was clear she wasn't going to get through to Burton at this point. Her best bet was to chat with her lawyers again and have them press Burtie and the station on negotiations for a new contract. Her current one expired at the end of March, and so far the only water-cooler rumblings she'd heard about salaries involved the staff taking pay cuts, not getting raises. But her situation was different, wasn't it? She was a fixture in this town . . . unless Burton had decided it was time for the fixtures to be changed. Damn it, but she wasn't about to let herself get steamrolled like Sandy Chase!

Her chin up, Carla strode through the maze of hallways, careful to step over the cables that snaked out of the studio as she made her way toward Makeup. On the inside, she seethed. *Damn Burton and his latest blonde ambition!* She hoped she could stop shaking and cursing before she shot her promos or she'd look like she had Tourette's.

Not a few station employees she bypassed called out to her in a perky kiss-ass fashion, "Good morning, Ms. Moss," and Carla somehow managed to smile and return their greetings. She couldn't risk alienating anyone these days.

When she reached the makeup room, she threw herself into her chair and stared glumly at her reflection in the brightly lit mirror. She opened her eyes as wide as they'd go, then narrowed them. She fluffed at her collar-length layered 'do, pinched the tip of her nose, and then pulled the skin of her jaw toward her earlobes.

Was she truly replaceable at forty-five? She didn't feel old, not unless she was speaking on the campus of Washington University, surrounded by an audience of giggling college coeds. Truly, she felt better than she had at thirty-five. But Burton must be keeping track of every line on her face, she thought, or he wouldn't be pushing Amber on the evening anchor desk so quickly.

Was it time to start contemplating one of those fast mini face lifts where everything was pulled back with fishing line? It sounded totally gross; but, hey, if it got her a new contract, she was up for it. When she met Kat and Elise at Brio tonight, she'd ask Lisie about it. Lisie was a dermatologist, after all. Wasn't that something she could do in her office during lunch?

"Good Lord, Mossy, what on earth are you doing? Let go of your cheeks this instant! If I'm not mistaken, that's skin you're tugging on, not Silly Putty."

A familiar face peered over her shoulder, and Carla blinked at her longtime stylist, Jesse Wyman. He looked positively elfin with his pointed chin, tiny nose, and bright eyes with their brows plucked so high they gave him an air of perpetual surprise.

"Must you call me 'Mossy'?" she sighed, and dropped her hands to her lap. "Isn't moss something that grows on old stones? Or maybe that's Rolling Stones, though they're old, too. I can never get it straight."

He chuckled and cuffed her on the shoulder. "Quit with the pity parties already. You're so not anywhere near Mick Jagger's age. Speaking of ancient ruins, did I mention doing Joan Rivers last year?"

And by "doing her," Carla knew he meant makeup, not sex.

"She was here promoting some books," he went on, waving a hand in the air. "Not that she wrote them, of course, but it's her name on the cover anyway."

"You might've mentioned your Joan experience a mere hundred times or so, but don't let that stop you," she teased.

And he didn't. Arms gesticulating, he exclaimed, "Lord, but that woman's addicted to plastic surgery! She's beginning to look like that freaky Cat Lady in New York City. Oh, and she's the first to admit how many needles and knives she's used to petrify her puss, although I wish she'd cut it out, no pun intended. She's close to becoming her own wax figure at Madame Tussaud's. I'm surprised she doesn't melt in the summer heat."

Carla wanted to laugh but all that came out was a sad little sigh.

Jesse cocked his head, bending low over her shoulder to squint at her mirror image. "Okay, girlfriend. What's got you so down this morning? You didn't have a run-in with that prig of an ex-husband again? How'd you guys ever stay married for more than a day without seriously maiming each other?"

"Xanax. Lots and lots of Xanax," Carla told him with a straight face before she began plucking nonexistent lint from her skirt. "You've heard he's promoting that silly blond reporter, haven't you? Apparently, it's common knowledge around the station, although I only heard about it fifteen minutes ago. He denies any underhanded plots to replace me, of course, but I've got bad vibes that say he's grooming her for my anchor spot. Not that it should shock me," she said softly, "since I'm probably the oldest news-caster in the corn belt."

"Please! You're the goddamned Queen of the Media, and don't you forget it." Jesse grabbed her shoulders and hissed in her ear, "Amber Sue doesn't have as much class in her whole body as you have in your pinky! She's one hundred percent Hoosier, believe me. Have you listened to that husky voice? If she's not giving phone sex on the side, I'd be surprised. She's probably got shots of her boobies on MySpace."

"Nice try." Carla grinned and patted his hand. But her mind was hardly at ease.

If she didn't take action soon, Burton would doubtless "Sandy Chase" her, relegating her to lame special assignments until she resigned. She'd be stuck covering the Route 66 flea market and birthday parties for the longest living residents at Delmar Gardens.

Shit. She would rather die on air than fade away.

"Aw, don't let that ass Burton get you down, sweetie." Jesse played with her hair, raking his fingers through it and flipping her part to the right and then the left. "How about I cheer you up with some sexy makeup and tousled hair that says, 'I just had a quickie on my desk?'"

Carla's eyes went wide. "How did you—"

"Darling," he cut her off, tapping the side of his nose. "You're definitely a woman with balls, but I know you don't wear Hugo Boss cologne." He picked up a comb and wagged it at her. "So someone got a little randy this morning, did she?"

"He's not so little," Carla said, and bit her lip.

Jesse clutched the comb against his heart. "Mossy! You're so naughty!"

"God knows, I try," she said, but he'd coaxed her out of her Burton-inspired funk, at least temporarily.

"So how about we eradicate whatever you've put on this morning and start over with soft pink cheeks and earthy browns on your eyes, maybe pale gloss on your lips."

"Perfect." She settled back in her chair. Calmer now, she stared into the mirror, watching Jesse as he pinned up her hair so he could tackle her face.

She studied her reflection and began finding a bright side to her postforty appearance. Her pores *were* still tight, thanks to regular facials at Elise's office, and her auburn hair still worked well with her green eyes and pale skin (which she'd kept out of the sun for decades). Her full eyebrows were subtly arched and didn't need pencil filler. Her crow's-feet were barely visible unless she grinned, and only vague laugh lines had been etched into either side of her mouth. Or rather "smile parentheses," Jesse called them, which made them sound a lot better than "wrinkles."

Unless someone looked very closely at her hands or at the tendons in her neck, she could pass for thirty-five on a good day if the lighting was right, she decided, and sat up a little straighter. Though that didn't exactly make her stiff competition for Burton's latest project, did it? Amber Sue had been in diapers when she graduated from K.U.

She frowned, thinking, Jesus Christ.

Jesse gave her arm a gentle squeeze. "Quit dissecting yourself. You're gorgeous, and you always will be."

A sudden rush of tears dampened Carla's lashes. "What're you trying to do, make me cry?"

"Better before I work my magic than after," he quipped, and dove into the fishing tackle box that held his battery of makeup, while Carla sniffled and grabbed a tissue to pat her cheeks.

"Do you want to hear about Kimora Lee Simmons's trip back to the Lou, and how she was hours late to every event?" Jesse started to prattle, and she didn't have the heart to remind him that, yes, she'd heard that story several times before.

"Please," she said instead, wondering as she always did why he stayed in flyover country when he had countless celebrity clients on either coast willing to pay big bucks to jet him east or west on a whim. Whatever the reason, she was glad he hadn't moved.

Carla didn't know what she'd do without him. If Jesse ever left her, it would be worse than any divorce. She was terrified to go shopping without him, much less appear anywhere on-camera unless he'd done her makeup first. And no one else she knew could dish as much dirt.

"So what are you shooting this morning?" he asked as he came to the end of his story. "Station promos or PSAs? Lord knows it's nothing for PETA."

"Ha ha." Carla cracked a smile. "They're plugs for my interview with the vice president."

"Ooh, spill," Jesse said as he used a tiny sponge to smudge foundation from her forehead to her chin and then cheek-to-cheek. "I was in L.A. when you shot that bit! So did he hit on you? I heard he's a flirt."

"He's a terrible flirt, but he's way too old for me," Carla replied as he dabbed at her skin. "I haven't been with an older man since Burton."

Jesse swatted her gently. "Well, of course you haven't, cupcake, especially since you've promised to leave the sugar daddies for me." He sniffed. "You know I'm still dying to become a kept woman."

Carla laughed. "Well, a girl's gotta dream."

<u>ELISE</u>

**Dr. Elise Randolph's
"Tips for a More Youthful You" from *Alive* magazine:**

If fillers and Botox are overdone, it creates a distinctly plastic look. The goal is to achieve a natural appearance so women feel good about themselves at any age. But if you're afraid of needles or want a less expensive path to a youthful glow, nothing does the trick like great sex with someone you love!

Chapter Five

ELISE Randolph didn't feel particularly middle-aged except when she looked at herself full-on in the bathroom mirror before she'd had her morning coffee. Long gone were those good old college days when she could roll out of bed, throw on a pair of jeans, run a brush through her curls, and confidently stroll across campus to class.

At forty-five, being ready to face the world meant a moisturizing from head to foot and carefully applying enough concealer and powder to cover the tiny veins and red spots that had seemingly appeared overnight. After a light touch of eyeliner, mascara, and a natural-looking pink lipstick, she was good to go. Elise didn't believe in overdoing it. Nothing added ten years to a woman's face like cracks in her foundation (so to speak). If she felt under more scrutiny than most, it was because her job entailed a healthy if not youthful appearance. No one wanted a dermatologist who wasn't a shining advertisement for her practice.

Although appearing fresh and pulled together every day had been so much easier in her thirties, before her bad habits had come back to haunt her. Back in her teens and twenties there'd been no one to warn her that the sun was not her friend. Elise couldn't even count how many times she, Kat, and Carla had slapped on baby oil and prostrated themselves by the pool every single day of summer vacation. Then the years crept up, she hit forty, and—*bam!*—hello, sun damage. Now she wore SPF-50 and took vitamin D religiously.

Maybe motherhood and devoting eighteen years toward raising a son had stripped her of her vanity. Whatever the reason, Elise typically felt satisfied with her looks, unlike her old pal Carla Jean, who showed up at her office every other week. "Just keep me in the game," Car would say, though Carla was as beautiful as she'd ever been.

"Being on TV has screwed up your brain," Elise liked to tell her, although maybe some of that was due to Carla's mother. Genevieve had always presented herself as the quintessential socialite, dressing in skirts and pearls, acting imperious, and dismissing her daughter—and her daughter's friends—like they were irritating waifs. It was no wonder Carla had always felt like she had to try harder than everyone else just to be good enough. "Relax," Elise had advised Car a hundred times. "There's more to Carla Moss than just a talking head." Maybe now that Kat was back, she could drum some sense into their looks-obsessed friend.

Ah, Carla and Kat, Kat and Carla.

Elise had them both on her mind after getting a quick morning phone call from Mary Katherine Maguire herself. She'd been tickled pink to hear that Kat had moved back to town and wanted to reconnect.

"Can you meet me and Car at Brio at seven?" she'd asked.

Elise hadn't even hesitated before telling her, "Yes, yes, yes!"

It would be the first time in years that the three of them were in the same place at the same time. Somewhere postcollege, after Elise had wed Michael and given birth to Joey, after Kat had uprooted to Manhattan, and after Carla's marriage—and divorce—to Burton, life had gotten complicated enough for each of them that they'd slowly drifted apart. Elise liked the idea of reestablishing their friendship. Kat was good for her and Carla both, kind of like the glue that held them all together.

It'll be wonderful having Kat in St. Louis, Elise thought with a smile as she rubbed a palm on the bathroom mirror and cleared a space so she could see her reflection. Michael had left the room steamy from his shower by the time she hung up the phone and made it to her side of their double vanity. Through the half-open door she could hear drawers banging and doors slamming, like Michael was hell-bent on getting dressed in a hurry.

Before Elise had finished brushing her teeth, Michael was yelling from the bedroom, "Elise! Did you pick up my shirts from the cleaners? And did you ask for light starch this time? I hate when the fabric feels too stiff."

Her mouth foaming with Colgate, she hollered back, "They're hanging on the back of your closet door!"

"What about the buttons on my Armani coat? Did you have those repaired?"

"It's in the front hall closet!"

For Pete's sake!

Tension tightened the back of her neck as Elise vigorously rinsed and spit. Lately she felt more like Michael's valet than his wife. With Joey a freshman at UT-Austin since last August, they finally had the house to themselves again after eighteen years. Only instead of spending the last seven months rekindling the passion, it was more like two ships passing in the night, or two harried people brushing past each other in the mornings. Sex? What was that? Elise wondered how long a person could be celibate and still remember how to do it without using something that required batteries.

When Joe had called home the other night, and she let him know his father wasn't home—that he seemed often to be working late these days—her son had played Dr. Ruth, suggesting, "Make a play for him, Mom. You know, surprise him some night. Otherwise he'll just ignore you for his other wife."

Elise had freaked out for a second, and not just because her barely grown-up child was obviously suggesting she entice her husband with sex. She was wondering what exactly Joe knew that she didn't. "What do you mean his 'other wife'?"

"His *job*, Mom," her son had said with a laugh. "Dad's always been married to his practice."

"You're right," she'd told him, because that was all too true. Michael had missed more of Joey's parent-teacher nights at school, hockey games, soccer practices, whatever had been going on at the time, because of his work.

Joey, Joey, Joey. Sometimes kids were wiser than adults.

Elise felt her heart tug, thinking of her son living hundreds of miles away in Austin. Every time she passed his empty room, she wanted to weep. She didn't need a therapist to tell her she was suffering from a severe case of empty nest syndrome, missing all the things that used to aggravate her: the loud rap music, the smelly hockey gear, the empty carton of milk put back in the fridge, the dirty towels on the floor, the constant texting through dinner, and all those weekends when he'd straggled in an hour after curfew.

Elise found the silence in the house so deafening at first that she'd worked longer hours than ever, staying at her desk to finish dictation and review biopsy reports until well past dark. Michael seemed perpetually absent as well, so that for weeks on end they rarely glimpsed each other after awakening in the morning until it was time to go to bed.

Is this part of empty nest syndrome, too? she wondered, feeling like she'd lost a child *and* a partner.

With a sigh, she turned on the shower and stepped in. Squirting Kiss My Face gel on her scrubber, she breathed in the lavender scent and tried to clear her head. Instead of imagining a beach somewhere with lapping waves upon the sand, she ended up going over her schedule for the morning: 8:00 A.M. mole biopsy, 8:30 A.M. dermabrasion, 9:00 A.M. glycolic peel, and so on and so on all the way through six o'clock.

When she stepped from the shower, she wrapped a towel around her torso and another around her head. Back at the sink, she rubbed a gentle cleanser into her palms before slathering the creamy mixture on her face. *Never, never use bar soap*, she liked to tell her patients, *it's too harsh, especially on aging skin.*

Aging skin, like her own.

Elise felt as if she'd sailed past forty overnight. Talking to Kat this morning made her realize how fast the years had gone by, how different her life had become than she'd imagined.

If she closed her eyes tightly, she could still envision her, Kat, and Carla sitting on a giant rock in the woods behind Kat's house. Kat's brown hair in pigtails, her cheeks tan and freckled; Carla with bangs and lip gloss and a training bra, already looking older than eleven; and she with her mop of gold curls in a handmade halter top and denim shorts, sunburned legs full of bug bites. They had clasped hands in the center of their circle and made two promises: to always stay close and to never become old and boring.

Kat may have broken the first part of their pact by moving to New York, but Elise knew she had thoroughly shattered the second part. Not that being a dermatologist was dull work, not for her; but she'd devoted so much of herself to balancing Joey and her job, pretty much forsaking all others, that when her son was gone, it was like the breath had been sucked out of her. If she was tired all the time, how was she supposed to catch her second wind?

Where was the joy in her life? She needed to find that spark again; although she was pretty sure that eating dinner alone in the den, watching *CSI* reruns, and waiting for her husband to come home would not bring eternal happiness.

Egads, how simply awful that sounded, like a grim fairy tale, she thought, and had a sudden urge to cry.

"Ah, there you are." Michael popped his head through the master bathroom door in time to catch her with a face full of goop. "I've got a tricky breast augmentation this morning so I'd better run."

Elise blinked as cleanser stung her eyes. "You're not having breakfast again?" she asked, talking even as she flipped water over her face and reached for her towel.

"No time."

She peeked at him through the towel as she patted her skin. "Will you be home for dinner?"

"You'd better eat without me." He tugged on his suit jacket and adjusted his tie.

"You look nice," she said, "very chic."

"Why thank you." He winked at her before he turned toward the mirror, checking himself out.

Elise stared at the dapper stranger in charcoal pinstripes and pale pink shirt with coordinating pink, gray, and black striped tie. Michael dressed really well these days, more conscious of labels than she, which seemed funny since all through med school he could barely match his socks, much less his shirts and ties.

She watched him fiddle with dark hair that seemed to have turned salt and pepper overnight. He was styling it differently. A Caesar cut, she thought it was called, which pretty well disguised his receding hairline. Elise wondered if he was trying to appear younger and hipper to keep up with Phil. His surgical partner was thirty-five, single, and about as slick a dresser as she had ever seen.

"Hey, sweetheart, did you hear me? I said I've got consultations booked until eight again, and Phil wants to have drinks and talk business afterward."

"Oh, okay," Elise said, before she put the face towel away, murmuring as she did, "Lucky Phil. He sees you a lot more than I do these days."

"Things at the practice are crazy. You'd think with the economy people would be saving their money, but you wouldn't know it by our calendar. We're booked solid for months."

Elise wanted to remind him that she wasn't exactly loafing around either, that her practice was busy, too. But she let his superior tone slide.

"Say hi to Phil for me," she replied benignly. She didn't mention that she was meeting Kat and Carla at seven. What was the point? He wouldn't get home until ten or eleven, she wagered. He'd never even know she'd gone out.

"Take care," he said, and leaned over to kiss her firmly on the brow. Then he patted her shoulder and was gone.

"'Bye."

Elise stood in her towel, breathing in the scent of the Gio cologne he'd taken to wearing lately—which made her want to sneeze—and she remembered when Michael couldn't stand to leave the house until he'd kissed her squarely on the lips, and kissed her good. When Joey was little, Michael used to get home early enough to help her fix dinner. They'd turned on the radio and danced around, using wooden stirring spoons as microphones, while Joe laughed like they were the silliest things. Michael would pat her butt, or steal a smooch in between browning garlic for the pasta. The way he touched her now was more like a friend than a lover.

She exhaled slowly and looked at herself dead-on in the beveled mirror.

He's having an affair, she decided, and not for the first time. He's having an affair, and I don't want to know anything about it.

She stepped back from the tumbled marble vanity and pulled the bath towel apart so she could better see her body. Her thighs carried most of the weight she'd gained through the years and were decidedly softer and plumper than before she'd had Joey. Never large to begin with, her breasts had gone up a cup size with her pregnancy and sagged thanks to gravity. But Elise liked that they were real even if Michael had suggested once upon a time that his partner, Phil Bernstein, could make them look like teenage boobs again, if only she'd let him. She had already caved once to Michael's wishes, getting a tummy tuck a couple years after Joey's birth. The gentle rounding of her postbaby shape hadn't mattered as much to her as to him. It was as though he'd wanted her to become the gangly adolescent girl he'd fallen in love with, only that wasn't ever going to happen.

Elise touched the vague scar across her lower abdomen and wondered if she looked too maternal to please him anymore. He was surrounded every day by females whose bodies he practically rebuilt, from faces to breasts to buttocks and bellies. How could she compete with a Bionic Woman?

Fleetingly, she found herself wondering, If I let Phil do my chest, would that change anything? Or was her body not really the problem?

"Aaargh." She let out a cry of frustration, knowing all her worrying wasn't doing her any good. If she wanted an explanation, she needed to confront her husband. Otherwise she had to stop beating herself up. She was still the same Elise she'd always been. If anyone had changed, it wasn't her: it was Michael with his Armani coats and lightly starched custom-made shirts.

Elise tugged the smaller towel off her head, shaking out her still damp curls.

Then she got to work applying her makeup and blow-drying the wave from her hair. In another fifteen minutes she was dressed and in her Audi sedan, the classical music station turned up loud enough to drown out even her most negative thoughts.

Chapter Six

ELISE slipped in a rear door marked PRIVATE and entered her office on the fifth floor of Building D at the Missouri Baptist Hospital campus. She glimpsed a full waiting room through the open reception window when she poked her head up front to tell her staff "Good morning."

Dropping her purse behind her desk in back, she flung open the louvered doors on the closet that hid half a dozen starched white coats with DR. ELISE RANDOLPH embroidered in blue across the left breast. Briskly, she donned one and headed up to the front desk. She heard the soft rock music her receptionist turned on in the mornings as she approached the ledge where a stack of charts sat neatly arranged in order of appointments.

"Who's up first?" she asked, and her nurse emerged from the file room, answering her question before Lindy, the receptionist, could.

"We had a cancellation," Jenny told her. "I just refiled Mr.

Rodriguez's chart, and I made one for the new patient." She crossed her slim arms over her purple smock and jerked her chin toward the first exam room door, which was closed. "I put him in Room Three."

"Please tell me it's not genital warts," Elise said, only half joking.

Jenny cracked a smile. "Nope, it's a very cute guy with a sports rash on his upper back. He thinks his hockey pads are rubbing, and the OTC hydrocortisone he's been using isn't working."

"Perfect." Elise winked at her then headed off.

The tap of her high heels muffled by the carpet, she walked up the brief hallway and bypassed several empty exam rooms. Soon to be occupied, she knew, as her patient load only seemed to get heavier all the time. She paused in front of the next door, which was closed. The patient's chart sat inside a plastic sleeve on the wall, and she plucked it out, glancing over the history sheet before she knocked twice.

"I'm coming in," she said clearly before she turned the knob and entered the room. "Hello, Mr. Lawrence, I'm—"

"You're Elise Randolph," a graveled voice interrupted. "Joey's mom, right?"

Paper crackled as jeans-clad legs slid off the table, and her patient towered over her. The space wasn't large, so they were virtually nose-to-nose; or rather, the top of her head reached his nose. He stood a few inches above six feet, and Elise felt small beside him despite her two-inch heels. He smelled like Ivory soap and wore a University of Minnesota hoodie. His lean face framed by shaggy dark hair looked familiar somehow, but Elise wasn't sure why. She saw so many patients, too many to keep track.

"It's me, Evan," he offered when she drew a blank. "Evan Lawrence. I used to coach Joe's summer youth hockey team when he was in middle school and I was in college."

"Oh, my God," Elise said as a flood of good feelings and memories washed over her. For an instant she was rinkside, watching Joe skate, her ears cold and her voice hoarse from yelling. "You're really and truly Coach Evan?"

"I am."

"Wow." She pictured him as he was then: a lanky, dark-haired, athletic young man with thick-lashed brown eyes, an impossibly square jaw, and an endearing lopsided grin. All the boys had looked up to him, and all the hockey moms had crushed big-time on him, herself included. Somewhere in the last decade his shoulders broadened, his lean cheeks shed their baby fat, and his thighs turned into well-muscled tree trunks that strained against washed-out denim.

So he was in his late twenties, she figured, and even more attractive than when the desperate housewives had fawned all over him. If she'd been more like Carla, she probably would've said something mildly suggestive, like, *My how you've grown.* He had definitely filled out in all the right places.

"Time flies, huh?" he said.

"You're telling me." She held his chart against her chest, trying to still her quickening heartbeat. "I remember when Joe broke his nose after a nasty high stick."

"Damn!" He rubbed his stubbly chin, shaking his head. "I was hoping you would've forgotten that."

"Hey, he considered it a badge of honor," Elise said, and laughed, because it was true. To this day Joey loved telling the story of why his nose seemed slightly off center. "He never wanted it fixed, not even with his dad a plastic surgeon."

"Joe always used to say you yelled louder than any mother at the rink," Evan went on, and Elise winced.

"I did?"

"Hey, it was great," he assured her. "Might've embarrassed Joe a little, but I loved how you got so into it." He scratched his jaw again. "Joe's dad never came to games much, did he?"

"No." That was something she used to get on Michael's case about, because she knew it bothered Joey not to have his dad see him play. She had never missed a game.

"Where's Joe now anyway?"

"He's a freshman at the University of Texas," Elise said, and the smile returned to her face. It sounded weird saying it; she still had trouble believing it herself.

"Is he a winger on a team down there?"

"No, he's not into sports at the moment," she replied. "He's way too into frat parties and girls."

"As well he should be." Evan grinned and sat back down on the exam table, the white paper crinkling beneath him. His long legs reached the floor even without the step-up. He had on beat-up black Pumas, and they looked about a size thirteen.

And you know what that means! Carla's voice filled her head again, and Elise focused her eyes on his paperwork.

"So are you involved with anyone—um, any one of the youth hockey teams now?" She blushed, realizing what she'd nearly asked.

"I'm still involved in local hockey, yes." His dark eyes sparked with mischief.

"So you're coaching?" Elise asked, and glanced down at his chart, fumbling through all the HIPA forms, registration, and history pages, trying to find what she was looking for.

"No, I play for the Blues as of two weeks ago. They just brought me up from Peoria after they got me on waivers from Minnesota last fall. I had knee surgery, and some folks had me down for the count." He rubbed his left hand over the aforementioned joint and shrugged. "It feels almost good as new, but sometimes it's more the perception that matters. I'm glad anyone took a chance on me at all."

"You're a St. Louis Blue? No way!" Elise exclaimed, sounding like a teenager. She wondered if Joey had kept track of Coach Evan and knew that he'd become a pro. It had been a while since she checked the sports pages, much less the rest of the local newspaper. Michael had stopped their subscription when rolled-up *Post-Dispatches* started stacking up in the garage recycle bin like so many logs.

"Do you ever get downtown for the games?" Evan asked.

"Not in a while." She shook her head. "I haven't been to see the Blues since Joe was in junior high school."

Come to think of it, she hadn't been much of anywhere since Joey had left last fall; but that wasn't a news flash she cared to share with Evan Lawrence.

"Well, we'll have to change that." Evan patted his thighs, giving her that lopsided smile that had every youth league hockey mom swooning. "I'll fix you up with seats, Doc. You'll have to come see me play."

"That would be cool," Elise said, and meant it.

"Great." His espresso-brown eyes crinkled happily at the corners, and his natural charm tugged at her like a magnet.

She glanced at his ring finger and saw nothing there. He doubtless had groupies, like a rock star; lots of blondes with big boobs who hung around the ice rink at St. Louis Mills during practices and waited for him after games.

"So you want me to strip down?" he asked, catching her off guard.

"Strip down?" Her chin came up and she dropped his file to her feet. Oh, God, way to act professional, she chastised herself silently.

"I'll get it." Evan hopped down to grab it for her, allowing her a bird's-eye view of broad shoulders and thick ink-dark hair. He straightened up and handed her the chart. "My rash isn't *that* bad, Doc," he joked. "You don't have to be afraid of me taking off my shirt."

It wasn't the rash that unnerved her. Elise set aside his chart so she wouldn't drop it again. Then she crossed her arms protectively, backing up against the cabinets. "I'm just having déjà vu, seeing you again after all these years."

"Well, you haven't changed a bit," he declared. "If anything, you look even prettier."

"Stop it," she said, a hand automatically going to her hair, straightened into a classic soccer mom bob. "Flattery won't get you a discount on your bill."

"Well, crap," he joked, then took a step back and sat down again on the exam table. He stared at her for a minute. "It's crazy, huh? Small world and all that."

Elise looked up into his soft brown gaze and nodded, her pulse racing faster than it had in a long while. "Yes, a very small world," she agreed, thinking sometimes that wasn't such a bad thing. She cleared her throat. "Okay, *now* you can take off your sweatshirt."

"Here goes nothing," he said, and pulled the hoodie over his head, followed by the T-shirt underneath it.

Elise took in an eyeful of Evan: sculpted chest, well-defined pecs, and shoulders ropy with muscle. If he noticed that she'd stopped breathing for a full ten seconds, he didn't show it. Maybe he was used to being looked at, and, well, she *was* a doctor.

Tossing the bundle to an empty chair, he sat upright and looked at her expectantly. "Should I lie down or anything?"

Yes, tell him to lie down! Carla's voice popped into her head. *But ask him to take his pants off first.*

"No, you're fine," Elise said, and turned to the sink to wash her hands. Then she moved around the exam table to a swing-armed lamp and shifted the neck, switching on the light so it clearly illuminated the red spots on his bare back. Before she touched him, she pulled a pair of latex gloves from her pocket and rolled them on. "Do you wear a clean shirt underneath your pads every time?"

"Yeah, Under Armour."

"Do you wash with unscented detergent?"

"I haven't been." He shook his head and looked at her over his shoulder. "Should I?"

"Try it," she told him as she ran a hand gently over his upper back, deciding it wasn't anything worse than low grade miliaria. "I'll give you samples of a prescription 2.5 percent hydrocortisone cream. Rub it in a couple times a day after you shower, okay? Don't leave your gear on for any longer than you have to. Wash up right away. And make sure you're spraying your pads with an alcohol solution to kill the bacteria."

His thick eyebrows arched. "You mean Lysol doesn't do the trick?"

"Lysol?" She laughed as she peeled off her gloves and swung the light away from him. "Please, tell me that's not what you've been doing all these years, or it's a wonder you've got any skin left at all."

"Hey, it keeps the hockey bag from stinking up," he told her with a grin, and folded his arms across his chest, causing his biceps to bulge.

"Go ahead and put your shirt back on, and I'll get you the samples." She tossed away her gloves and opened the cabinet to pull out half a dozen small tubes of the HC ointment. "Let me know if you're still having problems in a week or so, okay? If the rash hasn't cleared up by then, I should see you again."

"Maybe I'll make another appointment, just in case."

"Okay."

"Okay," he agreed, and that boyish grin slipped across his mouth again.

Tufts of dark brown hair stood up from his head, charged by the static from slipping his T-shirt and hoodie back on. She had an itch to go over and smooth it down, only thank God her hands were full of tiny tubes of hydrocortisone cream. She offered him the freebies. "Give these a shot."

"Thanks, Doc." Evan's fingers touched hers as he took the tubes from her, and Elise felt a frisson of excitement rush up her arms.

Aha! Carla's voice trilled. *Cougar bait!*

Elise stepped away, scooped up his chart and headed toward the door. "It was really nice seeing you, Evan," she said as she reached for the handle and pulled.

"It was great seeing you, too."

She refrained from glancing over her shoulder and got out of there as fast as she could, shutting the door behind her. She leaned against it for a moment, feeling flushed and unsettled, wondering what the heck was wrong with her. Wasn't she too young still for hot flashes and too old to be feeling like a horny teenager?

"Dr. Randolph, are you okay?" her ponytailed assistant asked, appearing from out of nowhere. "You look kind of, I don't know, agitated."

"I'm fine," she assured her, exhaling a held breath and looking around her, forgetting where she was supposed to be going.

"Carl Morrison," Jenny reminded her, "the chest mole biopsy. Exam Room One."

"Of course, thanks," Elise said, squashing thoughts of Coach Evan from her mind as she walked down the hallway to the first closed door and plucked the file from the plastic bin. As soon as she flipped it open and glimpsed the digital photo of the pencil-eraser-sized mole below eighty-year-old Mr. Morrison's left nipple, her pulse rapidly slowed down and all her flustered feelings evaporated.

Calmly, she rapped on the exam room door and said, "Hello, Mr. Morrison, you ready for me?" She waited for his feeble, "Yes, Doctor," before she put a pleasant smile on her face and went inside.

KAT

Kat Maguire's Facts of Life
for Women over Forty:

The older you get, the harder it is to find a single man your age who isn't either: (a) married or gay; (b) divorced with insurmountable baggage; or (c) looking for a girl half his age.

Chapter Seven

BRIO was hopping by the time Kat arrived promptly at seven. The piped-in music and hum of voices enveloped her as she stepped through the second set of double doors into the foyer. She must've been the first of the three to make it there, as she didn't see any sign of Carla or Elise crowding the benches near the hostess station.

Still, she took a shot and walked up to the chic blonde standing behind the podium and asked, "By any chance, has Dr. Elise Randolph arrived yet, or Carla Moss? We're meeting for—"

Drinks and dinner, she left unsaid as the woman perked up instantly at the mention of Carla's name and quickly snatched up several menus.

"Ah, so you're one of Ms. Moss's friends. She phoned earlier, and I've got her favorite table reserved."

"I didn't think you took reservations," Kat remarked, since she'd called and tried to make one.

"Oh, no, we don't usually," the woman said, her plucked brows narrowing as she leaned toward Kat and whispered confidentially, "but for Ms. Moss, we make an exception."

"I see." Kat struggled to keep from laughing, feigning a cough into her hand.

It was like high school all over again, with Carla always getting the best seat at the best table in the cafeteria, the cutest guy on the football team, and the coolest car when she turned sixteen.

"Please, follow me," the hostess said, efficiently scooping up menus and trotting away from her station, high heels click-clacking across the floor.

Kat fell in step behind her, ending up at an empty table set just across from the bar area. It was, in fact, the only empty table in sight. The dinner crowd already packed the place, and the bar was filling up as well, with most patrons shoulder-to-shoulder.

Kat settled into a chair and looked around. She hadn't been at Brio in a while, not since her last trip home. The place appeared as she remembered, one of the nicer chains in town, with its crisp white tablecloths, square pillars and arches, marble counters, potted palms, and Tuscan-inspired plaster walls. The seated clientele had that well-to-do, well-coiffed, well-dressed vibe of the Frontenac and Town & Country "ladies who lunch."

However, when Kat swiveled around to take in the scene at the lengthy bar, she noticed plenty of men, mostly clean-shaven guys in their twenties and thirties wearing button-down shirts with their ties loosened at the collar, their jackets tossed casually over the back of their bar chairs. They were put-together so well she might've guessed they were gay if they hadn't been so obviously flirting with the fashionable yet mature-looking women perched between them on the bar chairs.

Ah-ha. So Brio was a Cougar watering hole, she realized. No wonder this was Carla's favorite table. No doubt Channel 3's top anchorwoman came here for an occasional drink and inspection of the local eye candy, and Kat couldn't blame her. The view was pretty nice.

As if reading her thoughts, a guy with short blond hair in a brown crew-neck sweater looked over his shoulder, meeting her eyes. He smiled broadly and tipped his green Peroni bottle in her direction.

Talk about stinking cute.

Kat realized she was staring, and blushed, quickly glancing down to unbutton her coat, her heart skipping a few beats. God, she was so out of it after three years with Roger. Was flirting like riding a bike? Would she remember how to do it? When she looked up again, the blond guy had his back to her as he sipped his beer and conversed with a dark-haired man on his other side.

She sighed and shucked her tailored coat. Her hair crackled with static as she unwound the scarf from her neck. Tucking the thick strands of brown behind her ears, she drummed her fingers on the table for a minute before she tugged up the cuff of her cashmere sweater to check her watch: it was five past seven.

"Would you care for a drink?" the waiter in crisp white shirt and black trousers asked, appearing out of nowhere.

"A margarita, please, no salt and lots of ice," Kat said.

"You've got it." He smiled pleasantly and returned with her drink in two minutes flat.

Kat plucked out the skinny red straw and took a long, satisfying sip. She felt the tequila warm her throat down to her toes, and caught an ice cube in her teeth before she set the glass down. She tried to study the menu but her gaze kept flitting toward the doors, expecting Carla and Elise to walk in at any moment. She felt oddly nervous, and her pulse raced like a girl afraid of being stood up on a first date. Just to be safe, she did a quick scan of messages on her BlackBerry, but didn't see anything from either Carla or Lisie.

They'll show, she told herself, knowing her two oldest friends wouldn't let her down. They weren't the ones who'd fled St. Louis in the first place, ditching everything to run off to the bright lights, big city; suffering from some crazy "if you can make it there, you'll make it anywhere" syndrome.

Well, she was back now, wasn't she? And she had no plans to leave.

A sudden burst of high-pitched laughter caught her attention as the front doors flew open, ushering in a gust of winter wind and a gaggle of chattering women. For a moment Kat thought they were all part of the same group, until a curvy blonde separated herself from the mix and paused to look around, her fingers tentatively working the buttons on her hooded coat.

"Lisie! Over here!" Kat almost knocked her chair over as she stood, and she waved her arms like a stranded sailor flagging down a passing ship.

Elise glanced up and a wide grin broke out across her round face as she spotted Kat. Within seconds the blonde had crossed the slick floor in her pumps, without tripping, and Kat found herself enveloped in her friend's arms.

"Oooh, wow, it's so good to see you!" Elise gushed in her ear as they rocked back and forth, not wanting to let go.

"God, you look great," Kat said as they finally drew apart. "Seriously great."

Elise's wheat-hued hair had been worked into a straight, collar-length bob instead of the loose mop of curls, and tiny creases defined the corners of her wide blue eyes and her mouth, the fine lines undisguised by her very soft, barely there makeup; but otherwise she appeared much the same as she had the day she'd stood with Michael in Graham Chapel exchanging vows. Could that really have been twenty-three whole years ago? It felt like yesterday and a lifetime at once.

"You've hardly changed at all," Kat remarked. She reached out and touched the straightened hair. "Except for the missing Meg Ryan curls."

"I think even Meg Ryan's missing her Meg Ryan curls these days," Lisie said, dimples flashing as she smiled. She caught Kat's hand in her own, squeezing hard. "You're beautiful as ever, Mary Katherine."

"I think only you, Car, and my mom, still call me that."

"Now that's a select group," Lisie replied with a laugh.

"This is just so unbelievably cool." Kat hugged her again for good measure before plopping back into her chair. She waited all of ten seconds as Elise tucked gloves into pockets and draped her coat over her chair before she pounced. "So, how's life? How's the practice? How are Joey and Michael?"

"First things first," Elise said, and pushed at her silverware to lean forearms on the table. "Joey's doing fantastic. He's in his second semester at UT-Austin."

"Did he go through fraternity rush?" Kat asked, wanting to know everything. "Does he have a girlfriend?"

"Yes and yes, Aunt Kat." Elise set her chin in her hands and sighed. "He's a Phi Delt, and he's dating a Kappa named Honey, of all things." She arched dark blond brows. "He's so enamored with her that he hardly comes home anymore. He was here for three days at Christmas and spent the rest with her family in Dallas."

"Well, damn him for growing up," Kat teased.

"It just goes by so fast, doesn't it? It's like I blinked, and all of a sudden I was a middle-aged empty nester." Sadness darkened her pale eyes for a moment, and the dimples disappeared from her cheeks.

Kat reached across the table and touched her hand. "Hey, are you okay?"

"Yeah, I'm fine," Elise said, her front teeth catching on her lip. "I'm so awfully glad you came back, hon. I thought you'd forgotten us here in St. Louis."

"I've been a bad friend, haven't I?" Kat sat back in her chair, dumping her hands in her lap. "I should've made a bigger effort to stay in touch. It's like the last three years with Roger are a blur in my mind."

"We each had to make choices for ourselves, and our paths were all different," Elise replied. "There's no harm in that, not if you end up where you belong and it makes you happy."

Kat looked around her, noting how relaxed people seemed, how open their faces and unguarded their laughter. It felt so different from Manhattan, where it was practically verboten to say hello to a stranger on the street, much less smile at him, and where sometimes she'd felt like a tiny ant racing alongside other ants with only shadows of skyscrapers above her, not open sky.

"I feel rooted again," Kat said, nodding. "Once a Midwesterner, always a Midwesterner," she remarked, and glanced down, fiddling with her knife and spoon, lining them up just so. "It's like I can finally take a deep breath and let it go without being so pressured."

"What about Roger," Elise gently pressed. "You're sure you won't go back to him? Are you certain it's over?"

Kat squirmed in her chair. "Not that I'm psyched about being suddenly single, but it was time to go. Roger and I weren't in the same place. He still had a bunch of oats to sow, and I'm looking for real commitment." She blew out a breath, ruffling her bangs. "Though maybe I'm better off just avoiding relationships for a while."

"Right," Elise said with a thin smile. "I'm glad to hear you're over Roger. I agree about that oat-sowing part. When you brought him back that Christmas, I didn't tell you about this but . . . oh, geez, how to put it?" She winced, biting down on her lip.

"He hit on you?" Kat blurted out the first thing that came to mind, thinking of catching Roger with the college-age cleaning girl and finding him at his desk with his fly open, getting off to live porn on his laptop. And those were just the indiscretions that she knew about.

"He made a pass, yeah." Elise looked surprised that Kat seemed so nonchalant. "This isn't news to you, is it?"

"Not really," Kat murmured with a shake of her head, and a cramping sensation gripped her stomach. "I wish I'd realized sooner that he couldn't be faithful. I would never have moved in with him."

"I should have told you—"

"Hey, don't feel guilty," Kat said quickly, stopping her from going on. "You were trying to protect me. Besides, I had to find out on my own."

"He's young, that's all," Lisie remarked, as if youth excused cheating.

"And very spoiled," Kat added. Roger had always gotten what

he wanted without having to work too hard to get it. When she first met him, at a party in SoHo, he'd had women hanging all over him. Maybe the reason she'd caught his eye was because she completely ignored him. It's too bad he hadn't let her go then instead of pursuing her. Then again, she probably wouldn't be back in St. Louis now if Roger had been the perfect guy: sympathetic and understanding and loyal.

"You'll find someone else, someone better," Elise insisted. "You just haven't met him yet."

"I hope I know him when I see him," Kat murmured, and took another slow sip of her margarita, wishing someone had pointed out sooner what a self-centered egomaniac Roger was beneath his *GQ* appearance. Well, anyone but Megan. If Meg suggested she zig, she instinctively wanted to zag.

"Everything happens for a reason, right?" she mused aloud before she focused on Lisie again. "God, enough about me, okay? I want to hear what's up with you. Well, we covered the Joey part already, but how's Michael? When I saw you both two years ago, he seemed kind of stressed out. I'm sure the plastic surgery biz is insane these days, huh?"

"Hmm, how's Michael," Elise repeated. "Not an easy question to answer these days." Her eyes downcast, she shook out her napkin and smoothed it over her lap. "Maybe I should get a drink first?" she said, and looked around for their waiter. "Or should I hold off until Carla gets here?"

"Please! I didn't wait for her," Kat replied, and held up her half-empty glass. "That girl was never on time for anything."

Elise let out a delicate snort. "What am I saying? You're right. She's chronically late. The only time I ever see her is when she needs some work done, and even then she makes *me* wait."

"Can I add bossy to the list, too?" Kat cracked.

"Oh, Lord." Elise rolled her eyes. "Even when she's not around, I sometimes hear her voice, telling me what to do. It's like we're sixteen again, and she's the ring leader, whispering in my ear, egging me on." She tried to mimic Carla's smooth unflinching tone, "'Don't be so shy, Lisie, go for it!'"

Kat laughed, knowing just what she meant.

"Worse still, she has the gall to look more fabulous than she did in high school, although the way she talks half the time, you'd think she's turned into a raging hag," Lisie said with a snort. "Carla Jean is extremely well preserved."

"Is that thanks to you or to the Botox?" Kat asked, only half teasing, and Elise put a finger to her lips.

"Shhh, we don't talk about such things. We pretend it's magic, like Tinker Bell with her fairy dust," she said, and they both burst into giggles as the waiter appeared from out of nowhere, asking, "Can I get anything else for you ladies before Ms. Moss arrives?"

"Yes, please." Elise gratefully ordered a gin and tonic with extra lime, and then began to study the menu before her with fierce intensity. "I haven't eaten since noon, and I'm starving. Michael's practice isn't the only one that's busier than ever."

"Maybe I should call Carla and see what's keeping her," Kat suggested, and reached for her bag, which was exactly when the front doors to Brio flew open, letting in another gasp of frigid air and sweeping Carla inside along with it.

The hum of conversation seemed to cease for an instant as a different kind of rustle rippled through the restaurant. *"It's Carla Moss!"* Kat heard people saying, their voices rising above the piped-in music, and she watched nearby diners craning their necks to get a look at Carla as the anchorwoman air-kissed her way toward their table.

So Carla still hadn't mastered the art of subtlety, Kat thought with amusement. Back at Ladue High School, she'd sashayed into home room after the bell, clad in the letter jacket of the captain of one varsity team or another, with such an air of entitlement about her that no teacher had ever deigned to give her a tardy slip or even a verbal reprimand. Carla had "it," whatever that meant.

"Can I take your coat, Ms. Moss? Should I fetch you a vodka martini?"

The wait staff followed behind her like goslings behind a fur-clad Mother Goose.

Kat watched the approaching parade and thought with amusement, She couldn't get away with real mink in Manhattan. Not without the risk of getting doused with red paint by animal rights activists.

Carla had rightly inherited her love of luxury. Kat remembered plenty of occasions as children when they'd delved into Genevieve's closet—when Car's very strict mother wasn't home, of course—striking poses before the full-length mirror in designer shoes too big for them, silk Hermès scarves wrapped around their necks, and hats nearly obscuring their faces.

As Carla approached, Kat eyed the black mink more closely. *Is that what I think it is?* She could swear it was a vintage 1960s piece that Car had worn to a Christmas formal back in high school, borrowed from her mother. It made her feel better anyway to think that no new minks had died to keep Carla warm throughout the winter.

"My God, it's true! Kat Maguire is alive and well and living in St. Louis!" Carla exclaimed, and dramatically paused with arms outspread. Her heavier on-air makeup only added to her theatrical appearance. Her green eyes flashed fire, the red in her hair glowed, and her cheekbones seemed carved in stone. "Come here and give Carla Jean some love," she insisted.

"Car, you're such a rock star," Kat said as she came out of her chair and found herself caught up in a mink-soft bear hug. "And, you're gorgeous as ever, I see," she added as they drew apart.

Carla slipped her mink into the waiting arms of a Brio employee, who quickly disappeared, obviously to squirrel it away somewhere safe.

"Why, Mary Katherine, you're as observant as ever, I see," Carla teased, and her glossy lips curved like the Cheshire cat. "Hey there, Lisie," she acknowledged the blonde, who slowly rose from her seat for Carla's air kisses.

"Hey, Car." Elise raised her newly arrived gin and tonic. "It's nice spying you outside the office for a change."

Carla ignored the gentle dig, instead turning her full attention upon Kat. "My my, let me look at you, Kitty-Kat!" She clasped her hands atop the triple strand of pearls that dangled between her breasts and gave Kat a thorough once-over. "What'd you do, stop eating or something? My God, you're positively bony!"

She didn't *feel* especially bony; just plum worn-out. "I like to call it the Get Canned and Break-Up Diet," Kat quipped. "I've been too stressed out to eat."

"Well, we'll have to put some meat on you now that you've returned to the homeland." Carla plucked at the sleeve of Kat's cashmere sweater. "That skeletal look might work in Manhattan, but St. Louis men like their women to have boobs sticking out of their chests, not collarbones. Just ask them." Carla gestured toward the bar area. Not surprisingly, several men shouted, "We love you, Carla!" when they caught her looking, and she blew them exaggerated kisses.

Kat saw the blond guy watching her again, and quickly turned back to Carla.

"Fans of yours?" she asked.

"More like dessert," Carla joked, her mouth curved devilishly. "Too bad I have to go back to work tonight." She slid gracefully into the chair the waiter had pulled out for her. "Sometimes I come here for a drink, just to enjoy the scenery."

"It is very pretty," Kat agreed, daring to glance at Peroni Guy again.

"You should take advantage of that, Kitty-Kat, now that you're footloose and fancy free," Carla suggested.

"No, no, no"—Kat waved her off—"I'm done with dating for the time being. I've decided to pull a Sister Mary Katherine and wear my reconstituted chastity belt for a while until I figure out what I'm doing with the rest of my life."

"So you're going cold turkey," Carla said, the dry edge to her voice unmistakable. "Let me know how that works."

"I'll take two-to-one odds this vow of celibacy doesn't last a week," Elise added to the ribbing. "Still, that's better odds than I'd give Carla, who wouldn't last a day. Even Kat's got more will-power than you when it comes to men."

"Lord, who doesn't?" Carla laughed.

Elise tapped a finger to her chin. "Seriously, Carla Jean, I don't remember you ever being without a boyfriend, not through junior high, high school, or college."

"Only I remember she dated older men. I used to think she had a daddy complex," Kat teased.

"Oh, please." Carla sniffed.

"You're right. She was hooking up with seniors when we were freshmen." Elise cocked her head, as if studying the strange species that was Carla Jean Moss. "When you married Burton, I figured that you just liked them mature."

"But I did, when I was a neophyte," Carla said, wrinkling her slim nose. "However, as I grew wiser, my men got younger."

Elise groaned. "You'll never get married again at this rate."

"Better for my health if I don't," Carla insisted. "Quitting Burton was like giving up cancer sticks. I'll live twice as long without him. Being someone else's ball and chain is definitely a bad habit I don't want to repeat."

"Really, Lisie, everyone doesn't find the love of her life with the first guy she sleeps with," Kat lightly needled, only to see Elise's blue eyes cloud and close off. She looked like she wanted to cry.

Wow, what did I say?

Was there trouble in paradise? Elise never had gotten around to answering her question about Michael. Maybe there was a reason. Before Kat had a chance to ask if everything was okay, the waiter reappeared.

"Ms. Moss, your drink." He handed over her vodka martini—always with two olives—placing it reverently down before Carla. She smiled at him, offering up a sugar-sweet, "Why, thank you, Frankie. Now could you pop on back in about five to take our orders, please?"

With an adoring smile and obedient, "You've got it," he vanished.

Carla shifted her gaze from Elise to Kat. "So, where were we? And by 'we,' I mean the two of you. You were chatting up a storm when I walked in, and I don't want to miss any scoop."

Elise shot Kat a warning look, as in, *If you bring up my remark about Botox, I'll kill you.*

"We weren't gossiping about you," Kat told her, maybe too quickly. She pinched her fingers together then set them a smidge apart, adding, "Okay, maybe this much. I was asking Elise about her family life, and she was telling me how much better off I am without Roger."

"Well, she's right about that. Your little boyfriend actually pinched my ass at your parents' Christmas party two years back," Carla said pointedly.

Kat groaned and dropped her head into her hands.

"Consider yourself fortunate to be rid of him." Carla picked up her martini, socking back a healthy sip. She set the glass down and sighed. "I just wish I could jettison Burton without moving halfway across the country. He's become more of a pain than those injections Lisie shoots into my forehead."

So much for not mentioning Botox, Kat thought, and burst out laughing.

Elise groaned though Carla merely looked perplexed.

"I'm not sure what you think is so funny about that, Kitty-Kat," she murmured, giving Kat a sideways glance as she plucked an olive from her glass, sucked it between her teeth, and chewed.

CARLA

**Carla Moss in her cover feature
for *St. Louis Woman* magazine:**

*If you're new to dating younger men, it's okay to use the
"Don't ask, don't tell" policy. If he asks your age, just smile
and say, "How old do I look?" That'll shut him up, guaranteed, so you'll never have to tell unless you want to.*

Chapter Eight

BEFORE Carla could elaborate on the latest way her ex-husband was torturing her, their waiter resurfaced and began reciting dinner specials. Once they'd all ordered—chopped salad for Kat, the wood-grilled salmon for Elise, and the artichoke and herb-crusted pork chop for Carla, plus another round of drinks—Kat leaned toward Carla. Her freckled cheeks ruddy, and her dark eyes gleaming, she looked fit to pop. It was the same back in high school. Kitty-Kat always wanted to be first to hear any gossip.

"So what's going on with Burton?" she asked. "I'm dying to wallow in someone else's drama for a change."

"Yes, do fill us in on the latest episode of 'As Carla's World Turns.' I'm sure it's *way* more interesting than anything going on in my dull little life," Elise chimed in.

"Why am I flashing back to the three of us gossiping at our lockers? Only then it was all about guys, makeup, clothes, and parties."

Carla shifted her gaze from one to the other, feeling a little choked up as she realized all three of them were truly together again. "Oh, wait, that's still what I want to talk about." She chuckled.

"So, dish the dirt, girl," Kat said, and tapped the table so their silverware rattled. "What evil is Burton Echols up to now?"

"Other than trying to nudge my lovely backside out of my anchor seat, you mean?" Carla asked, and her smile evaporated. The mere memory of her verbal slugfest with her ex made her jaw clench. "He's plotting behind my back to bring me down," she said through gritted teeth.

"You're kidding, right? He's trying to pull a Sandy Chase on you?" Kat made a noise of disbelief. "He's got some nerve."

Elise set down her drink. "Are you sure he's not just yanking your chain again, Car? Remember the last time when your contract was coming up, and he delayed negotiations until zero hour. I thought you were going to blow a gasket."

"Oh, I'm sure this time," Carla said, and her lips puckered, the taste in her mouth extremely bitter. "It's karmic punishment, isn't it? All those years ago, I jumped at the chance to take over poor Sandy's seat the moment Burton dangled it like a carrot, and now it's coming back to haunt me."

"Please, it's not karma," Kat scoffed. "It's called growing old in a youth-obsessed society, and it reeks."

With that, she yanked a piece of bread from the basket and shoved it in her mouth. She talked as she chewed, something for which the Queen Mum would've rapped Carla's knuckles.

"I guess being a forty-something female isn't any more acceptable in St. Louis than in New York," Kat got out before swallowing. "Kind of a shock to the system, isn't it, finding out that you're dispensable?"

"But in your case, it brought you home," Elise reminded her, nearly erasing the annoyed expression on Kat's face. "You wouldn't be here otherwise, right? You'd still be caught up in the rat race, while Car and I muddled along without you."

"Muddle sounds about right," Carla said, only half kidding.

Kat shrugged. "I know there's a silver lining to every cloud and all that, but it's sad thinking how different the world is now from the one we grew up in. My father worked for the same company his whole life, but no one does that anymore."

"Um, yeah, but the world we grew up in didn't have cable TV until we were in high school, either, or the Internet and cell phones," Car reminded her.

"I could live without all of those," Elise said with a decisive nod. "No wait," she reconsidered, holding up a finger. "Except for my CrackBerry. I don't think I could live without that."

"Everyone's on CrackBerry these days." Carla sighed. "We're all so hooked up that we don't think we have to deal with each other face-to-face anymore."

"Makes it easier to trade us in for newer models because we're just a cell number or an e-mail account, not real people," Kat added with a wince. "I wish I could describe how surreal it was, being told I could leave D&M with their lovely exit package and save face, or accept a position I'd worked my way out of fifteen years before. It was like a slap in the face."

"Rotten buggers," Carla agreed, knowing all too well how she felt. "That's like asking Marie Antoinette if she'd prefer the guillotine or eating cake in a dungeon suite with rats as companions for the rest of her life." She leaned over to touch Kat on the shoulder. "I'm sorry your boss treated you so shabbily, sweetie. It's not exactly comforting knowing we're both getting screwed."

"Can't you sue for age discrimination?" Elise asked, shifting her gaze from Carla to Kat. "If that's what it is, it only seems right."

Kat sighed, plucking at another slice of bread until she'd disemboweled it. "They didn't exactly put a gun to my head, so the decision was mine."

"Still, it's firing you without firing you." Lisie made a face. "It sounds underhanded."

"I have contacts here in town, if you're looking to get back in the ad game," Carla offered, but Kat shook her head, summoning up a halfhearted smile.

"I've been asking myself what I would do if I could do anything, and I think I'd like to do something else." Kat looked up almost shyly. "You know how I loved volunteering at the Art Museum during high school, and I took drawing classes during college, although I was never very good." Her voice got more confident as she talked. "I spent almost two years at my friend Rosalie Moore's gallery in Tribeca before I started working at D&M." Kat gulped in a breath before getting to the point. "Okay, I'm considering working at a gallery for a while until I can open my own someday."

"Oh, Kat, that sounds wonderful!" Elise visibly brightened. "I remember how much you loved to sketch when we were kids. And you could whip us at Masterpiece. Heck, you could peg a Jackson Pollock back when the rest of us just thought the painting looked like monkey scat."

"I'm very friendly with several gallery owners in Clayton and Ladue," Carla said, wanting to help Kat in any way she could. "If you'd like me to give them a call and set up appointments, I'd be more than happy to do it."

"Thanks, Car." Kat grinned, and it was like the sun coming out from behind a cloud. "I might very well take you up on that. I'd like to find a place to live first, and I figure I've got a lot of options since square footage here is so much cheaper than Manhattan."

Carla tapped her chin. "Hmm, I believe you could buy a town house in most any of the 'burbs around here for less than you'd pay for a closet on that little island you've called home these past twenty years."

"You're right." Kat laughed, and Carla's insides warmed at the sound.

"Hell, I might even be joining you on the job hunt soon"— Carla sniffed—"if Burton gets his way. Apparently, his pet project, the one he's propelling toward my anchor spot, is a fledgling reporter named Amber Sue. Randy informed me they're already exchanging bodily fluids."

"Ugh," Lisie murmured, and began to twist a strand of blond around her finger, as she'd done so often when they were kids.

"The girl did traffic reports on the sunrise show until Burtie started humping her," Carla went on. "All of a sudden, he's got her doing special assignments for the evening newscasts. I know his M.O. It's just a matter of time before she's in my chair."

She left out the part where Burton delivered the infamous line about *You're here as long as you want to be,* which was as good as a kiss of death. Instead, she told them, "Did I mention she has a voice like a phone sex operator, and she's got hooters the size of Nebraska? I wonder if Michael did them, Lisie."

"He did yours, didn't he?" Kat cracked, reminding them all that, yes, Elise's husband had seen Carla's boobs and even manhandled them (or was that doc-handled?).

Lisie blushed but said nothing.

Carla just kept talking. "Burton gave me the spiel about what a fabulous news reader she was, as natural as I was when he plucked me out of the Kansas cornfields," she said dryly. "He swore up and down that any changes he's making to showcase his newest bimbo won't affect me at all, but I don't buy it. He nudged out Sandy weeks after she hit the big four-oh, and I'm five years past that already."

"Burton sounds like Hugh Hefner with his teenage girl-friends," Elise said, and her cupid bow mouth pressed into a tight line. "The older and grayer he gets, the more nineteen-year-old twins he pretends to bag."

"I don't care if this Amber Sue looks like a goddess, she'll never replace you. Never," Kat insisted, hand over her heart. "The people of St. Louis will revolt."

"They didn't revolt when Sandy left the air," Carla reminded them, "and she was as beloved as the Budweiser Clydesdales."

"Which might be why she started shilling for the brewery," Lisie replied, nodding. "She was their public affairs person for a while, and she was practically in every ad they ran. It was sort of like she'd never left the air until she retired for real." Elise squished up her face as if trying to remember something. "I believe she lives in Grafton, up on a bluff above the marina, and she's taken up painting bald eagles, or so I've heard."

"Speaking of bald, what's going on with your co-anchor?" Kat asked Carla head-on.

Carla squinted. "What about him?"

"Jesus, Car, Don Davidson must be close to sixty, and no one's shoving his ass out the door, are they?" Kat asked.

"That's true," Carla agreed, thinking of her weeknight co-anchor who was fifty-two but had the wrinkled puss of a life-long chain smoker. If she had aged anywhere near as badly, she would've been stuck long ago doing farm reports at 5:00 A.M., until her contract was up and her career was dead and buried.

"Burton can't just dump you out on the street, can he?" Elise inquired. "I mean, he won't refuse to offer you a new contract and toss you out like a used-up Dixie Cup?"

Used-up Dixie Cup?

Good Lord.

Carla shook her head. "If he knows what's good for him, he'll do it gently, in stages," she replied, hoping Burton couldn't be so blinded by Amber Sue that he didn't realize her own popularity was as high as it had ever been.

But then, why wasn't he cooperating with her attorneys? They'd been putting some pressure on Burton to get at least a two-year deal negotiated, although the bastard hadn't yet agreed on anything and time was running out.

"You're right, I haven't a clue what's going to happen," she said, exhaling softly, suddenly devoid of appetite.

"But you're an icon in this city." Kat stabbed the air with the knife she was using to butter bread. "What in the world is he thinking?"

"With his penis, I'm afraid." Carla began twisting her napkin in her lap.

"That sucks," Elise said, commiserating.

"I just have to hang in there, keep doing the best job I can until Burton sees the light." Carla realized her hands were shaking and laced her fingers together to still them. The idea that she might lose her job drove her crazy. It was more than just work to her. Hell, it *defined* her.

"Screw Burton," Kat said, shaking her head. "I knew he was no good when he made you keep that ancient 'honor and obey' line in your marriage vows, and he hasn't changed a lick."

"Well, you know how well that stuck." Carla smiled thinly, and Kat kept a straight face for about two seconds before she started laughing.

Elise watched the two of them and shook her head.

"How about we switch topics," Car suggested, and turned her attention to Elise. "Dear Lisie, I believe it's your turn to tell all."

"About what?" A pale hand shot up to twist a blond strand around a finger.

"For one, how's your very talented husband?" Carla asked. "I used to run into the two of you at charity events now and then, but it's been quite a while."

"Yes, how's Michael?" Kat echoed. "You never got around to telling me what's going on with him. Is his practice still growing by leaps and bounds?"

"Michael's so busy nipping and tucking that we're practically strangers," Elise offered, sounding less than thrilled. "He's got consultations till late again tonight, which is why I'm ecstatic at being here with the two of you. It seems like he's never home these days, and the house is so empty without Joe around." She pouted. "Boy, do I miss my kid."

"Well, it's no wonder Michael's working 'round the clock. So many faces to lift, so little time, eh?" Carla said, but her internal radar began to blare like a tornado siren. Could it be that Michael and Elise's picture-perfect marriage was hanging a little crooked? Not that it surprised her. It seemed, in her experience, that dual career couples who were both wildly successful at their jobs were doomed to fail at love.

"Michael's crazy to let you out of his sight so often, Lisie," Kat remarked, and shook her margarita glass, empty except for ice. "He should be insane with worry that some hot young thing's gonna steal you away."

Elise squirmed, like she was sitting on thumbtacks. "The closest I get to meeting any hot young things are high school jocks who show up in my office with sports rashes and faces full of acne." She attempted a smile but it flitted across her lips and didn't stay. "Besides," she added more quietly, "it's not Michael who's doing the worrying."

Carla glanced at Kat, who mouthed, *Uh-oh.*

Keeping her voice low, Kat leaned over the table to ask, "What's going on, Lisie? You think Michael's stepping out on you?"

"Do we really need to discuss the state of my marriage now? It's our first time together in forever, so let's not spoil it," Elise begged, and her eyes got all misty.

"Sweetie," Carla said softly, "are you all right?"

Elise took her napkin from her lap and dabbed at damp lashes. "I'll be fine, I promise. Michael and I aren't fighting or anything. I didn't even notice until Joey was gone how much time we spend apart." She forced a tentative smile on her lips. "I'm sure it's nothing that most married couples don't face after twenty years together, especially when their schedules are as busy as ours. We'll figure it out."

"Let him know how you feel," Kat suggested, concern etching commas into the corners of her mouth. "You two used to be able to talk about anything."

Carla remembered pushing the pair together during their junior year in high school when Lisie kept whispering about the quiet boy in her science and math classes. Brilliant Michael had been afraid of sports and deathly afraid of girls, and Carla had nudged Elise into asking him to a Sadie Hawkins dance.

"You were two peas in a pod," she remarked, thinking back, "both studious and smart and so pretty to look at."

"Then we had Joe, and for the last eighteen years all we ever talked about was him, or maybe it was me doing all the talking and Michael just listening," Elise said, and her fingers reached for the infinity circle dangling from her neck, like it was some kind of talisman. "Right now, he's been spending more time with his surgical partner than he spends with me."

"Could he cut back on his schedule?" Carla asked gently. "Can't all those saggy breasts and imperfect noses do without him for a week so you can take a vacation?"

"A vacation?" Elise let out a sharp laugh. "Ha, like that'll ever happen in this century. I can't seem to make Michael come home for dinner anymore. I doubt I can get him to fly to some tropical island."

"Just be sure to find a little time now and then to, you know," Kat said, only to elicit a strained face from Elise in response.

Carla balked. "You are having sex, aren't you?" she asked with far less tact. Why else would Elise constantly be giving sound bites to the *Post-Dispatch* and *Alive* magazine about getting nookie as a way to keep skin youthful if she wasn't getting any herself?

"It's, um, been a while." Elise shrugged, glancing down at her lap.

A while? Carla mouthed to Kat, who gave her a warning look.

Now *this* was news. She had never seen Elise so off-kilter. The woman defined calm and collected. If Elise had a bad day, she rarely showed it. She was a modern-day Donna Reed, living the perfect life, raising the perfect children, married to her high school sweetheart. Though it hardly sounded like an idyllic marriage if Elise wasn't getting laid. Hell, she personally viewed regular sex as a God-given right. What the eff was wrong with Michael?

"Can we change the subject, please," Elise said plaintively, her blue eyes begging; her teeth gnawed her bottom lip.

"All right, the subject is tabled," Car assured her, and reached over to pat her arm. "But always know that we're here if you need us, right, Kat?"

"Right," Kat said, tucking dark hair over her shoulders, "because I'm not going anywhere for the next forty-five years of my life, once I actually find a place to live, that is."

"Thank God for that." Elise relaxed, nodding gratefully at them. "I do love you both."

"Ditto," Kat remarked, looking a little weepy herself.

"Let's have a toast then, shall we?" Carla picked up her martini and waited until Kat and Elise both had their drinks in hand before she offered, "To the three of us and to our friendship, which has survived men and careers and God knows how much other crap. Here's to our enduring sisterhood. May it bind us together more tightly than the Lycra in my Spanx underpants."

"I'll drink to that!" Kat laughed.

"Cheers!" Elise chimed in, the spark returned to her eyes.

They touched the rims of their glasses, eyes meeting eyes as they each took a sip, and Carla wished she didn't have to go back to work that night to face Burton again. She wished she could stay here with her two best friends, catching up and leaving the rest of the world behind for a while. It had been so long since she felt like anyone was there to watch her back.

"Ladies, your dinners." The waiter appeared with a round

tray. Efficaciously, he began dispensing hot plates in front of each woman.

"Yum," Kat said, picking up knife and fork and digging into her salad.

Ravenous, Carla attacked her pork chops, though she noticed that Elise seemed too preoccupied to do more than pick at the piece of pink salmon on her plate.

Chapter Nine

MUCH as hanging out with Kat and Elise had warmed the cockles of Carla's heart—whatever the hell cockles were—she couldn't stick around Brio for long. She had the ten o'clock news to co-anchor and couldn't afford to get caught in traffic on the way back downtown. Once she'd slipped behind the wheel of her Lexus sedan and shot east on Interstate 64/40, she made good time, enough to floss her dinner from her teeth and touch up her face before getting miked.

With minutes to spare, Carla settled behind the anchor desk, a giant panorama of the St. Louis city skyline behind her. Only Don Davidson's seat beside her remained empty, and they were set to go live in mere seconds.

"Where's Don? Has anyone seen Don?" she kept asking, though no one on the set gave her an answer until she heard Burton in her ear, talking to her from the control room.

"Uh, Don's got a touch of food poisoning," he said, sounding as cool as a cucumber. "But I've got it covered, Car, so don't panic. Help is on the way."

A gray-haired production assistant in a Channel 3 sweatshirt and headset scrambled over. "Sorry, Ms. Moss, but your pearls are rubbing against the mike," she said, and proceeded to fiddle with the tiny black clip on Carla's lapel, which kept her from seeing more than a shadow beside her as someone took Don's seat.

"Thirty seconds," a voice called out, and Carla thought her head would explode until the sound lady stopped fiddling with her lapel mike and muttered, "All set," before scurrying away.

" . . . five, four, three, two, one, you're rolling, Carla," she heard in her ear, and she plastered on her best TV smile. She gazed dead-on at the glowing red light above the camera angled in front of her. Once Burton said, "Go," into her earpiece, she smoothly began to read from the rolling teleprompter.

"Good evening, St. Louis. This is Channel 3 'News at Ten.' Our top story involves the shooting of a man in North County after a wild police chase that resulted in a host of fender benders and a car fire." She paused as she got to the part of the script meant for Don and inclined her head right.

"Our other top story involves a student teacher who became romantically involved with one of her charges," said a throaty voice, clearly feminine, that was as far from Don Davidson's as Carla could imagine.

Carla's heart nearly stopped at the sight of the bright and shiny girl perched in her co-anchor's chair, looking like she owned it.

Well, if it isn't Amber Sue Double D! Carla's brain screamed. Damn you to hell, Burton!

" . . . and we'll have a sneak preview of our own Carla Moss's interview with the vice president. She was the only local reporter allowed to speak with him on his trip to St. Louis. Isn't that right, Carla? *Carla*?"

Carla blinked and snapped back into action. The smile that slid from her lips for an instant quickly eased back in place. "That's correct, Amber Sue. I *was* the only anchor in town allowed access to the vice president, and we had an amazingly in-depth conversation. But more on that after the break."

As soon as they'd gone into a commercial, Burton was yelling in her ear, "What the fuck was that, Car? You looked like a goddamned deer in the headlights!"

Why, you dirty, rotten, back-stabbing bastard, she wanted to scream, but she didn't. Despite what he'd told her this morning, Burtie was pushing his bimbo up the food chain faster than even she had imagined.

"You're looking pale, sweetheart. If you're not up to this, we can let Amber fly solo," Burton threatened, and it took all Carla's might to sit still.

What was he doing in the control room anyhow? Playing Professor Higgins to Amber's Eliza? Was he that afraid his latest creation would fuck up on-air if he didn't monitor her every move? She would have dearly loved to take him up on his advice, duck out of the desk, and let Air Bimbo crash and burn.

But instead of yanking the receiver from her ear and walking off the set, she decided to show Burton what a pro she was. Below the dark wood of the anchor desk, she curled her fingers to fists and inhaled slow, deep breaths. Above the waist, she smiled as if she didn't have a care in the world.

" . . . three, two, one, you're on, Carla," a voice counted down in her ear.

Carla smoothly read off the teleprompter, "We're back with a heartwarming story about the newest zoo baby," like it was any other broadcast. Somehow, she managed to keep her anger in check throughout the broadcast until Dave did the weather forecast, Randy had reported on the Blues latest road trip, and Amber Sue's graveled voice had breezed through a fluff piece about ice sculptures in Forest Park.

Right on cue, Carla closed with her signature line, "Good night, St. Louis, and good news."

The moment the red light on the camera went off, she stood. She tried to work the microphone from her lapel but her hands shook so much she couldn't get the damned thing off.

"It was a pleasure sitting beside you tonight, Ms. Moss. I learned so many things that they never teach in J-School," Amber Sue said, and Carla couldn't tell whether she was being sarcastic or sincere. "It's going to be hard filling your shoes. You're like an historical monument around here."

Did she just say I'm an historical monument?

"Don't worry, darling," Carla replied slowly, taking in the girl's kewpie-doll face and overplumped lips, wondering how much of her was real and how much was fake. "Trust me. I'm not going anywhere anytime soon, no matter what you've heard. Besides, you've got a lot still to learn before you're wearing my Manolos."

Amber Sue's chin jerked up, but her unlined face appeared nonplussed. "I know how you must feel, wanting the world to stand still so you can stay on top, even though everything's changing around you. Don't worry about me," she said in that smoky voice, "I'll be around for a long time."

"And you should use that time wisely," Carla advised as her mind darted back to the past, to a similar night over a dozen years before. She remembered Sandy Chase's expression when Sandy had finished her last broadcast and she approached her afterward, gushing sincerely, "I'm so honored, Ms. Chase, to be taking your seat." And Sandy had looked at her as if she had two heads, replying, "Dear girl, you may be sitting in my chair from now on, but you're hardly my replacement. And God help you if you actually believe you've earned it."

What comes around goes around, she heard a tiny voice in her head, mocking.

"Ms. Moss?" The gray-haired sound tech stepped up beside her. "Let me help you get that mike off."

"It's okay, I'll do it," Carla said, and waved her away.

Randy handed over his mike and leaned in from her left, whispering, "Babe, are you okay? You look fit to kill. You want me to come over tonight and give you a body massage?"

He smelled deliciously of Hugo Boss, and he looked so pretty in his custom-made suit and paisley tie that normally she would have invited him over without a second thought.

"Not tonight," she told him. She wasn't in the mood.

In fact, she was seriously trembling as she finally got the damned microphone unclipped and the pack off her waist. She dropped them on the anchor desk and looked up, spotting Burton in his shiny silk suit, sauntering over to Amber Sue.

"You were fantastic," he told his new best girl, and Amber Sue beamed like she'd won a Pulitzer.

Much as Carla hated to bust up their happy reunion—okay, truly, it was her pleasure—she had a bone to pick with her ex and she wanted to pick it now.

"Burton! Might I have a minute of your time?" she said so loudly that everyone on the sound stage stopped what they were doing and turned to stare at her.

"Aw, no, babe, *don't*." Randy clamped his bear paw of a hand on her shoulder. "Let's get out of here, okay?"

But Carla shook him off and stomped over a phalanx of cables to plant herself three feet from her ex-husband and his latest creation.

"Save it for tomorrow," Burton said before she'd had the chance to get a word out. His jowls drawn into a scowl, he added, "If you know what's good for you, sweetheart, you'll go home and get some rest. You looked like crap tonight."

Though he kept his voice low, Amber Sue stood too close not to have heard every word. To her credit, she didn't openly gloat. Instead, she said, "C'mon, Burton, let's go home," and tugged at his arm.

"That's a brilliant idea." He set his beady eyes on Carla and grunted, "I'll see *you* later."

Then he turned his back to her and started to leave.

Carla swallowed hard. Heat emanated from her every pore as she silently seethed. She opened her mouth to hurl all sorts of vicious words his way when she felt Randy's firm hand on her shoulder.

"Please, don't say anything you'll regret, promise me?"

But Carla hardly heard him. "Look at them," she murmured, shuddering as she watched Burton depart with the blonde who was half his age. She felt like she'd just been squashed beneath his heel like a bug, and she wanted to chase after him, knock him to the ground, and pummel him until he cried uncle.

"Let him go, Car," Randy said again, giving her a little shake, as if he knew she wasn't listening.

"He's setting me up for a fall, Randy." She moved to face him, her hands clenched into fists, and still she kept shaking. "You can see that, can't you?"

"Forget Echols," the young sportscaster leaned down to whisper in her ear. "You're worth a million of him, babe, and the station's not going to let him throw you under the bus just because he's general manager. He might think he's God, but Burton still has to answer to Graham Howell, and he knows it. So he's using Amber to piss you off, figuring you'll throw a hissy fit and walk, but don't let him get his way, okay?"

"Well, if you put it *that* way," she told him, and cracked a smile. Randy was no dumb jock. She hoped he was right and Burton was just trying to bait her. Only, Randy didn't know her early history with the station's owner. Graham Howell had never been her biggest cheerleader. He might even feel fewer warm fuzzies toward her than Burton.

"How about we get out of here?" he suggested.

"Is that offer for a massage still open?" she asked.

"Hell, yes," he said, and set her hand in the crook of his arm, leading her across the cables and through the winding cubbies of the newsroom, out into the lobby and down the elevator to the garage.

He followed her home in his Range Rover, and Carla made her way to Highway 40. The radio off, she drove in silence, her mind replaying what had gone on this evening, listening to Kat talk about being shoved out the door by D&M, seeing the unknowing in Lisie's eyes as she revealed that her marriage stood on shaky ground at best, and having Amber Sue Nobody call her an "historic monument" to her face.

Randy was right. Burton didn't just believe he was God, he

was firmly convinced; and he was playing her and Amber Sue both, pitting them one against the other just as he'd done with her and Sandy Chase all those years ago. But if there was one thing she was sure of, she was no Sandy Chase, and she wasn't about to give up her career at KMOK without a fight.

There had to be a way to beat Burton at his own game, and she was going to figure out how if it killed her.

ELISE

**From a profile on Dr. Elise Randolph
in the *West County Suburban-Journal:***

*Sometimes it's difficult to separate the professional woman
from the woman. But I try hard not to forget that my private life is every bit as important as my practice. I want to
be happily married, not married to my work.*

Chapter Ten

TEN o'clock had come and gone by the time Elise arrived at her home in Chesterfield. She'd stayed with Kat at Brio for longer than she'd intended, drinking coffee and chatting well after Carla dashed off. She'd checked her PDA for messages before she pulled out of the parking lot, but there was nothing from Michael and she wasn't about to call to check on him. She was his wife, she reminded herself, not his mother.

"Home, sweet home," she whispered as she pulled into the driveway and her headlights swept across the two-story façade. She'd once loved this house beyond rhyme or reason. It was the first place she and Michael bought together, and they'd moved in when Joey was an infant. Back then the rooms had echoed with his boisterous giggles and shouts of "Mommy, Mommy!" The air perpetually smelled of Play-Doh and baby powder. Without Joe around, the place felt way too big and way too empty. She had been having thoughts recently about selling it.

As she gazed through the windshield now, the whitewashed brick and black shutters had the sleepy look of closed eyes, with all the blinds drawn. Part of her hoped that Michael was already inside; that he was sitting in the living room, reading a book, and he would glance up as she entered, very glad to see her.

Only the place didn't appear any less dormant than every other weeknight when she rolled into their cul-de-sac after a twenty-minute ride west on the interstate. Before the garage door had rattled all the way open, she knew this evening was no different. The only lights on inside would be those that worked on timers, and no one would be waiting for her.

"Where are you, Michael?" she said aloud, and sighed.

If he was having drinks with Phil and discussing the practice, it was no wonder he'd lost track of time. Phil didn't have a wife to go home to, much less a family, only some kind of little barking dog—a cockapoo, she recalled—who clearly didn't wear a watch.

She slipped her Audi into the garage beside a space marked with an oil smear from Michael's previous Saab. When he traded up this time, he'd gotten a canary yellow convertible, which she had thought was kind of flashy; but at least it wasn't a little red Corvette.

With the press of a button, Elise shut the garage door and listened as it rumbled closed. She turned the dead bolt as she entered through the mud room, hanging up her coat in the dark. Scant moonlight through the windows made the stainless appliances shimmer in the kitchen. The light blinked on their landline, though she didn't pause to check for messages. Everyone who mattered had her cell number. Those who didn't were either strangers or robocallers.

She dropped her keys and handbag on the granite countertop. Then she peeled off her velvet gloves and left them there as well. She thought about making a pot of coffee, but she was out of decaf and didn't want to risk being up half the night.

Besides, her mind still raced with conversation, all the things that had passed between her, Carla, and Kat tonight, so much shared within a few short hours. Now they knew her deep dark secrets, how alone she felt without Joey around and how nervous she was that her marriage was crumbling around her.

Before she'd parted ways with Kat, her friend had asked her point-blank, "Are you okay, Lisie? You want me to follow you home and stay for a while? It's not like anyone's expecting me back at my borrowed condo."

"I'm all right," she'd said, even if it wasn't altogether true.

"Call if you're lonely," Kat had suggested. "I'll probably be up for a while."

"I will," she'd promised, although she knew that she wouldn't.

Instead, she walked over to the cabinet closest to the sink and drew out a brown vial. She shook a single Valium into her palm and turned on the faucet. She didn't bother with a glass of water, just placed the pill on her tongue and let it dissolve a little before sipping from the tap.

Now it would be easier to fall asleep if Michael didn't show up by the time she turned in. Sometimes she'd hear him return halfway into *David Letterman*. If she wasn't too groggy, she would drag herself downstairs and curl up on the sofa, asking him how his day went.

He'd pitch his suit jacket across the nearest chair, roll up his sleeves, and mumble something about a particularly exhausting tummy tuck or rhinoplasty. Then he'd pour himself a snifter of Courvoisier, something Phil had gotten him hooked on, and he'd kiss her on the cheek before disappearing into his paneled den; finally coming to bed long after she headed back upstairs and nodded off.

Ding. Ding.

The grandfather clock chimed at the quarter hour, reminding Elise how late it was and how her tired feet ached. She crossed through the dark first floor of their tastefully decorated Colonial and hesitated in the foyer. Grabbing hold of the balustrade, she toed off her high heels and then clutched them in her left hand. The patterned runner soft beneath her soles, she marched up the steps, her right palm skimming the banister.

She didn't pause until she entered the bedroom and her gaze fell upon the king-sized bed. For an instant she wrinkled her forehead, trying to count how many nights she'd slipped beneath the sheets alone. How sad that she couldn't remember.

What was it that Kat had said? *Everyone doesn't find the love of her life with the first guy she sleeps with.*

She had never been with anyone but Michael, and maybe that was part of the problem. What if all the years while she was juggling her growing dermatology practice and driving Joey to hockey games, or volunteering for the PTO and skipping lunches to attend parent-teacher meetings, Michael had started to look elsewhere for affection? Could he have found someone who pleased him in a way she couldn't? He'd never been comfortable initiating intimacy, usually waiting for her to make the first move. That was something she'd done less and less once she had Joey. Motherhood had filled her life in a way their relationship couldn't; and, until Joey left, she wasn't consciously aware of how long it had been since Michael actually touched her like a lover. More and more, it was a pat on the head or a kiss on the brow, very sweet and very platonic.

An old Diana Ross song floated through her foggy mind. *Baby, baby, where did our love go?* Because that was exactly how it felt these days.

She exhaled, the noise so loud against the quiet. Desperate for companionship, she switched on the television, setting it on Channel 3, only to find the station at a commercial break.

She padded toward the walk-in closet to put away her shoes and toss her dress in the "dry cleaners" pile. The music from a Burger King ad filtered in as she stripped off her slip and stockings, and snatched her flannel nightgown from its hook on the bathroom door.

Wait a sec. She stopped herself and rehung the Lanz of Salzburg gown. She heard Joey's words running through her brain. *Make a play for him, Mom. Surprise him some night.*

Maybe tonight was that night.

She slid open the lingerie drawer in her closet bureau, withdrawing a silky peignoir, which she shrugged over her head. She tugged it down over her breasts and hips, smoothing her hands over the clingy fabric.

What if she gave it the old college try and did her sexy best to get Michael's attention? If she could get him in the mood, maybe they'd both remember what it was they'd been missing.

Pleasantly mellowed by the Valium, she hummed quietly as she pulled her hair back in a clip and washed her face, taking care to remove her makeup. Once she'd patted dry, she slathered on a gooey Aveda moisturizing mask. While it sat for five minutes, she brushed her teeth and tried not to swallow any of the goop as she rinsed and spit. When she wiped the mask off, her skin felt as soft as a baby's butt. Still, she faithfully smoothed on her night creams: one for her eyes, another for her neck and décolleté, and still another for between her eyes and around her mouth.

Squinting at herself in the mirror, she gave a nod of approval, deciding so far, so good. She might inject women like Carla with Botox and fillers, but it didn't mean she was ready for either.

"I feel a burning, yearning, burning inside me," she softly sang as she removed the clip from her head and shook her hair out. The steam from the sink had undone her straight blow-dry, turning the chin-length bob into messy kinks.

She ran her hands through it, wondering if Kat was right about missing her curls. She felt sexier anyway when everything didn't appear so tidy and perfect.

After she smoothed Burt's Bees on her lips, she shut off the bathroom lights and padded toward the bed. Another glance at the clock—ten-fifteen—and still Elise heard no sounds in the house other than the yammer of TV talking heads.

She propped her pillows up against the headboard and drew up the silk sheets and down-filled duvet, fluffing her hair out, anticipating that Michael would straggle in any minute.

" . . . thanks for that closing piece, Amber Sue." Standing next to the bed, she heard Carla's remark as her gaze went to the TV screen. "I don't think I've ever seen an actual interview with a circus elephant before."

Oh, my God, it's Carla's worst nightmare, she thought, and stood in front of the television, stunned.

There was Carla Jean seated beside a very pretty made-up girl with incredible posture and incredible breasts, barely contained within her navy blue sailor jacket with bright brass buttons.

Amber Sue looked all bright-eyed and bushy-tailed and more like Carla's daughter than her equal.

Good Lord, so Burton really did it, she thought, knowing Carla had to be fit to pop despite that chummy smile plastered on her angular face as she uttered, "Good night, St. Louis, and good news."

Poor, poor Car. Elise shook her head and zapped off the TV, thankful she didn't have a buxom babe waiting in the wings to push her out of her practice. Most of her patients wouldn't care that she got older so long as she could still clear up acne, remove moles, and shoot collagen into wrinkles.

As the screen went black, the room turned dark again, and Elise could hear the wind whistle around the house, rattling the windows.

She climbed into bed and plumped the pillows beneath her head, shifting position several times before she settled on her back and closed her eyes. Still her mind raced, flashing with images of patients, diagnoses, and verbal exchanges with her staff—the usual detritus of the day—before it finally turned blank and her pulse eased to a gentler rhythm.

She fell into REM deeply, lids flickering over closed eyes when she sensed a shadow above her. A newly familiar scent tickled her nose: warm and male, clean like Ivory soap. A feather-light touch caressed her cheek, strong fingers gliding across the curve of her jaw, thumb softly brushing the fullness of her lips.

"You're so pretty, Elise," the shadow whispered. "Prettier than I remembered."

Before she could reply, his mouth covered hers and he kissed her so sweetly.

His touch moved down her body slowly, from shoulders to

breasts; slipping inside her negligee so his fingers could tease her nipples. She arched against him as his kisses became deeper, possessing her, and his right hand eased her nightgown up her thigh and settled in between. She gasped and turned her head against the pillow, her heart beating crazily.

Bam, bam! Bam, bam!

The slam of a bough against the siding jerked Elise awake, and her eyes flew open. She came bolt upright and stared into the dark of her bedroom, breathless and dazed. Such a heat pulsed inside her that it took a moment to convince herself that what she'd just felt had not been real but imagined. Reaching out a hand, she patted the space beside her, but no one was there.

It was only a dream, she realized, and slid back beneath the sheets.

The red numbers on the alarm clock glowed against the black: 2:00 A.M. But she didn't wonder where her husband was. She wasn't thinking of Michael at all.

Chapter Eleven

BEEP *beep beep beep!*
The cry of the alarm clock snapped Elise out of sleep so deep that she could hardly find the damned button to smack off. She groaned and rubbed her eyes, peeling crust off her lashes. Groggily, she blinked against the slivers of sun streaming through gaps in the drapes. She looked around her, but Michael was nowhere in sight.

Demoralized, she leaned against the padded headboard, staring at the empty space where he should have been. Had he even slept in the bed at all, or in the guest room, where he sometimes went "so I don't wake you"? For all she knew, he might not have come home.

Damn it. She let out a strangled cry. How much more would she take before she got up the nerve to confront him?

She threw the covers back and stormed from the bed, yanking her sexy negligee over her head as she stomped toward the bathroom. Once she'd freed herself from it, she wadded it into a ball and threw it with all her might.

Thanks for nothing, La Perla!

She stood in her panties, chilled despite the heated tiles on the floor. A frustrated cry escaped her lips at the sight of her lingerie lying rumpled on the floor, a visible symbol of how rejected she felt.

Unable to stand the sight, she walked over and picked it up to shove it in the hamper. She hesitated when she realized Michael's pink shirt from yesterday had been piled atop the wicker lid.

So he did come home, she thought. Only he'd snuck in like a thief, never disturbing her, fleeing before she'd even opened her eyes.

What a coward!

She grabbed up his socks and undershirt, nudging up the lid to toss them in the hamper. Then she picked up his shirt, about to place it in the dry-cleaning pile, when she realized how nasty it smelled.

Drawing the button-down closer, Elise sniffed it. The hint of Michael's Gio cologne lingered, as did other less appetizing smells, like cigarette smoke. Ugh. She wrinkled her nose and took another whiff, detecting a scent that was musky and sweet. It seemed familiar and alien at once. All she knew for sure was that it damned well didn't smell like her.

Consultations my ass!

Where had he really been last night? Had he gone with Phil to a bar or a club? She imagined somewhere with lots of willing women in tight clothes who didn't have stretch marks or breasts with nipples pointing vaguely south.

"You're a liar, Michael," she said, and tossed his clothes into a pile at her feet.

Trembling, she turned to the mirror and hugged her arms closely over her chest.

So what did she do now? Give up? Insist on counseling so they could patch things up? Did she really want to be single again when being married had always felt so cozy and safe?

I don't know, she realized. I honestly don't know.

She thought of Carla and Kat at Brio, discussing their respective rugs being pulled out from under them, and she blinked at her reflection. *Dear God, am I having a mid-life crisis, too?*

Maybe it was catching.

ELISE PUSHED HER first appointments back to nine-thirty, determined to take charge of her life again, starting that morning.

Donning a T-shirt beneath a gray fleece warm-up suit, she tied the laces on her barely worn New Balance sneakers, threw on her coat, and drove several streets over to the area rec center where she used to take "Mommy and Me" classes with Joey when he was a toddler. Then when he'd started preschool, she did Jazzercise with Barb and Kim, two of the neighborhood moms she'd been friendly with. But once Joe was in the first grade, she went back to her practice full-time, and stopped coming altogether.

Barb and Kim had tried to keep in touch, sending e-mails about their book club or a scrapbooking class. Elise had gotten too busy, wrapped up in her work and her son's afterschool schedule, and pretty soon they'd disappeared from her life completely.

When she'd gone through the mail with her coffee and toast, she found a flyer from the rec center with a full winter schedule.

There was a stretching and toning class at eight-thirty, and she decided that was the perfect place to start working on her new self-image. She had to get moving again, had to tone herself up so she had faith in her body again, had to reconnect with the outside world.

About ten other cars had parked in the lot by the time she arrived, five minutes before class. She unzipped her down coat and hung it on the rack in the lobby. When she walked into the gym, she took a quick survey of the several groups of women gathered around the colored mats lined up on the floor.

Most of them looked so young, with pink cheeks and pony-tailed hair. She figured they were mothers with preschoolers. Few seemed old enough to have a boy in his first year of college. Two with gray hair sat side by side on mats, doing vague stretches as they talked.

"Two minutes, ladies," a woman in yoga pants and fitted purple top called from the front of the room as she fiddled with an iPod and speakers.

Elise walked toward the nearest unoccupied mat, which is when a voice called out, "Elise Randolph? Is that you?"

It was one of the gray-haired women. She pulled herself up to her feet, brushed off her hands, and walked over. Her blunt-cut bob framed a strong-boned face with heavy-lidded eyes and thin lips. Grooves dug deep into her cheeks as she smiled, and permanent lines were drawn between her eyes.

"Hello," Elise said, wracking her brain for a name but drawing a blank.

"It's Barb," the woman reminded her. "Barb Holton. We used to take Jazzercise together when our kids were small."

Oh, my God. Elise nearly keeled over. *This* was Barb? But Barb Holton was her own age, and this person standing before her looked sixty, if a day.

"Forgive me," she apologized, trying not to stare. "I should've recognized you but it has been a while. Is Kim here?" she asked, hoping to hell the other gray-haired matron who held a mat for Barb in the middle of the room wasn't the other mom she used to pal around with.

Barb waved a hand. "Naw, Kim moved about five years ago. Her husband got a job in Minneapolis."

"Ah." Elise nodded. She couldn't even remember what Kim's husband's name was or what he did for a living. "I feel so bad about losing touch."

"Well, it is all your fault," Barb said, and smiled tightly. "You got so wrapped up in your patients and all your son's sports and clubs that we didn't ever see you anymore."

"How's your husband, um—"

"Matt," Barb filled in for her. She frowned and leaned nearer. "The bastard left me for some skinny bitch he trained with at HammerBodies. She's probably twenty-five, tops, and she sure as hell hasn't popped out three kids."

"I'm so sorry." Elise felt a pang in her gut and wished she hadn't had two cups of coffee.

"Don't be," the woman said dismissively. "I got the house at least." She smiled again, accentuating the deep grooves in her cheeks. "Even better, he's going to have to pay alimony for the rest of my natural life, and I plan to live to a hundred just to spite him."

"Wow," Elise remarked, staring blankly, wondering if that was how Michael saw her, as an out of shape, wrinkled matron who was no competition for a pretty young thing with a butt so tight you could bounce a quarter off it.

"Ladies! Take your places, please, and let's get started," the instructor called from up front, and clapped sharply several times.

"Gotta scoot, but we'll talk later," Barb promised, and headed back toward the empty mat next to her chum.

Elise heard an intro beat before the music started: a loud dance tune with an oversynthesized female voice that might have been Britney Spears. She didn't stay to figure it out.

Instead, she took off just as the instructor was shouting for everyone to stand with their feet hip-wide and stretch overhead. She grabbed her coat from the hanger in the lobby, pulled it on and zipped as she pushed out the doors into the cold. Why, she wondered as she drove the few blocks home, did hanging out with Car and Kat make her feel young again, and seeing Barb made her feel so unappetizingly old?

When she ducked into her office an hour later, she felt in control. Putting on the white coat always calmed her, no matter what was going on in the rest of her life. Once she'd buttoned it over her wrap dress, she felt like a different person, in charge of her world.

"Good morning, everyone," she greeted the front office with a smile, then went about her daily routine, picking up the chart outside the first exam room and glancing over Jenny's jotted notes about history and symptoms. She knocked before she entered, as she would ten more times in the next two hours.

She skipped out for a minute to visit the ladies' room, only to be confronted by her nurse the minute she slipped back through the private rear door.

"Hang on a minute, Dr. Randolph!" Jenny's ponytail swung back and forth as she held up a hand, stopping her. Then Jenny jogged up to the front desk and returned clutching a white envelope. "This is for you." She waved it like a flag of truce. "We got so busy that I forgot to tell you about the messenger dropping it off."

Not much was ever messengered unless it was urgent lab work. Elise could tell from the lack of a return address that this wasn't anyone's biopsy results.

"Thanks, Jen," she said.

Her scrub-wearing nurse smiled before turning on a heel and sauntering back toward the front desk.

Elise took the envelope into her office. Her name and address had been written on the front in neat block letters. There was nothing overt to reveal what it was or where it came from.

She picked up her letter opener and slit the back. Then she dumped the contents onto her desk. Several colored slips of paper fluttered out, and she turned them right side up. Her eyes went wide when she realized what they were.

"Holy cow," she said.

They were hockey tickets, and not just *any* tickets: prime lower bowl seats behind the home bench at Scottrade Center for a Blues game that evening at seven-thirty.

She blew open the envelope, checking for a note, and found a small yellow Post-it stuck inside. The neatly penned message read:

I think it's high time you saw a Blues game again—Evan

Elise bit her lower lip, thinking of Evan Lawrence, all grown up, taking off his shirt in her office yesterday, and that giddy feeling rushed through her.

Impulsively, she picked up her phone and dialed out, waiting through several interminable rings before being sent straight to voice mail.

"Hey, Kat, it's Lisie," she said, unable to keep the excitement from her voice. "Any chance you'd want to go to a Blues game tonight?"

KAT

**From Kat Maguire's
"Twenty-five Things" on Facebook:**

*I can't cook worth a damn
I won't buy clothes made in China
I'd rather go to the gyno than the dentist
I believe everything happens for a reason*

Chapter Twelve

KAT peeled one eye open and winced as sunlight seeped into her brain.

Ay-yi-yi! She lifted a hand to rub at her face, like that could erase the throbbing ache. *How many margaritas did I drink last night?*

Two with dinner, she clearly recalled, and then another two after at the bar? Okay, okay, she should've gone straight home when Elise had taken off; but Peroni Guy stopped her outside the ladies' room before she'd even buttoned her coat. And was it wrong that she'd found him too cute to resist?

"I'm Cameron," he'd introduced himself, "and I'd love to buy the prettiest woman in the place a drink before she goes."

Her endorphins did a high-five the moment she accepted. Sipping margarita number three, she'd sat beside him at the bar, chatting about everything and nothing in particular; and mostly, she'd snuck looks at him, trying not to drool. He had an all-

American-boy-meets-*GQ* appearance that screamed, "I'm hetero-sexual but my socks match," from his crisp white shirt beneath the long-sleeve chocolate brown sweater to the scuffed-up Cole Haan loafers on his feet. In fact, he met all the vital criteria on her Eternal Hubba-Hubba list:

> *Must smell good and have clean nails*
> *No "Mother" tattoos*
> *No comb-overs*
> *Good teeth*
> *Absolutely no wedding rings*

His pale blue eyes and killer dimples were icing on the cake.

Was it any great surprise that "a drink" had turned into two drinks, not to mention several straight shots of tequila? Not that she was a lightweight with liquor. Roger had turned her on to Patrón early in their relationship. But she hadn't exactly been eating like a horse since her escape from Manhattan. No wonder she'd had trouble getting her coat buttons into the right holes when she finally decided to leave.

"Give me your keys, and I'll drive you home," her new friend had offered when Kat had snagged her quilted Chanel bag from the bar and promptly spilled half its contents on the floor (thank God, no tampons).

"I'm perfectly fine," she'd assured him, although even her ears had heard something more like, "Ahm fer-pectly fine."

"Hey, Cam, everything okay? You want me to call her a cab?" the hostess in black had asked, clearly keeping an eye on him, and Kat couldn't blame her.

"It's cool, Jeannie," Cameron had told her. "I'll come back for my car later."

Kat might not have had all her wits about her, but with the few that remained intact, she figured she'd be safe in Cameron's hands. If the restaurant knew his name, then he was a regular, so he couldn't very well be a serial killer, could he? At least that's how she'd drunkenly rationalized it.

"Drive safe," the hostess had said, and Cameron gave her a quick wave on their way out the doors.

Kat remembered his steady arm around her, guiding her outside into frosty air that burned her lungs and sobered her up a little. He'd settled her onto the soft leather of her Jaguar's passenger seat and made sure she was belted in before he slipped behind the wheel. She told him where she lived, and he drove straight to her building, like he'd been there before. He parked in the condo's reserved spot in the garage and nodded to the security guard as he stepped into the elevator alongside her, going up to the fifteenth floor. Like a Knight in Shining Armor, he unlocked the condo door but didn't enter.

Instead, he placed her keys in her palm and told her, "Go on to bed, pretty lady. I'll call a cab from downstairs."

What the hell kind of hook-up ended before the actual hooking-up part?

When he leaned over to kiss her sweetly on the lips, Kat had caught his shoulders and whispered, "Do I really have to go to bed alone?"

Or as Carla used to say, *Cue my inner slut.*

He'd hardly resisted, as though he'd known all along what would happen. She'd been played by a player.

Kat groaned softly, pushing the heel of her hand against her aching brow, as the bright light of morning made everything crystal clear.

Did he think she was one of those desperate Cougars who placed ads on Craigslist looking for a hot young stud game for a little mature, experienced action?

Ugh!

She hated that stupid "Cougar" label and wished like hell that whoever came up with it would be marinated in beer au jus and dropped in a hungry lion's den as punishment.

She tugged the sheet up beneath her chin and swallowed hard, remembering how aggressive she'd been with Cameron, pulling him through the door. She kissed him hard and had barely let go as they shed coats and clothes and stumbled their way toward the bed. Much fumbling and groping of naked body parts had ensued, though most of the specifics fell into the shadowy abyss of her tequila-pickled brain. She was fairly sure they'd had sex. She lifted the sheet to peer beneath. Yep, she was bare-assed, her first night out of flannel since she'd been back in St. Louis.

Hey, it's okay. I'm of age—and how!—and I'm unattached, she told herself, refusing to feel guilty for indulging in a one-night stand, no matter how skeezy it sounded.

Had Cameron slipped out already? Was he still there?

Kat held her breath and listened, hearing a tiny whistling noise that didn't belong to her. She rolled over as gently as she could and saw the back of his head buried in the feather pillow; the outline of his body beneath the blanket.

She gently came up on an elbow, noticing the way the sunlight that slipped into the room between linen shades made the whiskers on his jaw glow like peach fuzz. His ear was a perfect pink shell, and she recalled how he'd moaned when she ran her tongue along the curves.

Cradle robber, she heard her sister's disapproving voice, and imagined her tight-lipped frown.

Aw, screw it!

With one glance back at Cam, still snoozing like a baby, she quietly slipped out of bed and tiptoed around the trail of discarded sweaters, jeans, socks, and underwear.

She tracked down her purse, retrieved her BlackBerry, and took it with her into the loo, locking herself inside. Pulling on her robe, she sat atop the toilet tank, placing her feet on the lid as she dialed.

One ring, two rings, three . . . ah, thank God, Carla's there!

"This had better be important, Kitty-Kat, because I feel like hell," Carla grumbled in lieu of *Hello.*

Kat gnawed on the inside of her cheek, wishing she'd called Elise instead; except Lisie was a married woman (happily or not), and Carla was sleeping with the hot young sportscaster (this month anyway). "Car, are you all right?"

"I doubled up on my Xanax last night and started snoring on Randy in the middle of a full-body massage," she said, and sighed.

"So Randy's there?"

"He's taking a shower, and I've yet to get out of bed. I feel like death warmed over, only without the warmed over part."

"Did something happen with Burton at the studio?" Kat took a stab in the dark, seeing as how that was all Carla could talk about at dinner.

"I take it you didn't see the ten o'clock news, or you wouldn't be asking that," came her testy reply.

"Sorry I missed it. I was a little, um, preoccupied."

"Well, guess who sat in Don's chair right beside me? And I'll give you a clue: it wasn't Don. It had much larger ta-tas."

Kat gasped. "Not Burton's girlfriend?"

"Oh, yes, Amber Sue Double Ds." Carla sighed again, sounding even more depressed, if that were possible. "Lord, but he's so damned arrogant! I wanted to have it out with him, give him a piece of my mind, but Randy put the kibosh on my histrionics."

"Good for Randy," Kat said, adding, "Burton might've canned you on the spot."

"Oh, honey, I almost quit."

"I don't think you want to do that, Car."

"It would've been worth it, just to stick it to him." She snorted. "You don't know how tempted I was to tell him off. I would've loved having the crew an eyewitness to my suggesting Burtie kiss my ass."

Kat winced. "Wait till you sign your new contract before you do that, okay? I'd hate to see both of us unemployed at the same time. Who'd pay for dinner?"

"You're right, of course, Kit-Kat," Carla sighed. "I need to have a chat with my lawyers today and see why it's taking so damned long to get that bastard to put something tangible on the table. Their office is in Clayton, not far from where you're shacking up, girlfriend. So how about I tend to some business and then we do lunch at Remy's, say, at one?"

Remy's was a cozy little Mediterranean café and wine bar in Clayton. Kat could walk there without too much trouble.

"Sounds like a plan," she told Carla, shifting her feet on the toilet lid. "I'm sorry about Burton being such a jerk, Car, really I am. You deserve better," she said, then wondered if that sounded lame considering how often it had been said to her lately.

"Where are you, Mary Katherine? I'm hearing echoes. You're either in the toilet or the Grand Canyon."

"I'm sort of hiding out," Kat confessed, keeping her voice low—not that her bed buddy was even awake, or could hear through the walls if he were. "I had an interesting postdinner evening as well."

"Let me guess," Carla said. "While I was getting screwed by Burton, you were getting screwed, too. I just hope yours was a hell of a lot more satisfying."

"Carla Jean!" Kat nearly fell off the toilet tank.

"So who was it?"

"Remember Peroni Guy . . . um, the cute blond at the bar?"

"Funny, but I don't recall seeing any priests drinking imported beer at Brio last night, and I clearly recall hearing Sister Mary Katherine take a vow of chastity."

Kat groaned, dropping her head and rolling her brow against the heel of her hand. "Rub it in, why don't you?"

"So I take it the vow didn't stick?" Carla asked.

"Not so much," Kat murmured.

"Please, my darling, there's nothing wrong with rebound sex, even if it's drunken rebound sex. After putting up with a snake like Roger, I'd say you've earned it! So long as it was good. I mean, it *was* good, wasn't it?"

"I guess so." Kat didn't recall having any complaints, although some of last night was still a bit fuzzy.

"And you did play it safe? Because you never know where his junk's been before you, and besides, you're not menopausal yet, right?"

"Um, no, I'm not menopausal, but thank you very much for suggesting it," Kat told her, and pressed a thumb between her eyes. *Good God.*

"Then you could still have a few dusty old eggs just waiting for some supersperm to swim upstream, and wouldn't your mother love that," Carla snickered. "I can see Eileen Maguire praying for a miracle as we speak. That woman wants a grandchild so bad she could kill for it."

"Thanks for the reminder," Kat said flatly. "Although I don't think my mom's going to get that baby from me anytime soon. My dusty old eggs and I aren't stupid."

They had used a condom last night, hadn't they?

Kat gazed down at the wastebasket beside the toilet, hardly willing to poke around to find it. She couldn't imagine she was so drunk she wouldn't have made sure Cameron wore one. No matter, she was damned sure *he* wasn't that drunk.

"Of course you're not stupid, Kitty-Kat," Carla replied sweetly before squawking, "so quit with the freaking out, would you? It's not like you have to marry the guy. Didn't we have this chat back in college?"

"He's still here," Kat whispered, as if Cameron could hear her from behind the closed door, through his snores. "I thought he might be gone, which would've been easier."

"Well, wake him up, and shove him out," Car instructed matter-of-factly. "Men have done that to women for centuries. Just because we're playing the same game as the boys now doesn't mean the rules have shifted."

"But that's rude—"

"Life is rude, Mary Katherine, so get over it!"

Ouch. Kat winced, wishing now that she'd phoned Elise instead. Lisie never yelled at her.

"Quit acting like a repressed Catholic schoolgirl who got her first French kiss and actually enjoyed it."

"I'm Presbyterian, Car," Kat said, massaging a crick in her neck.

"It's what it was and nothing more," Carla said, "a good old-fashioned fuck."

"Oh, my God." Kat heard a knock on the bathroom door and froze.

"Hello? Are you still there?" Carla trilled.

"I've got to run," Kat whispered into the phone. "I'll see you at Remy's," she added, and ended the call, slipping her BlackBerry in the robe's right pocket. Impulsively, she flushed the toilet and ran the tap water for a few seconds before she opened the door.

"Hey," she said, meeting Cameron's sheepish expression with one of her own.

"Hey, yourself." He rubbed his grizzled jaw and glanced past her shoulder, like she was hiding something in there. "Mind if I—"

"Oh, no, go ahead," she told him, and got out of his way. He'd put on his boxers, she noticed, as he brushed past her and into the bathroom. That was almost too bad. He had a really nice butt.

Once he shut the door, she sprang to action. She ran around the room, throwing the duvet over rumpled covers, picking up clothes, tossing hers onto a chair and his onto a corner of the bed. By the time he emerged, she was in the kitchen, microwaving water for green tea, pretending this was a morning like any other morning.

He had his overcoat on, buttoned up to his collar, plaid scarf around his neck. One hand grasped his cell and the other jangled keys in his coat pocket. "I've got a cab on the way, so I'll head down, I guess. But, man, I hate to leave this place," he added, glancing around them at the open living space and view of the Arch on the horizon that seemed right out of *Architectural Digest*. "You've got amazing taste."

Kat's eyebrows went up, and she had to stifle a laugh. "You think this is mine?"

He scrunched up his boyish face. "It's not?"

"I'm just the lowly house-sitter," she explained, "at least until the condo sells. It's on the market, by the way, if you can afford a three-million-dollar mortgage."

"Really? Oh, wow"—he suddenly made a big deal over checking his watch—"look at the time! I've gotta bounce. Thanks for last night, Kat," he said, "it was fun."

"Yeah, fun," she echoed, rubbing her arms and smiling awkwardly at him.

"Well, good-bye," he said, and covered the space between them to give her a quick kiss on the cheek.

"'Bye."

He nodded at her. Then he made a beeline for the door.

Kat wasn't sure whether to follow him or not, though he was moving so fast she would've had to sprint to keep up.

The door clicked shut as she walked toward it. With a sigh, she locked the dead bolt and rubbed her aching head, whispering, "Welcome back to the meat market, Mary Katherine Maguire."

God help me.

She washed down two aspirin with a cup of green tea before she headed straight for the master bath. Stripping off her robe, she turned on the shower, hoping the water pressure would cure what ailed her. As soon as she stepped in, spray exploded from the cloudburst head, and four body jets pummeled her in the most incredible ways.

She let out an obscene moan. She closed her eyes and turned around so the spray could hit her from every angle. The pounding in her head eased along with the kink in her neck. It was almost better than sex, she decided. *Almost.*

The shower itself had no doors or curtains, just a wide opening beyond the granite-tiled wall that boxed her in. A plush terry towel hung on the heated rack beyond. She wasn't sure she'd ever leave. If she'd had $3.2 million handy, she'd snap this place up in a nanosecond.

Kat arched her back, working shampoo into her hair, feeling generous enough to admit she owed Megan for putting her up in this amazing place. She even considered giving back the diamond stud earrings Meg thought she'd lost when she moved out of the Godwin house and in with Billy.

Naw, she mused as she squished her eyes closed and rinsed the shampoo out. She'd grown kind of attached to those earrings.

She could have stayed in that shower forever, but didn't want to use half the water in Clayton. Reluctantly, she shut off the spray. Hair dripping on her shoulders, she stepped out onto the plush mat and snatched a towel from the heated rack.

As the vent hummed, diminishing the steam clouding the beveled mirrors, Kat took in her body as she patted dry. Carla was right. She seemed leaner than ever. The nervous energy that plagued her since leaving New York had kept her from eating as much, and her hips and belly looked less curvy, more boyish. Even her ribs seemed more defined beneath her breasts.

She figured her "Get Canned and Break-Up Diet" had cost her five pounds, maybe ten, though she had no desire to weigh herself. She didn't like scales; she never had.

You're getting a little cheesecake on the back of your thighs, and you know I don't like cheesecake, she heard Roger say in the back of her brain, remembering how he'd critiqued her as she walked naked to the bathroom after sex.

I'd like to buy the prettiest woman in the place a drink. Yep, she liked Peroni Guy's line much better. Kat smiled hesitantly at her reflection. Even if she didn't ever see him again—*it was what it was,* as Carla had so aptly put it—he'd restored her faith in her dating skills, if she could call it that. He'd shoved Roger further into her past as well, and that was a definite plus.

Kat felt the pieces of her life coming together again, and realized that having Car and Elise around had a lot to do with it. She could feel something changing inside her, shifting and settling, making her lighter. She was already in a better place just by coming home.

The mat turned soggy beneath her feet, and she shivered as her damp hair dripped on her shoulders. She bent over and was vigorously wiping the towel through her hair when she sensed the stir of motion outside the bathroom door.

" . . . all three bedrooms have en suite baths, though this master bath is particularly dramatic—"

She stood up as the door flew open, and her suit-wearing sister stepped into the bathroom with a stranger in tow: a tall gray-haired man with wire-rims who wore a heavy overcoat, a plaid cap, and a sizable grin.

"Jesus, Kat, you're naked!" Megan shrieked.

Kat hastily unfurled the towel, pressing it against her torso, trying to cover up her bits and pieces. "I'm usually naked when I take showers," she shot back. "It's not like I was expecting company." She jerked her chin to remind Meg that they weren't alone. "Why didn't you call?"

"I did!"

As they squabbled, the older man stood at Meg's elbow, looking like he was enjoying every minute.

"Mr. Neiderman, would you please step into the bedroom for one sec?" Meg nudged her client out and closed the door.

"God, girl, you scared the living crap out of me!" Kat put the towel back on the rack and pulled on her bathrobe.

"What're you doing here?" Meg hissed, and stabbed her fists on her hips, looking spitting mad. "I called your cell twice and you never answered! I thought you'd gone out already, looking for a job or a new place to live!"

As Megan went off on her, Kat ignored the urge to fight back. She'd done enough arguing about the unimportant with Roger, and she refused to be lured back into that pattern, not even with her sister, who had bickering skills uncontested in the Maguire family.

When Meg had finished her tirade and paused for breath, Kat said, "Hey, look on the bright side, Meggie. If you'd come, like, fifteen minutes earlier, I could've introduced you to Peroni Guy."

"Peroni Guy?"

"His name's really Cameron something or other. I met him last night at Brio."

"And you brought him *here*? Mary, Mother of God." Megan's eyes bulged. She looked fit for a seizure. "You know what, Kat? This isn't going to work at all. You can't stay here any longer. You need to find a place to live pronto."

"Jesus, Megan, calm down," Kat suggested. She'd only been minding the place for a week, and she'd done nothing wrong except forget to lock the shower door. "I'm sure the old guy has seen boobs before."

"I want you packed and out of here by the end of the week," Meg instructed, glaring at her, before marching out and slamming the door behind her.

Puh-leeze, Kat thought, and rolled her eyes, reminded of the fights they'd had growing up over clothes and curling irons, despite the seven years that separated them. It never got old, did it?

Well, she was hardly going to let Little Miss Priss ruin her day.

She went over to one of the glass bowl sinks and peered at her face in the mirror.

Her deep-set eyes stared back at her from angular features, and her skin glowed pink against the smattering of pale brown freckles.

Not bad, Mary Katherine. Not bad at all.

She took her time rubbing in moisturizer and then hung her head upside down to blow-dry her hair. She started singing "You Shook Me All Night Long" as she dabbed mascara on her lashes and slicked Really Rosy gloss on her lips.

Before she met Carla for lunch, she figured she'd call on half a dozen of the classified ads for rental apartments in the area, see if she couldn't find something she liked before Megan tossed her out on the street. It needed doing anyway, and maybe getting a kick in the pants from her sister wasn't such a bad thing.

Kat had pulled on a pair of pink panties to match her pink bra, and was digging through her suitcase looking for a favorite butter-yellow sweater to wear with her jeans when she heard her BlackBerry twitter.

She scooped it off the bedside table, only to realize that Meg was calling. She considered ignoring her—being bitched out once this morning was plenty—but changed her mind.

Kat didn't even bother with *Hello,* and instead said in a rush, "Please, don't yell at me again. I had no clue you were coming over, and I already apologized besides—"

"I'm not going to yell," Megan told her, though it was more like *not . . . going . . . yell,* since the connection seemed a little sketchy.

"Where *are* you?" Kat asked, putting a hand over her other ear and straining to hear. "You're kind of fading in and out."

"I'm on that patch of 40 where . . . can't hear . . . heading back to the office . . . Mr. Neiderman just made an offer for the condo . . ."

Kat interrupted. "The guy I just flashed?"

"Yes . . . he's surprising his wife . . . thinks the place is sexy."

"*It's* sexy? Sure he didn't mean me?"

"Don't make me vomit."

Kat couldn't help laughing. "Do I get commission?"

"On a three mil condo?" Meg suddenly came in loud and clear. "Ha! I'm thinking maybe I should have you flash all my clients."

Was Megan actually being funny?

Before Kat could exclaim, *Who are you and what have you done with my uptight sister?* Meg hung up on her.

CARLA

From the
Ladue Horton Watkins High School Yearbook:

Always Seen or Heard
Carla Jean Moss: Never a hair out of place and always the
center of attention.

Chapter Thirteen

EVEN after hanging up with Kat, Carla made no move to get out of bed. She merely propped herself up on two fluffy pillows, lying there like a lump as Randy shut off the shower and eventually emerged from the bathroom. His short hair was damp and curling at his nape, and he wore only a towel tucked around his lean waist.

Usually the sight of his rippling abdomen and chiseled chest made her want to growl and attack; today, she merely sighed, making sure the sad sound was loud enough to draw him over.

"Babe, get up," he said with a clap, ambling toward her. "It's time to rise and shine. I'll fix you breakfast."

Carla watched him approach. He walked like a football jock, loose limbs, tree-trunk thighs, his broad shoulders as wide as a yardstick.

"You've got eggs and bread, don't you?" he asked as he paused bedside and reached down to ruffle her hair, instead encountering the silk of her sleep mask, propped on top of her head.

"I might have bread," Carla said. As far as she was aware, she hadn't bought fresh eggs in months. Whatever remained in the carton stuck at the back of the fridge was probably as old and dusty as the fragile stockpile in Kat's ovaries (not to mention her own, if she had any left at all).

"I just want coffee and toast," she said listlessly.

Randy settled down beside her, the mattress dipping with his weight. "You're not still sulking over Echols?"

"Of course I am!" she grumbled. My God, what did he expect? That she'd awaken like Sleeping Beauty, completely oblivious to the fact that her witch of a stepmother (in this case perfectly played by Burton Echols) had poisoned her apple (aka putting that blond worm Amber in Don Davidson's seat)? "He played me for a fool," she insisted.

"Well then, you've got to put on your jockstrap, wear your best game face, and get ready to snap the ball," he instructed, sounding like her coach and not her friend with benefits.

Carla stared in amazement, waiting for him to blow a whistle and tell her to run a quarterback sneak or throw a Hail Mary pass while she was at it.

"What's with that look? You don't like my advice? Or have I got you bug-eyed because I'm so hard to resist?" he teased, and bent over to plant a wet one on her lips.

All of the above, she wanted to say, but her mouth became otherwise occupied.

He tasted yummy, clean and minty fresh. Her hand slipped over his bare shoulders, holding onto him and making the kiss last a little bit longer. Normally, she would've yanked off his towel and gotten down and dirty with him posthaste; but she wasn't in the mood for a morning quickie.

She pulled away, and he didn't seem any too happy about it.

"Don't you want to—" he started to say.

"Not right now," she cut him off, and smiled coyly, running a finger up and down the ropy length of his arm, his skin smooth from the shower and lightly covered in downy hairs. "I've been thinking, sugar—" she started, only to hear him groan.

"No, no, no, don't *think*, Carla, please. Because when you do, it's usually bad news for somebody," he protested. "Like when you were pissed off at Mitch because he kept taking your parking spot and you started thinking of ways to get even."

"Well, he's not even the first-string meteorologist!" *Good Lord, did that even merit an explanation?* "He's second tier all the way, the guy who's called in at two A.M. to wait for updates to tick in and report on tornado watches expiring. He's *supposed* to park on the lower level."

Randy waved off her protests. "Babe, you wanted me to bribe the guys on set to change Mitch's green screen for blue to match those shirts he always wears so he'd look like a disembodied head."

"It was brilliant!" Carla grinned and clasped her hands. "Too bad you didn't follow through, scaredy-cat. It would've been pretty funny."

"You need to learn to let bygones be bygones," he said, exasperated, leaning over so they were nose-to-nose. "Just stick to doing what you do best and everything else falls into place. Don't mess with anybody's head just because they mess with yours. You'll let the other guy win if you beat yourself first."

"What?" She pressed her palms against his bare chest, holding him at bay. "Who told you that crock of shit? Your college coach? Or did you read it in a fortune cookie?"

"You're hopeless," he said, and fell away. Exasperation clouded his eyes. Still he ended up asking, "So what evil plot do you have in mind, and what's my part in it?"

Carla squealed, gleeful at how fast he seemed to be falling in line. She crawled out from beneath the covers in her purple silk nightie and sat on her heels in front of him. "You'll help me?"

His gaze fell to her breasts, her cleavage amply displayed by the deep V-neck of her nightie. "Depends what you want."

"It'll be easy, sugar, I promise," she said, though maybe that was stretching the truth a little. She caught her fingers in his wet hair, playing with the natural curls as she told him, "I know for sure that Amber Sue's only sleeping with Burtie because he's got her sold hook, line, and sinker on his plan to make her the next star anchor of Channel 3. And I'm damned certain she's not enjoying herself in the sack with him, no matter how much Cialis he's popping these days."

She paused to make sure Randy was following along. His eyes seemed vaguely glazed, so she ran a finger around his right nipple, noting how his jaw muscles clenched. Yep, he was paying attention.

Carefully, she continued, "If dear Amber Sue isn't already getting it on the side, she's got to be dying to bump uglies with a hot young guy, someone so pretty he has women sexting naked photos on his iPhone from all over the city."

"You can't be serious." He squinted at her, catching her hand and putting an end to her nipple-teasing. "You're asking me to seduce her?"

"God, no, Randy!"

"Good," he grunted, the tension in his brow easing, "because I won't do it."

Carla bit her lip, figuring out how to phrase precisely what she was driving at. "What I'd like you to do is *befriend* her," she started slowly, "inspire her confidence. You got a ride with her to that interview yesterday so she obviously already likes you. And who wouldn't?" She arched her eyebrow appreciatively. "Just flirt with her, out of Burtie's sight, of course, and encourage her to send you naughty pictures of herself, or even better, a risqué video where she's talking dirty."

Randy's Adam's apple bobbed in his thick neck. "You want me to use Amber Sue so you can blackmail Burton?"

"Yes"—Carla nodded, not giving him near enough credit sometimes for having brains—"that's it exactly! I'm sure she's sent hundreds of naked photos of herself to men before, so for you this little assignment will be a piece of cake."

Randy blinked, saying nothing for a moment. Then he made a noise of disgust and gently pushed her away. "No," he said, and stood, shaking his head emphatically. "You're crazy, Car. I won't use anybody like that." He started to walk away but turned around, hands futilely grabbing air. "I don't understand it. You're a beautiful, amazing, intelligent, sexy woman. But when it comes to Burton Echols, you get totally mental."

"Hey, what did I say?" she asked as he stomped away.

"Randy!" Carla scrambled after him. She reached out and grabbed the towel from around his waist. It came off in her hand, but he kept right on going, and she watched his bare-naked backside as he strode into the bathroom.

Ditching the towel, Carla followed him, across the polished limestone floor, past the soaking tub, and into one of two walk-in closets, both full of her clothes, though she'd made a tiny space for a few of his things.

"Sweetie pie?" she called gently.

She found him pulling on his Armani underwear. He glanced at her briefly but kept his mouth in a grim line. Then he shrugged on a Mizzou T-shirt and gray sweats before sitting on her velvet-covered bench. His gaze downcast, he pulled on his socks and cross-trainers, paying her no mind.

"Look," she said, standing there in her tiny nightgown, long legs exposed, arms tucked under her breasts, "I'm sorry if I was out of line, but it's not like I'm asking you to compromise your, um, integrity for me. I just need something to work with, a kind of job security." She exhaled impatiently when he didn't even look up. "C'mon, Ran, I just want to get Burton off my back."

He slowly raised his eyes. "You really don't like other women much, do you?" he asked.

"Excuse me?" Carla had to grab one of her shoe shelves so she didn't fall over. "I have no clue what you mean."

He leaned his arms on his thighs, his square jaw earnestly set. "You see other chicks as your competition, never as your homies. You always think someone's out there, wanting what you have."

"I am not paranoid," she insisted, jerking up her chin.

"Hit too close to home, did I?" His thick eyebrows peaked.

"No, you didn't. Oh, I get it." Carla shook a finger at him, letting out a coarse laugh. "You want me to play nice with Amber Sue Nobody, don't you? Take her to lunch, be her buddy, share all my secrets for staying on top, and pat her on her empty head when she takes over my spot."

"She's not your enemy," he said.

"The hell she's not," Carla snapped, hardly appreciating the turn their conversation had taken. She had grown up with a woman who could hardly bear to be in the same room with her. If it was jealousy or dislike or something else entirely, she would never know for sure. But *she* was nothing like Genevieve. Her reasons for mistrusting Amber Sue had nothing to do with envy. It was survival, pure and simple.

"Babe, didn't anyone ever tell you about catching flies with honey?"

"I thought one caught flies with a glove?" Carla said dryly, while Randy threw up his hands. "And you're wrong about my not having female friends," she defended herself. "Two of my closest pals are girls I've known since grade school."

"Really?" he said, apparently surprised to hear it. "And I thought you only had a GBF."

"In English, please," she demanded, hating modern slang with a passion.

He patted his thighs. "In your case, gay best friend," he said, and got up.

Carla prickled. "Do you have a problem with Jesse?"

"No, God, of course I don't!" His face reddened. "That's not my point. You just don't get it, do you?"

The last thing she needed at the moment was an ex-football jock yet to reach his thirtieth birthday lecturing her on the state of her female relationships, or lack thereof. What did men know about women's friendships anyhow? *Nothing*, she decided with a sniff. Guys talked sports and lawn mowers and sex in locker rooms and bars, but they had no earthly idea what it meant to really trust someone not to stab you in the back.

"Listen, sugar," she said, and planted herself right in front of him, hands on her hips. She'd had enough of this back and forth.

If Randy wasn't going to help her, so be it. She'd find another way. "Someday, when you're a forty-five-year-old woman with your career on the line, you can tell me how to behave, all right?"

"Whatever." He threw up his hands. "It just seems to me that insecurity will get you nowhere. Confidence is the name of the game."

"Seriously, do you do a lot of Chinese takeout?" She grimaced. "Where do you come up with this stuff?"

"That one's a Randall Mossbacher original," he replied, and bent to kiss her, but this time it was less than passionate.

Carla figured she'd ticked him off, though it was hard to tell with Randy. His personality ran the gamut from mellow to more mellow. "You headed to the gym?"

"Yeah."

"But you just took a shower."

"Yeah," he said, and gave her a curious smile, like it made perfect sense to him. "I'll see you at the station later?"

"I guess," she said without enthusiasm.

He shook a finger at her. "No tricks, promise me."

She held up three fingers. "Girl Scout's honor."

"Ha!"—he laughed—"like you were ever a Girl Scout."

He came over and embraced her, kissing her slowly, deeply. Then he left her standing in the middle of the closet with several hundred pair of shoes and more clothes than she'd ever wear, and she felt a pang of self-pity, like a cramp in her belly.

I am not paranoid, and there's nothing wrong with only having two close girlfriends and one best gay friend, she thought, deciding she'd rather have three people in the world that she could trust than thirty she couldn't.

She felt worn-out after her exchange with Randy and shuffled back through her bedroom suite, crawling back beneath the covers. She'd just settled in, folding the duvet beneath her chin, when she heard the most annoying sound.

Tweeeet. Tweeeet.

She let her landline ring until her old-fashioned answering machine picked up. "Where *are* you, Carla?" It was Angie, the personal trainer from hell, screaming, "Do you want to lose all your muscle tone? We'll have to double your workout tomorrow, you know!"

Carla barely had time to recover from that one when the phone twittered again.

This time, at least, the voice was soft and less frightening: "Um, Carla . . . Ms. Moss . . . it's me, Deidre. You're usually at the station by now, and I wondered if you were coming in this morning. I left that invitation on your desk yesterday—you know, the one asking if you'd keynote at the Women in Journalism awards dinner in April—and I wasn't sure how you wanted to respond. Give me a call when you get this, okay? They'd like an answer ASAP."

Carla smashed the sides of the pillow against her ears, wishing everyone would just leave her alone for a few hours. She thought of Elise and of her ordinary life in the suburbs, of how undemanding it must feel to pop zits for a living and then go home each night, never fearing that someone might take away your job just because you'd outlived forty. She was even mildly envious of Kat, suddenly footloose and fancy free, contemplating a career change and hooking up with the Peroni-drinking hottie from the Brio bar, completely string-free.

She closed her eyes, envisioning her office at KMOK and all the regional Emmys she'd won, not to mention the dozens of plaques that filled her walls, like her "Best St. Louis Anchor" awards from the *Riverfront Times* and *St. Louis Journalism Review*, and her "Media Person of the Year" tributes from the Press Club.

"It's going to be hard filling your shoes," she could hear Amber Sue saying. "You're like an historical monument around here."

Breathe, Carla, breathe.

It wasn't even that she wanted to be twenty-five again. She'd already played the role of fresh-out-of-J-School-wide-eyed-reporter years ago, and she wouldn't want to hoe that row again if it were offered to her. She just wished she could keep what was hers without having to sic her legal eagles on Burton.

All I want, she told herself, *is another two-year contract so I can continue doing what I love.*

Flipping onto her side, she punched a fist into her silk-cased pillow, imagining it was Burton's face and feeling slightly better for it. Randy was right about one thing: she could not—would not—let Burton beat her down like this.

It was enough to propel her out of bed anyway. She was dragging herself into the bath for a shower when her doorbell exploded.

Dingdongdingdongdingdongdingdong.

Had the mailman stroked out and fallen on the button, for God's sake?

"Mossy! Mossy, open up!" she heard a familiar voice yelling in between the ringing bell and the pounding of fists.

Carla descended the stairs from the second floor as fast as she could under the circumstances, her bare feet touching down on polished wood and her right hand skipping along the carved banister. Light glowed like jewels through the Tiffany stained-glass window at the landing, but she didn't pause until she'd reached the foyer. She didn't even bother to switch on the chandelier overhead, simply squinted through the peephole to confirm it was Jesse out there before she unlocked the heavy door and let him in, along with a burst of icy wind. She rubbed goose bumps from her arms and stepped back as he entered.

"Holy hell! What're you doing all shut up in here, Mossy? The lights aren't even on, and you've got a pile of mail on the floor. Your little assistant told me you hadn't shown up at the station this morning, and she freaked. Now I'm freaking, too."

"Deidre tends to overreact," Carla murmured, "and so do you."

"Please, Burton's turned you inside out, and you know it." He bent down to retrieve the slew of invitations, bills, and magazines scattered around his feet beneath the mail slot. When he came upright, he plopped the pile on the console table and faced her again with his hands on his hips. "You, my dear, look like you're channeling Gloria Swanson from *Sunset Boulevard,* or is that the latest in bag-lady boudoir chic from French *Vogue*? Whatever's going on, it's got to stop."

Carla glanced down at her bare feet and rumpled silk nightgown, then touched her head, feeling her forgotten sleep mask tangled in the rat's nest of her hair. She was a hot mess, wasn't she?

"I was taking it easy this morning," she told him, which wasn't entirely the truth. "Okay, yes, I've been sulking after that stunt Burtie pulled on me last night, and you know when I pout I do it right," she added as she locked the door behind him.

"Well, cut it out," Jesse instructed, peeling off a puffy black ski jacket, which he tossed onto the circular settee centered beneath the unlit chandelier. He set his hands on his hips and jutted out his pointed chin. "Now let's commence with the cheering up."

He slung an arm across her shoulders and gave her a squeeze. "I've decided to play hooky for most of today. So get dressed, and I'll do what I can with your hair and makeup. I've already called Laurie Sollet, and she's putting aside a shit-ton of new arrivals from L.A. just for you to try on. After the ten o'clock news tonight, I'm whisking you off to the Loading Zone to let loose."

"Jesse, no, seriously?"

The Loading Zone was his favorite gay bar in the Central West End, always filled with handsome med students and physicians from Barnes Jewish Hospital.

Someday, Jesse would make a great doctor's wife, but Carla wasn't in the market for a gay husband.

"You'll be the most popular girl in the room," he assured her.

"Quite possibly the only girl," she murmured, scratching her uncombed head.

"Look, don't even think that far ahead. First, we'll play at Plaza Frontenac, okay?" His impish eyes lit up. "C'mon, Mossy, a trip to Saks always makes you perky. Don't you want to try on some new Donna Karan?"

"Sure, I mean, what the hell." She yanked the sleep mask off her head and clutched it in her fist. "I might even find a new pair of Louboutins."

"That's the spirit." He held out his hand. "Now let's scoot upstairs and you can shower while I pick out something for you to wear. We'll skip Laurie's boutique and go straight to Plaza Frontenac to browse so everyone can fawn all over you and ask for your autograph. Like that"—he snapped his fingers—"you'll forget all about that prick Burton Echols."

Carla wished it were that easy. Images of Burton dissing her last night kept flitting through her brain, until she began to ponder a hundred different ways to murder the man. Perhaps she could buy a tubful of those little Asian fish that ate the dead skin off people's feet and let them get a taste of Burton's whole chubby body, or maybe she could toss him into the Muddy Mississippi right at the site of a riptide and see how quickly he sank without Amber Sue's double-D floaters to grab onto.

Suddenly, Carla was grinning.

Jesse paused on the steps, picking up the change in her demeanor, and he squeezed her hand. "Now, that's my girl," he said. "Keep thinking those happy thoughts."

"Oh, I will," she told him. "I will."

Chapter Fourteen

AFTER spending the rest of the morning with Jesse, wandering through the upscale shopping haven that was Plaza Frontenac, Carla felt like a new woman. From the moment they arrived, she'd started collecting knowing glances and whispers, and a group of saleswomen had huddled around her while she inspected a pair of black suede and patent Jonathan Kelsey pumps in the shoe department at Saks.

Jesse had kept a quiet eye on them as they fluttered up to her, asking, "Is there anything we can help you with, Ms. Moss? We've got tons of new pieces from Donna Karan's spring collection for you to look at. We can have them sent to your house if you don't have time to try them on now. Would you like some champagne, perhaps? Or Pellegrino?"

They'd drawn enough of a crowd that Jesse went into his "horse-tail" mode, as he called it, shooing away the flies, which Carla guessed made her the ass.

A posse of young mothers had followed them as they headed toward Louis Vuitton near the escalators, and one finally got up the nerve to call out, "Carla Moss? Is it really you? Can we have a picture?" That meant Jesse got to play photographer and shoot a few digital photos while Carla smiled and posed between two of the moms while the babies screamed at the top of their lungs.

Carla had nearly been smothered by a gaggle of giddy women at Neiman-Marcus, who'd surrounded her and chirped, "Carla Moss, we love you! You're so much better than Katie Couric!"

One of them even asked her to autograph a silver metallic Carlos Falchi tote with a Sharpie, which she obliged. At least she hadn't been asked to sign anyone's breast, which was what happened to Randy every time they went to a sports bar.

An hour had passed when Jesse herded her out of the chi-chi mall and toward his Mini-Cooper (aka the Clown Car) in the parking lot. Carla hated to leave, she was so flush with groupie adoration.

"See, what did I tell you? They worship you, Mossy, and they always will," he assured her before he dropped her back at her house.

Oh, how she wanted to believe him! It made Burton's maneuvering seem a little less threatening.

She spent the next hour holed up with her attorneys in their office on North Meramec in downtown Clayton. They all looked alike to Carla, in their sober-colored Brooks Brothers suits and sedate ties with their severely cut gray hair—if they had hair at all—and it felt more like a wake than a discussion about her status at KMOK.

"I hate to be the bearer of bad news, Carla," Andrew Snodgrass said to kick things off. "But we heard from Burton this morning, and he made an offer for a one-year contract that I agreed to present to you."

"Just one year?" she asked, disappointed on the one hand; on the other, she was happy Burton had finally made a move. Didn't that say something? "I wonder if the station got flooded with unpleasant e-mails about Amber Sue subbing for Don. She's still awfully green. I guess Burtie finally realized he can't afford to lose his number one anchorwoman."

Neither Snodgrass nor McNally made a peep.

"But I'm digressing, aren't I? So let's get down to brass tacks." She rubbed her hands together, relieved that Randy had kept her from smacking Burton upside the head during their showdown last evening. Maybe being patient would be worth it. "So what kind of carrot is he dangling, and by carrot, you know I mean money?" she asked eagerly. "If it's at least as much as I made last year, that's okay. I don't want to get greedy. I'd just be thrilled to keep my job."

Snodgrass cleared his throat and glanced beside him at his partner in the entertainment law firm. "Peter?" he said, like he was afraid to answer a simple question.

"Ah, yes, about the money." Peter McNally, who was equally stodgy and dour-faced, slipped a file across the conference table. "Maybe you'll want to take a look for yourself."

Carla wasn't sure what the big deal was, but she shrugged and reached for the manila folder. She opened it to find an e-mail from Burton at KMOK. As Carla read down the page, her eyes grew wider and wider.

She glanced up, blinking, tapping a finger on the pages. "What the hell is this about? That son of a bitch wants to knock my airtime back to four days a week at a twenty percent pay cut? Is he completely insane?"

Now it was McNally's turn to clear his throat. "Well, technically, it's not a cut in pay if you're being offered one-fifth the salary for one-fifth the work schedule. But, yes, it is below your annual salary per your current contract for the past two years."

"You must be fucking kidding me!" Carla had to fight to keep from shrieking. *Deep breaths, deep breaths,* she told herself, but it didn't help. Her heart beat a hundred miles a minute, and her neck muscles stiffened up like rebar.

"What we think we should do, Carla, is raise the stakes a little," Snodgrass insisted, pounding a pudgy fist on the table, his dark glasses low on his nose. Even angry, he appeared habitually constipated. "Let's subtly threaten the son of a bitch with an age and sex discrimination suit, then we'll go for the jugular, make him pay through the ass for a new two-year contract that keeps you on the air five days a week—"

"Stop," Carla said, effectively shutting him up. "I don't want to threaten to sue anyone, not even subtly, especially Burton. He'd see that as a challenge, and not in a good way. Besides, it's just plain bad for business."

Carla knew that Sandy Chase had quietly exited KMOK with a bonus in her pocket before she vanished from the anchor desk, and she'd heard that the latest middle-aged sacrificial lamb from Channel 5 had done the same. All that "womb to tomb" lawsuits did for an anchorwoman her age was make her look like a bitter and pathetic loser. And it often ended badly in court, with the ejected newswoman (or occasional man) winning just fifty percent of the time. That was hardly worth risking her sterling reputation.

"Gentlemen," she said more evenly, and shut the file so she wouldn't have to glimpse Burton's offensive missive. "I'd like you to decline Mr. Echols's insulting offer and insist I won't take any less than what I'm currently earning. If he continues to play hard-ball, he's going to regret it."

"But, Carla," McNally practically stuttered, his bald pate creating a glare as the overhead fixture beamed down squarely upon it. "The man seems to glory in putting you through hell. We'd be honored to squeeze his balls in court for you."

"At least let us go straight to Graham Howell," Snodgrass begged, clasping his hands against his chest. "He doubtless doesn't have a clue what Burton's up to, and he can't possibly want to lose his cash cow."

Cash cow. What a lovely image that evoked. But Carla shook her head, "No, please, don't go to Graham, not yet."

Graham Howell was the crankiest, most chauvinistic seventy-two-year-old man on the planet. To say that her relationship with him was "cordial" was being generous. She still vividly recalled when she'd started at KMOK and walked up to him at the annual Christmas party—after having been forewarned to avoid him at all costs—in order to cheekily declare, "One of these days, I'm going to anchor the nightly news."

He'd lowered his cut-glass of bourbon, stared at her straight in the eye, and said, "There's nothing I like less in this world than pushy broads. In fact, if I had my way, there wouldn't be a female on-camera in my newsroom."

She had mumbled, "Nice to meet you, sir," before she slunk away.

The next time she ran into Graham, she was co-anchoring the morning show, and he'd given her the evil eye, as if to say, *I'm watching you, and I hope you fall on your pushy ass.* All these years later, he still scared the crap out of her, and going to him to plead her case would be the last straw.

"I've got an idea, if you'll listen." Carla looked from one lawyer to the other. "There is something you *could* do to help my cause," she went on, deciding that sticking it to Burton where it hurts was worth another shot, even if Randy hadn't exactly endorsed Plan A this morning.

"You name it, Carla." Andrew Snodgrass's leather chair squeaked as he bent over the table.

"Yes, what can we do?" McNally agreed, his shiny head bobbing.

"Your firm employs private investigators, does it not?" she asked them, and the men glanced at one another before Snodgrass gave a nod.

"Of course we do. We have several excellent investigators on the payroll, former police detectives, as a matter of fact."

"Wonderful." Carla smiled, a bubble of hope rising in her chest. "Well then, I'd like to hire one of them and send him on a little information gathering trip to Amber Sue Evans's home town in Indiana. I need all the dirt that can possibly be dug up on her, and it's got to be pay dirt, you understand? If there's an old boyfriend with a sex tape, I want a copy. If there's a married man who had a fling with her, I want a notarized transcript describing every sordid detail." She paused, taking in their slack-jawed expressions. "Are you getting the picture here?"

"All too clearly," Snodgrass uttered, snapping into gear.

"Vividly," McNally declared.

"That's what I'd hoped to hear," Carla said, and left the manila folder with Burton's insulting offer on the table as she rose from her chair.

"We'll get right on it, Carla," Andrew Snodgrass assured her as they walked her from the conference room and down the hallway toward the lobby. "As soon as we have any information at all, we'll let you know."

"Thank you, gentlemen," she said sweetly as they punched the elevator's down button. "It's been a pleasure as always."

She smiled at them both as the elevator pinged and its doors opened. Stepping inside, she cocked her head and listened to the piped-in music. She couldn't help but sigh when she recognized a watered-down version of the Stones' "Under My Thumb."

Chapter Fifteen

CARLA found herself humming the tune as she drove her Lexus the short distance to another parking garage on Bemiston.

The hands on her Patek Phillipe showed five minutes past one when she crossed the street to Remy's and saw Kat wave to her from a windowside table. Once she'd made it past the hostess inside, Carla headed straight toward her friend.

Kat got up from her chair, looking adorable in a teal-colored jacket over a turtleneck and hip-hugging jeans.

"Hey, sweetie," Carla opened her arms as she approached and gave her a squeeze, offering air kisses as well before they both settled down.

"What're you drinking?" she asked, brushing wind-blown hair from her eyes and shedding her coat on the back of her chair.

"A sauvignon blanc, Angeline, I think she said, and it's lovely." Kat made a "yummy" face as she took a sip before setting her glass down. "I figured I'd treat myself since I've spent most of the morning looking at apartments."

"Find anything?"

"I saw two that were okay," Kat told her, hardly sounding madly in love. "One space is on the fourth floor of an old building on Washington in U. City, just off the Loop behind the post office." She wiggled her hand in a so-so gesture. "It's nice, but there's just a window unit in the bedroom, no central air. And the kitchen's really small, although it's not like I cook much. Roger and I did lots of takeout."

"That sounds like the perfect postcollege pad," Carla remarked with a roll of her eyes, "although I'd love for you to be that close to me."

Kat took another sip of wine and shrugged. "The Loop is amazing," she said. "It's like a little slice of Manhattan. I can walk to Cicero's and the Tivoli and a Starbucks."

"But you can come visit me anytime, and we can do that." Carla gestured impatiently. "What's the other one like? Is it more suitable for a grown-up?"

"A two-bedroom town house in Brentwood Forest," her friend explained. "It's not big, but it's nicely updated, plus it's a rent-to-own situation."

"Ooh, I like the sound of ownership." Carla rubbed her hands together. "It feels so permanent."

"It has central air, and the location's prime. There's a Whole Foods and Bread Company within walking distance." Kat paused, and frown lines appeared between her eyes. "I'm just not sure it's what I want either."

"My dad used to live in Brentwood Forest before he met Mother," Carla said as Kat's description sparked a memory. "It was called Audubon Forest back in the fifties, and it was apartments, not condos and town houses."

"So that's why the streets are named after birds." Kat's eyes widened. "It makes sense now, huh? The unit's on South Swan Circle and it's very pretty, with a deck overlooking the lake with all the ducks and geese paddling around."

"Sounds very serene if that's what you want," Carla remarked.

"I'm not giving up," Kat told her with a determined look. "I'll find the perfect spot if I keep looking. I figure I'll know it when I see it."

"Aw, don't worry about it, sweet cakes. You've only been back a couple weeks. You've got time."

"I've got less than a month, to be exact, now that Megan's sold the condo I'm bunking at."

"Well, you can always stay at my place for a while," Car reassured her, then leaned back in the chair, shaking her head, hardly able to believe this day had come. "Mary Katherine Maguire's planting her roots back in St. Louis after all these years. It's really happening." She got teary-eyed, so many emotions rushing through her at once. "This isn't a long, very pleasant dream I'm having, is it?"

"No," Kat assured her, reaching over and rubbing her arm. "It's as real as it gets. I'm not going anywhere, unless it's to Bermuda on vacation."

Carla resisted the urge to leap over the table and pinch her friend's freckled cheeks. "This calls for a celebration. How about a little champagne on me?"

"You don't have to do that—"

"I insist." Carla grabbed the bar list, immediately seeing a selection she liked.

"Oh, miss," she trilled, catching their waitress as she wandered past. "A half bottle of Taittinger La Francaise Brut, please," she ordered with a smile. "And bring it here tout suite."

Within minutes she had a full flute in hand and made sure a glass was poured for Kat as well. Then she raised hers in salute. "Here's to finding your new place, to living real, and to never settling for less than we deserve."

"What, no mention of Spanx?" Kat teased, referring to her toast the night before.

"Okay, okay, here's to Spanx. Long may it flatten our tummies," Carla said with a grin, and they touched rims.

Carla relaxed as she sipped and the sweet bubbles tickled her tongue, sliding down her throat. She took in the small space around them with its blue-painted walls and dark wood, cozy yet chic. Their table was next to the plate-glass window, so she could see out to the street, and to the cars endlessly streaming past, an occasional human bundled up for winter hurrying by as well. Inside the restaurant a few heads turned toward her, staring for split-seconds before looking away; but no one got up and came over.

She smiled to herself, enjoying moments like this when people respected her privacy almost as much as she did getting fawned over, as she had this morning in Frontenac. Each had its place. Right now the air of normalcy felt good.

"Oh, I had a message from Lisie," Kat said as she swiped too-long bangs out of her eyes. "She invited me to a hockey game tonight."

"A hockey game? Ah, yes, Elise was a hockey mom for years, wasn't she?" Car remarked, and squished up her face in thought. "I still find it hard picturing her as a pit bull with lipstick."

"More like a poodle in pearls," Kat suggested with a smile.

Carla swallowed more champagne, licking her lips when she'd emptied the glass, and began pouring another. "Or maybe a Labrador retriever," she said, rubbing lipstick from her glass. "They're blond and want so badly for people to like them. It's a good thing I never worried much about that."

"Except when you check your TV Q score," Kat pointed out, and set down her champagne. "You want the adoration of the masses but you're slow to trust on a personal level."

"Thank you, Dr. Phil. Actually, Randy was on my case about that this morning. He told me I'm not nice enough to other women." Carla rolled her eyes. "Oh, and get this, he wants me to buddy-up to Amber Sue Nobody."

"The old keep your friends close and your enemies closer trick," Kat said, and fiddled with one of the silver hoops swinging from her earlobes. "He's smarter than your average jock."

"And more sensitive," Carla added softly.

She didn't tell Kat about her attempt to get Randy to cozy up to Amber Sue. When she thought about it now, it did sound kind of crass, and, more to the point, why the hell would she want to push her lover toward a much younger woman? Randy was right. She was nuts! It wasn't like there were enough of the good ones out there to go around anyway.

"Speaking of men," she ventured to ask, "did you give your number to your hook-up? Think he'll call you?"

Kat pursed her lips and shook her head. "No and no again. When he realized this morning that I didn't own the three mil condo and was just house-sitting, he didn't stick around."

Carla clicked tongue against teeth. "Ah, sweetie, don't let that hurt your feelings. That's the trouble with the pretty boys at Brio.

They're desperately seeking sugar mamas. I learned that lesson the hard way, too. So now I just look and don't touch."

Kat nearly spit out a mouthful of champagne. "Cameron thought I was a sugar mama?"

"Well, darling, look at you," Carla said, waving a slender manicured hand at her friend. "You dress impeccably, your bag's real Chanel, and you're driving a Jag that's as well-preserved as you are."

"That's too bad," Kat remarked, setting her chin on her fist. "He was so pretty."

Carla shrugged. *"C'est la vie."*

"La vie," her friend said, and smiled, if a little sadly.

"So you and Elise are heading to a Blues game tonight," Carla prodded, shifting back to a safer topic.

"Yep."

"I wonder why she's not going with Michael?"

Her friend shrugged. "Maybe he's busy, or else she just wanted some girl-time. It'll be cool hanging out with Lisie. Maybe she'll loosen up a little more and talk about what's going on with her and Dr. Mike."

"You mean, what's *not* going on, from the sounds of it," Carla said, wondering how serious it was. "You think they're going to split?"

"What I think is that Lisie could use more fun in her life," Kat replied diplomatically.

"You're equating hockey with fun?" Carla looked at Kat like she'd lost her mind. "Watching a bunch of overgrown boys pummel each other with sticks? Do any of them still have their own teeth? How does that saying go, 'I went to a fight and a hockey game broke out'?"

"Aw, you're such a sissy, Carla Jean." Kat punched her lightly in the arm. "I used to see weekend games with my dad when I was a kid. I loved going to the Arena."

"They tore the old Arena down, you know, back in 1999 while you were gallivanting around New York City, searching for—" Carla hesitated and wrinkled her brow. "What exactly *was* it you were chasing again?"

"Hmm," Kat said, tapping her chin. "In 1999, if I remember correctly, I was chasing after Keith Wozniak. D&M was doing a campaign for an imprint of William Morrow, and he was an editor there. He ran marathons, you see, so I had to lace-up and run just to keep up with him."

"How very literary of you," Carla teased.

"Ha!"

"Come to think of it, that's the same year I filed for divorce to rid myself of Burton," Carla remarked, sighing at the less than pleasant memory. "So I was running away from someone, and you were running after someone else."

"And we both ended up right here, right now"—Kat patted the surface of the table, causing the glasses of bubbly to shake— "still single and trying to figure things out."

"So what does that say about us?" Carla asked, and placed a steady hand on her champagne flute. "That we're slow?"

"Hell, no," Kat replied without hesitation. "It says that we're women who've taken some hard knocks in order to realize what's important in our lives. There's nothing wrong with that."

Car smiled. "Did you practice that in the mirror?"

"Funny."

"I just hope the road ahead is a lot smoother than what we've left behind."

Kat leaned forward and placed her hand on Carla's arm. "You're thinking about Burton, yes?"

"Yes." Carla sighed, unable to get the thought of Burtie's insufficient contract offer out of her head. "All I want is to do my job, and he's making that more impossible each day."

"No one's going to let him get rid of you without a fight, trust me on this," Kat said with her freckled face so earnest, her voice so certain, that Carla wanted to believe her. "You're too important to the station."

"I hope you're right," she replied, wishing she was as sure.

"I know I am." Kat squeezed her arm before letting her go. "Just have a little faith, okay?"

"I'll try," Car said, because she wanted to have faith. Faith that the private eye her lawyers were going to sic on Amber Sue would unearth something in her past so embarrassing that Burton would agree to whatever contract terms she demanded in order to keep his girlfriend's secrets buried.

Hiring an investigator: $100 to $200 an hour. Pulling a fast one on Burton: priceless.

It was enough to bring her appetite back, and she picked up the menu, hungrily gazing at its offerings. "So how about we get some chow? Suddenly, I'm famished!"

ELISE

Dr. Elise Randolph on KWMU:

Trying to achieve natural beauty in an unnatural age is tricky. Just remember that true beauty should be more than skin deep. It's about loving what you do, never losing your sense of wonder, and living your life with childlike abandon.

Chapter Sixteen

ELISE glanced up at the clock as she finished dictating on her final patient of the day and signed off on her last bit of paperwork.

Six-thirty on the nose. She got up from her desk to grab her coat and scarf, checking her bag twice to make sure she had the hockey tickets. The rest of her staff had already gone and the cleaning crew had emptied wastebaskets and vacuumed; so she switched off the lights in her office before taking the elevator down and out of Building D at Missouri Baptist into the parking garage.

As she followed the exit arrows from the underground lot and began weaving through the medical center campus toward the light at Ballas Road, she dialed Michael on her cell phone.

"Elise?" he said, picking up after a single ring. "What's up?"

"Oh, hey, it's you!" she said stupidly, caught off-guard at hearing his actual voice. Nine times out of ten when she dialed his cell these days, she had to leave a voice-mail message. "Will you be home tonight for dinner?"

"Aw, sorry, honey, but I'm gonna be really late again, so don't hold off eating on my account," he replied, making excuses, as expected.

"I won't be home early, either," she told him, squashing her desire to yell *So there!* "I'm going with Kat to a Blues game, and it starts at seven-thirty. I'm picking her up now. I didn't think you'd mind."

"A hockey game, huh? Sounds great! Of course I don't mind. I'm glad Kat's back in town, and you're spending time with her," he said, way too eagerly. "You should be doing things with your friends instead of sitting home alone. Have a blast, okay? Just watch out for flying pucks."

"Uh-huh."

"All right, then," he said, clearly ready to hang up.

Only something welled up inside her, a rush of anger and disappointment that propelled her to blurt out, "Michael, do you love me?"

As soon as she'd expelled the words, she held her breath. Her heart hammered in her chest. She had no idea how he'd answer, whether he'd tell her the cold hard truth or lie to appease her.

He finally cleared his throat and murmured, "God, El, what a silly question. Of course I care about you—you and Joey both— and I always will."

"Oh," was all Elise could get out.

She felt like she had peanut butter stuck to the roof of her mouth. *Well, there it is*, she told herself. If she'd expected to hear him profess his undying love, *I care about you* hadn't exactly done the trick. But those few words said more than enough. He had changed more than she'd realized, and she hadn't changed along with him. Something was gone from their relationship, and it wasn't coming back, no matter how hard she wished it.

"I've got to go," he said. "Have fun at the game, and I'll see you when I see you."

"But, Michael, I—" She wanted to say something more, though she didn't know what. "Michael?"

It was too late. He'd hung up.

But, Michael, I feel really lost and confused. I don't know what you want from me anymore, or what I want. In other words, what the fuck are we doing?

Elise realized everything that was once so safe and familiar suddenly wasn't. A terrible ache filled her chest, and she was tempted to turn the car around and drive out to St. Luke's to confront him. But what would that accomplish other than making her look even sillier to him?

Get a grip, Elise, she berated herself. *You're not the only woman who's ever been through this. It's not the end of the world, for Pete's sake.*

Okay, but easier said than done.

For a long moment she stared at the dirty back end of the Subaru in front of her. She'd never imagined being in this kind of situation. Her parents had celebrated their golden anniversary the year before her dad died of lung cancer, and her mom from missing him just a year later. Elise felt almost glad neither of them was alive to see the wrong turn her relationship with Michael had taken. When Carla and Burton had divorced, she'd thought, Ha! That's what you get for not marrying for love. And now look what had happened to her. Even love didn't guarantee a damned thing.

I need a drink, she decided, wondering if they had gin and tonics at Scottrade.

She sucked in a deep breath and slowly let it out again before she speed-dialed Kat. "I finally got away from the office," she said, hoping the quiver in her voice would go unnoticed. "I'll swing by your building and pick you up out front in ten minutes."

"Yay, I'll be waiting!" her friend chirped.

At least someone's happy.

Elise dumped her cell into the nearest cup holder and inched the Audi ahead in the thick line of traffic, waiting for the light at the Ballas intersection to change. When it finally went green, she followed a string of cars turning left. Once she'd veered onto Ballas, she quickly shifted into the far right lane. In another few seconds she was on the ramp to the interstate, heading east toward Clayton.

She considered Kat and her perky mood, and reminded herself that her good pal had just gone through a major upheaval, yet she was dealing with it brilliantly. And Carla! Geez, she and Burton were like Godzilla and Mothra, locked in a constant battle to the death, and still Car held her chin high.

Elise sniffed back her pity party, deciding if her friends could be so strong despite the crap in their lives, surely she could face her own mid-life crisis head-on and come out the other side.

Buck up, she told herself, clearing her throat before doing what she always did for Joey when he'd been in a foul mood after school or a bad hockey practice. She started singing the goofiest song she could think of.

"'Hello, out there, we're on the air, it's hockey time tonight . . . the tension grows, the whistle blows, and the puck goes down the ice,'" she trilled loudly and off-key, but it was idiotic enough to get her grinning.

As she warbled, she gazed through the windshield at the stark landscape, which looked anything but cheerful. Slush followed the yellow highway lines, and mounds of dirty snow ran along the shoulder.

Her voice trailed off as soon as she realized she couldn't remember more than one section of "the good ol' hockey game" beyond the chorus. She reached for the button on the steering wheel to start a jazz CD then changed her mind. Instead, she switched on the radio, flipping to KSHE, the classic rock station, and caught the tail end of an old Bon Jovi tune. Buoyed by the music, she sailed up 170 to Forest Park Parkway and then exited on Forsyth into the heart of Clayton.

When she pulled the car around the circular drive in front of the high rise where Kat had set up temporary digs, she saw her friend push through the revolving door and wave. Kat rushed toward the Audi, looking chic and warm in snug-fitting jeans and boots, a down coat, gloves, and scarf.

"Hey, Lisie!" Kat said by way of greeting, her cheeks pink from the cold as she climbed inside, shut the door, and buckled herself in. "You ready to rock, girlfriend?"

"I'm gonna try," Elise replied, and put the car in gear, rolling back toward 170 and then to 64/40 East, about a ten-minute drive to downtown.

And for a moment it was as though they were sixteen again, headed to the Arena to see Journey and Styx on a 1980s "Gods of Rock" double bill.

"No waaaay!" Kat squealed when she heard the synthesized prelude to Van Halen's "Jump."

Before long, Kat was crooning along with David Lee Roth, "'And I know, baby, just how you feel. You've got to ro-o-oll with the punches to get to what's real . . .'"

What else could she do but join in, and Elise found herself grinning like a fool and singing, "'Might as well jump, go ahead and ju-ump,'" as they sped down the interstate, and they kept it up even as Van Halen segued to Def Leppard's Joe Elliott growling, "Pour Some Sugar on Me."

In fact, their eighties rock medley continued all the way to the Fourteenth Street exit, when the Audi settled behind a logjam of cars after turning left at the light. Ahead of them, traffic cops blew whistles and gestured, stopping traffic at the Clark Street intersection so Blues fans could cross the street. Though night had fallen, lights lit up the block around them. Scottrade Center loomed from the corner, advertising coming attractions on a jumbo-sized screen on the arena's façade. Beneath the glow of the streetlamps, men, women, and children in blue and gold Blue Note gear strode past on the sidewalk.

"Man, I don't think I've been downtown in twenty years," Kat remarked, staring out the windows with her mouth wide open. "It's nothing like Manhattan, is it?"

"That's just the way we like it," Elise quipped.

"Remember when Famous-Barr downtown used to do such cool Christmas windows?"

"Now it's Macy's," Elise said, "and there's no downtown store anymore."

"And the old Busch Stadium is gone." Kat made a moue of displeasure. "I hate when things change just for the sake of having something newer and flashier."

"That's progress."

"Right, progress," Kat said, sounding less than pleased by the idea.

"They're redeveloping the old Kiel Opera House, you know." Elise threw her friend a bone. "The guy who owns the Blues has a hand in that. So everyone's not into tearing down the old."

"Now that's a man after my own heart." Kat smiled and settled back in her seat. "Is he single, by any chance?"

"Not sure about that, but I know he's over thirty, which is *way* too old for you," Elise teased, and Kat swatted at her.

The black-booted cop at the intersection let out a shrill blast of his whistle, halting the flood of pedestrians, and Elise could finally take her foot off the brake and move ahead, toward the city lot off Fourteenth, which allowed event parking.

"This is so exciting," Kat said as Elise rolled down the window to pay the fee before they could proceed inside the iron gates.

"You *have* been away for too long if you think parking is exciting," Elise joked as she guided the Audi onto the lot, which already looked pretty packed. Mounds of icy sludge took up more than a few precious spaces, but she located a spot far across the lot. Pulling toward a wall of slush, she stopped before the bumper nudged it, then turned off the ignition.

"C'mon, slowpoke, let's go!" Kat cried, and hopped out of the passenger door before Elise got the headlights turned off.

Once she climbed out and locked the doors, the wind caught at her coat and whipped around her stockinged legs. She wound her cashmere scarf around her upturned collar, and still her teeth started chattering.

"Hurry, it's freezing!" Kat urged, as if Elise needed reminding.

Her friend had dressed appropriately in blue jeans and boots beneath her winter gear, and Elise had on the dress and pumps she'd worn at work. She didn't have a change of clothes at the office, and she'd figured scrubs would hardly be warmer than what she had on.

"I'm having fun, I'm having fun," she reminded herself as she shivered and hurried alongside Kat, quickly meshing into the stream of fans plodding toward the arena. Once they'd crossed the street and pushed inside the glass doors, she felt warmer air embrace her, and she stopped shivering as she waited for the quick inspection of her Prada bag by a flashlight-wielding security guard. She followed Kat through the gate, hearing a *beep* as her ticket was scanned.

"This way, Lisie," Kat said, catching a hand in the crook of Elise's elbow and guiding her left around the outer aisle of the arena, heading toward Section 103.

"Beer, ice-cold beer!" a vendor shouted, holding up silver cans, and Kat hesitated, dragging Elise to a stop.

"It's thirty degrees outside"—Elise was still shivering—"how can you even think of drinking something ice cold?"

"That's what the alcohol's for, Lisie, to warm us up," Kat replied, but Elise nudged her forward.

They kept winding through the crowd, looking above them for the numbered signs indicating each section.

"My legs are cold but my neck is five hundred degrees," Elise grumbled, and unwound her scarf so the ends hung down over either shoulder. She plucked off her velvet gloves next and stuffed them in her pockets. A hand instinctively went to her hair, sure the wind had blown it into a bird's nest.

"Hey, your curls are back!" Kat remarked, quickly adding, "They look good on you, Lisie. They suit you, just like those square-toed pumps."

"I wish I'd had flats at the office. I'm seriously overdressed." Elise felt self-conscious in panty hose and high heels and a Nicole Miller dress beneath her lined Burberry trench. She glanced sideways as a group of men in Blues gear and ball caps swaggered past, turning their heads in her direction.

"*They're* not complaining," Kat said with a laugh, leaning nearer. "Face it, Dr. Randolph, you're a hot mama."

Another gaggle of men approached, passing on their left, only this foursome was younger, with styled hair, button-downs, tailored jackets, and upscale bottled beer in hand, instead of giant cups sloshing twenty ounces of Bud.

"Speaking of hot," Kat murmured, and brazenly eyed the posse of well-groomed twenty-somethings.

"Hey, there, ladies," one of the four called out, and Kat uttered a bright "Hey, guys" right back.

Giggles tickled Elise's throat as she grabbed her friend's arm and asked, "What happened to swearing off men?"

"Ah, I didn't tell you about my post-Brio tryst, did I?" Kat grinned like a little girl hiding a secret.

"You had a tryst last night? How'd I miss that?"

"Please, *I* nearly missed it. I was sloshed on Patrón, and he drove me home and then—" Kat came to an abrupt halt in front of a stand peddling funnel cakes. "Oh, my God, am I dreaming?"

"What, you didn't have county fair crap in New York?" Elise snorted, wanting to hear the rest of the dish on Kat's one-night stand. Food could wait.

Kat flung a hand to her heart, as though she'd found a lost love, and breathlessly confessed, "I haven't had one of these since the VP Fair, like, a hundred years ago when it was still called the VP Fair. You want one, too, Lisie?"

Before Elise could even answer, her friend cut through the stream of Blues fans until she'd taken a place in line at the booth. Dodging a pair of large men in Blues jerseys, Elise scurried over to the wall and waited beneath the sign marking Sections 103 and 104. She watched the faces as they passed her, wondering if she'd see anyone that she knew—she didn't—until Kat reappeared with two funnel cakes on paper plates.

She shoved one at Elise and took at bite of her own, leaving a mess of powdered sugar on her lips. "Ummm, this is divine, way better than tiramisu," she said, and took another bite, dripping powdered sugar on her coat.

"Sweetie, you're a mess." Elise went into mother mode, brushing the telltale sugar off Kat's scarf and lapels and using her thumb to wipe off a smudge on Kat's chin. "There you go."

"What if I like being a mess?" her friend mumbled as she stuffed another piece of fried cake in her mouth. "It's better than trying to be perfect all the time. In fact, I think that's my new motto: I am a mess."

"Stand in line," Elise muttered. "Let's find our seats." She balanced her funnel cake in one hand, sliding her handbag into the crook of her arm so she could grab Kat and drag her into the tunnel.

Bah-bum-bah-bum-bah-bum . . .

As they emerged at the top of the rows positioned above the team benches, Elise heard the warning notes for the warm-up, sounding like the coming of *Jaws* on ice. Below, the rink with the huge Blue Note painted in the middle sat just beyond a partition of Plexiglas.

"Your tickets, ladies?" a young usher in a royal blue jacket and spiked-up hair stopped them to ask.

Kat shuffled her funnel cake into her left hand and reached in her pocket with her right, pulling out the ticket. Elise dug hers out, too, and the usher peered intently at them both before lifting his head.

"You're down to the right, row D."

"Great." Elise thanked him and descended the steps ahead of Kat. She didn't realize how close they were to the players until she slipped into her seat just as the horn blew and the Blues magically appeared from the tunnel, hitting the ice.

"Oh, my God, that was loud!" Kat said with a wince as she plopped down beside her. "Hey, it's cold in here. I'm glad I layered up."

But Elise wasn't listening. She stared ahead, transfixed, watching the team in navy and gold uniforms swirl around in a circle, hitting pucks to the goalie, while the Nashville Predators warmed up on the other side of the red line.

Joey would kill to sit here, she mused, thinking she should text him, tell him where she was, that Evan Lawrence had given her tickets to see him play. She could remind him of how they used to sit behind the home goal at rinkside, and he'd tease her about how she used to recoil, closing her eyes every time a puck hit the Plexiglas in front of them or a player checked another into the boards, causing the glass to shudder.

But she didn't text her son. She kept her BlackBerry in her purse, tucked against her side. The funnel cake sat on its paper plate, growing cool and forgotten in her lap, as she looked for

Evan out on the ice. Chilled air rose from the concrete at her feet, blowing up her legs and making her shiver.

Next time, I'll wear long underwear and jeans, she decided, her eyes locked on the moving circle of players. She read off the names on the back of the jerseys until her breath caught.

There he was! Or at least, there was a jersey with LAWRENCE spelled out in gold letters across the upper back. He followed the players before him and took a shot at the goal before coming around the corner. At just that moment he glanced up in her direction and did a double take. Had he not expected to see her?

He flashed a quick grin, and she saw the white plastic of his mouthpiece. Then he briefly raised his stick before he put his head back into the warm-up and caught a puck to shoot again.

He's glad I'm here, Elise thought, and blushed, getting that same giddy sensation she'd felt in the office.

"Are you having a hot flash?" Kat asked through a mouthful of funnel cake.

"No," Elise scoffed, though she wished she'd bought a program so she could fan her face. She did feel a little flushed.

"What's got you all red-faced, then?" Kat turned toward the rink and squinted at Evan's figure as he sailed around the ice. "You know him? That Lawrence guy?"

"He's a patient," Elise replied smoothly, "and he used to coach Joey's summer youth league team. He's the one who gave me these tickets."

"*Really?*" Kat peered at her intently. "Have you seen him naked, Lisie?"

"No, I haven't seen him naked," Elise said, and turned to Kat, giving her the evil eye. "Your mind's as dirty as Carla's."

"Well, he's very cute, even with all those pads on." Her friend smiled and raised her eyebrows, doing a fair impression of the Joker, with her mouth covered in white powder.

Elise sighed, wondering how they could both be forty-five when Kat still acted like a teenager. "You've got it all over your face again, Mary Katherine." She carefully dug in her purse, searching for a tissue since Kat had neglected to grab them some napkins. She spit on the corner of one, but Kat threw up a hand.

"Ew, no way you're putting slobber on my face. Would you loosen up, please? I'll go wash up in the bathroom after I've finished enjoying every fat-infused morsel."

"Sorry." Elise shoved the Kleenex in her coat pocket. "It's reflexive."

"Well, you don't have to mother me. I've got one already, and one Eileen Maguire is plenty." Kat nudged her with an elbow.

In another five minutes Kat had inhaled her entire funnel cake. She wadded up the plate and waxed paper, shoving it into her empty cup holder.

"So"—her friend jerked her chin at the untouched fried mess on Elise's lap—"are you going to eat that?"

Before Elise could reply, Kat picked up the plate from her lap and proceeded to demolish the second cake, too, or at least a good half of it.

Elise watched in astonishment. "How does someone so thin eat so much without exploding?" she wondered aloud.

"Sex," Kat replied with a powdered sugar smile.

"So about that tryst . . ." Elise started to ask, but her voice was drowned out as a foghorn blared through the sound system.

Egads! She clamped her hands over her ears until the noise stopped and peppy music ensued as the Blues began skating toward the tunnel, their warm-up over.

Elise forgot all else as she stared at the Plexiglas, watching as the players glided forward and then came off the ice. They disappeared one by one, heading into the locker room; though a few stayed behind, driving pucks into the cage until they, too, scurried off and out of sight. She got one last look at Evan just before he went in, and her heart beat a little bit faster.

"Beer! Ice-cold twenty fo's!"

A vendor with extra-tall cans of Budweiser brands came down their aisle, and Kat dusted off her fingers before flagging him down.

"You wouldn't happen to have Peroni, would you?" Kat asked, and the yellow-shirted beer man grinned from the aisle.

"No, ma'am," he said, then proceeded to reel off one Budweiser product after the next. Kat picked the Bud Select, and he immediately plucked one from his carton and began pouring it into a plastic cup.

"What d'you want, Lisie?" she asked as she balanced the funnel cake on her knees and dug a couple bills from her jacket pocket. "It's on me, too."

"I'm good, really," Elise told her. Though she'd craved a drink after talking to Michael, she didn't want one anymore. Being in the noisy arena, seeing Evan on the ice, it had all her senses waking up again, and she didn't want to dull them even a little bit.

"It feels like old times, doesn't it?" Kat said with a laugh, taking the twenty-four-ounce cup the man passed her. "I've got the booze, and you're the designated driver!"

"So much like old times." Elise sighed and closed her eyes for a minute, picturing herself behind the wheel of the boxy Volvo her parents had bought her when she'd turned sixteen. And there was Carla in the passenger seat, pointing out directions to a senior party they were crashing, and Kat in the back with a can of beer she'd stolen from her parents' fridge, saying, *Hey, don't worry about me! I'm not driving!*

"Dr. Randolph?"

Elise opened her eyes to see a young man in a dark blue sport coat and gold and blue striped tie standing in the aisle.

"Yes?"

"This is for you," he said matter-of-factly, and held out a folded square of paper.

When she reached out her hand, he plunked it into her palm. "Um, thanks."

"Are you supposed to tip him or something?" Kat whispered.

Elise shrugged. She'd never had a note hand-delivered to her at a hockey game before. Before she could fumble in her purse for money, the nattily dressed guy disappeared, so the point was moot.

"What does it say?" her friend asked, peering over her shoulder as Elise unfolded the notepaper.

Hey, Doc, you showed! Yell loud for me, okay? Evan

Elise smiled as she recalled Evan's comment in her office, about how Joey said she yelled louder than any mother at the rink. *Might've embarrassed Joe a little, but I loved how you got so into it.*

"So this Evan Lawrence is your patient, huh, Lisie? Are you sure that's all he is?" Kat asked, tipping her head as she watched Elise fold the paper and put it in her coat pocket.

"That's all he is," Elise repeated, though her cheeks warmed again as the blood rushed to her head.

"Uh-huh," Kat said dryly, "right. So who's the Cougar now?" she added in a singsong voice, and Elise tugged her hair. "Ouch, cut it out!"

"No, you cut it out."

A blast of music surged through the arena, and Elise looked up to see the Jumbotron flashing as the announcer did his best Ed McMahon, trilling, "And here's Charles Glenn!"

Elise turned to Kat to say, "Evan's a great guy but that's all," though her voice was lost in the noise of cheering and bellowing as a robust-looking Charles belted out the Blues version of "When the Saints Go Marching In."

Kat started singing along loudly, and Elise clapped to the beat, loosening up and getting into the spirit. Despite the cold near the rink, something thawed deep inside her, and a frisson of anticipation set off goose bumps on her skin. She ignored the images on the Jumbotron entirely, keeping an eye on the ice, waiting for the foghorn to bellow before the team came out and she could spot Evan again.

And when it happened—when the Blues players skated out and suddenly there he was—she forgot her troubles with Michael and any fear about the future. She could hardly stand still from the beginning note of the National Anthem until "the home of the brave" trailed off and the puck was dropped. She stomped her feet and chanted, "Let's go Blues, let's go Blues!"

She screamed like a woman possessed when the Blue Note with LAWRENCE on his jersey threw a Predator against the boards in a killer bodycheck, and she high-fived Kat, the usher, and half their section when T.J. Oshie ripped right past the Nashville defense and scored.

Three hours later, when the game ended and the Blues had won 3–2, Elise was hoarse from yelling, her legs were frozen, and she smelled beer in her hair. But it didn't matter. Being at the game had flipped a long dormant switch deep inside her.

She felt like she'd come alive again.

KAT

Kat Maguire on Sex and Dating:

Men are like shoes. You have to try on a few before you find a pair that won't rub you the wrong way.

Chapter Seventeen

I T was just after ten o'clock when they left the Blues game triumphant, and Kat had the brilliant idea to stop at the Ritz-Carlton for a drink before Elise headed back to the West County suburbs. Lisie didn't need much convincing.

Parking the Audi in the adjacent garage, they entered the hotel and wound their way past the ballrooms toward the Lobby Lounge, with its dark wood and chandeliered wall sconces. They settled in a pair of floral upholstered chairs around a small table on which a blue votive flickered.

Since the place was famous for having over two hundred types of martinis, Kat figured it would be a sin not to order one. So she decided on a pineapple upside-down cake martini, while Elise ordered a gin and tonic and the BBQ spicy chicken wings as an appetizer.

"Well, I'm hungry," Lisie declared. "I wasn't the one who in-haled two funnel cakes before the game even started."

"One and a half," Kat corrected, although it may as well have been two, as full as she'd felt. But she figured she'd used all that sugar up, as much as she'd jumped up and down, screaming and cheering the Blues on to victory over the Preds.

The bar was pretty quiet on a Thursday night, no live music and only small groups and couples enjoying the low-key setting; although Kat spotted a trio of men in suits drinking nearby. All clean-cut and several bespectacled with name tags pinned to their lapels, they were doubtless refugees from a winter conference of some kind.

One of them smiled, noticing her looking over, but she didn't offer him any hope. Stoically, she turned away. She was done with hook-ups and relationships with uncommitted men. From now on she'd stick to flirting and good old-fashioned dating. No more sex without strings. She wanted a soul mate, and for that she had to be patient. There had to be more to life than jumping in some hot guy's pants.

"What're you thinking about?" Lisie asked just as the waiter brought over their drinks and the plate of hot wings. "Sex?"

Kat nearly choked on a sip of pineapple martini. "Of course not," she lied, scrambling to change the topic. "I was remembering when we came here for tea one afternoon with Carla and Genevieve. I believe we were about eight—"

"Seven," Lisie interrupted as she licked barbecue sauce from her fingers. "And prissy Genevieve insisted we wear our Sunday best dresses and eyelet ankle socks with black patent Mary Janes."

"Oh, man"—Kat rolled her eyes—"I felt like I was in church, the way good ol' Genny kept instructing us under her breath to sit with our hands in our lap, ankles crossed, and no slouching."

"And heaven forbid we took a finger sandwich directly from

the serving plate instead of setting it on a napkin first," her friend remarked, and plucked up a wing with her pinky very properly extended.

"When Carla dropped a blob of jelly onto her Florence Eiseman dress, I thought the Queen Mum was going to clock her upside the head," Kat recalled with a wince. "I always felt kind of bad for Carla. Seems like whenever her mom gave her the time of day, she was on Car's case."

"I told myself that I'd never be like that with Joey," Lisie agreed, blond head bobbing. "He never had to beg for my attention, or act like a Stepford kid just to please me."

Although Kat thought Elise looked a little Stepford herself in her Nicole Miller print dress, a slim strand of pearls at her throat, her legs crossed, and napkin in her lap. The only thing Genevieve Moss would have frowned upon was Lisie eating her wings with her hands. *We are not Neanderthals*, Kat could practically hear Carla's mother chastising.

"Carla does have good table manners, I'll give her that," she murmured.

Elise chewed thoughtfully, swallowing before she added, "Having manners is one thing, but making your own child feel like they're never worthy of you is a horrible kind of punishment in itself."

"I'm glad my mom wasn't afraid of a mess," Kat said, and laughed. "Hell, I always thought of the Maguires as the Beverly Hillbillies of Ladue. My dad never was good at fixing up the house, and they were always too busy to hire someone else to do the work unless something was literally falling down. Half the time Meggie wore my hand-me-downs. We didn't care."

Lisie grinned, her lips slick with sauce before she dabbed at her mouth with her napkin. "Ah, but that made your house the most fun. Car and I knew that when we were under Eileen Maguire's roof, we could be ourselves. It was great."

"She's still that way."

"You're lucky, Kat, to have someone who loves you so uncon-ditionally, even when you're no longer sixteen or even thirty." Elise got quiet, pushing aside her plate and picking up her gin and tonic. She took a long, slow drink, nearly emptying the glass.

Her friend's girlish face looked so strained in the soft light, and Kat reached across the table for her hand. "How are you, Lisie? I mean, really and truly. Are things with Michael that bad?"

"Well, he doesn't beat me, and he doesn't call me names, and I certainly don't want for anything material."

"That's not what I asked," Kat said, letting go of her and lean-ing her forearms on the table, glad that Genevieve Moss wasn't there to do her *Mable, Mable, get your elbows off the table* rou-tine.

Elise sighed, dropping her hands in her lap. She pursed her lips before she replied, "I didn't put him first, not while I had Joey around, and I'm not sure I even put him second after I got back to work full-time, rebuilding my practice."

"You think he found someone else."

"He's changed, inside and out," Lisie said, her eyes downcast, avoiding answering directly. "I realized just the other day that his hair's different, and he wears clothes I can't imagine ever buying for him. He uses cologne that makes me sneeze."

"Twenty-three years is a long time," Kat remarked, trying to rationalize. "I'm sure neither of you is the same as the day you stood in Graham Chapel and said your vows."

"I don't feel like I've changed at all," Elise insisted, and her pale brows furrowed. "I don't think I'm any different than I was when we got married. Okay, except for the extra pounds and the cellulite on the back of my thighs and the wrinkles." She lifted her chin. "But if he doesn't like who I am anymore, he should speak up instead of just staying away. How am I supposed to know how he feels if he doesn't tell me?"

"How do you feel about him?" Kat asked, point-blank. "Do you love him now the same way you did when you were newly-weds?"

"Are you nuts?" Elise scoffed, flicking a hand in the air. "You can't keep that kind of passion once you've had a baby." She bit her lip and blinked rapidly, as if trying to figure it out. "Your love mellows, you know. It's comfy and warm like a Snuggie. Oh, hell," she groaned. "No wonder he's messing around."

"You don't know that for a fact," Kat tried to console her. "You need to go home tonight and talk to him, face-to-face. You're going to drive yourself mad if you let this go on any longer."

"You're right." Elise nodded at her before plucking her napkin from her lap and dropping it on the table. Then she glanced around the lounge.

"What're you doing?"

"Looking for the waiter so I can pay the bill and we can scram."

"Hey, I'll take care of it," Kat told her, getting up from her chair. "You do what you have to do."

Lisie got up as well, and Kat went around the small table and hugged her. She held on tightly for a moment, sensing the connection between them as strongly as she had when they were kids. She just wished she could do something more to help her friend.

"Thanks for the game. I hope it's the first of many."

"Me, too, now that you're home for real," Lisie whispered against her ear, and then drew away.

"If you don't mind, though, I think I'll stay and finish my drink."

"Stay?" Elise looked alarmed as she buttoned her coat and wound her scarf around her neck. "But how will you get back to the condo?"

"Please, it's across the street," Kat said with a sniff, "and I've got on enough layers to keep me warm for three hours at the hockey arena. Five minutes outside won't kill me."

"If you're sure—"

"I'm sure." Kat smiled as she picked up Elise's Prada clutch from the table and handed it over. "Hey, drive safely and good luck with Michael. Promise you'll call if you need me, even if it's three o'clock in the morning."

"I swear." Lisie gave her a backhanded wave and walked out, weaving through various sofas and chairs in the lobby area until she disappeared around the corner.

With a sigh, Kat sank down into Lisie's chair and reached across the tiny table for her martini. She decided not to let the rest of the chicken wings go to waste, either, and picked up one to nibble.

She glanced across the room at the bar and saw a well-dressed woman "of a certain age" nervously brushing highlighted blond hair off taut cheeks. Then she checked her watch and glanced across the lounge.

Ah, she's waiting for someone, but who? Kat wondered. She licked sauce off her fingers and surreptitiously watched the elegant blonde. Her husband, she decided, figuring at ten-thirty at night that was the only reasonable answer. They'd just come home from seeing a show at the Fox in midtown, and he let her off while he parked the car. They planned to have a nightcap before the bar closed at eleven and then they'd head upstairs to break out the Cialis.

The woman's chin lifted suddenly and a smile curved her painted lips.

Kat turned her head to see a man cutting his way through the cushioned sofas and chairs; and when the glow of the lounge lights illuminated his face, she realized it was a much younger man, no older than mid-twenties.

Probably the woman's son, she guessed, as he resembled a recent college grad with a navy blue hooded sweater, flat-front khakis, and loafers. He actually looked a little like her Peroni Guy from last night.

He settled beside the woman at the bar and leaned in for a kiss: a lingering smooch on the lips that left no doubt about their relationship. Kat grinned. The chic Cougar played with his short hair for a second before letting her hand land possessively on his arm. Then she summoned the bartender, ordering a drink for him; probably so he wouldn't get carded, Kat mused with a chuckle.

"You go, sugar mama," she said under her breath as she searched in her pocket for some bills and deposited them on the table.

She tugged on her down coat and tucked her scarf in front of her chin. Then she pulled on her gloves and took off into the cold, feeling the icy air bite her skin as she ducked her head and followed the sidewalk around Carondelet Plaza, heading toward the high rise just across the way. She reached the lobby of her building in about five minutes flat, although it felt like twice that, as cold as it was.

Kat used the key card Megan had given her to slip through the rear door. A buzzer went off as she went in and headed up a red-carpeted hallway toward the lobby.

She nodded at the night security guard at the front desk, peeling off her gloves and stuffing them into her pockets. She pressed the button for the elevator and stood there rubbing her hands, working the blood back into her fingertips.

"Ms. Maguire," the guard called to her, and she turned her head to see him rise from his chair. "There's someone here to see you," he said as she approached, which is when Kat realized a man was sitting on one of two tufted benches situated between potted palms.

She looked over as he stood, her brain not registering who he was until he got to his feet, ran a hand through his hair, and smiled cockily.

"Hey, Kat, long time no see," he said.

The elevator pinged, but she hardly heard it. All she could hear was the thud of her heart pounding as she swallowed hard and managed to get out, "Roger? What the hell are you doing here?"

<u>CARLA</u>

Carla Moss on
Helen Reddy's inadvertent Cougar anthem:

"I am woman, hear me roar?"
Please. Some days it's all I can do not to spit up a fur ball.

Chapter Eighteen

R ATS." Carla's breath hung on the air in icy puffs as she stuffed her cell back into her clutch after leaving a "Call me" voice mail for Randy. She missed seeing him tonight on-set, as he'd done his sports segment live from the Scottrade Center, interviewing Blues players after the game. She wished she could've been there, too, and maybe even introduced him to Kat and Elise.

Ah, well, that'll happen soon enough, she thought, thanking her lucky stars that at least Don Davidson had been back in his chair during the evening news broadcast, although Amber Sue's presence had been felt—Burton couldn't resist keeping the pressure on, could he?—reporting from a gubernatorial fund-raiser. Blondie had been all done-up in evening wear like a Miss America contestant. Carla had fought the urge to ask her on air if her lifelong dream was for world peace.

Jesse had been waiting in the wings for her the moment she

ended the half hour with her customary, "Good night, St. Louis, and good news."

"You said you'd go with me to the Loading Zone, and I'm holding you to it," he reminded her, pouting when she begged for a rain check.

"Not allowed," he told her, promising they wouldn't stay out late, just long enough for her to bask in the admiration of her fans and let off some steam.

So here she was, following Jesse from his parked car and walking through the freezing cold toward a gay bar on South Euclid. If she had an ounce of brains left, she should have been curled up in her toasty-warm bed, waiting for Randy to join her.

She wondered if Randy had left downtown yet. Would he stop by his apartment before he headed to her house? He'd been spending more and more time at her place lately, enough so that she was seriously contemplating giving him a key. Usually she panicked when a man left so much as a comb in her bathroom, but she didn't mind that Randy's pulsating toothbrush stayed plugged in atop her granite vanity. She felt strangely sanguine about his clothes invading her walk-in closet. If she didn't watch out, he'd start stashing his undies and socks in her bureau.

Carla wondered if she was getting soft in her old age, or, more likely, if she was getting soft on him. She shivered, although whether from the cold or the idea of Randy moving in, she wasn't certain.

"C'mon, Mossy, we're almost there. It's just the next block," Jesse said, impatiently waiting up ahead on the sidewalk. When she caught up, he linked his arm with hers to hurry her forward.

"I wish Randy were coming," she grumbled, hating how the hair in her nostrils froze and her throat burned from the frigid air. "But he's got his phone turned off, so he's probably still taping interviews with toothless puck jockeys."

"Honestly, it's for the best, sweetie," Jesse said. "He'd get hit on by every man in the place."

"You're right." Carla smiled in spite of the winter chill and how much her feet already hurt just from schlepping a block in stiletto-heeled boots.

"Here we are!" Jesse cried out, and dragged her through a door into a crowded space where the music was so loud Carla could feel the bass notes pound against her rib cage. "Isn't this fun?"

"Just super," she raised her voice to reply as Jesse started waving and shouting "Hi, hi, hi" at assorted gorgeous guys in turtlenecks and cashmere who milled about with drinks in hand, glancing up now and then at the enormous flat screens flashing music videos overhead.

Carla looked at all the pretty boys and felt very much like a diabetic in a candy shop. It wasn't fair to heterosexual women that the gays got such a large helping of the best-looking men. She figured the universe had a very black sense of humor.

Thank heavens she had a hunky guy at home and wasn't exactly on the prowl. Besides, tonight wasn't just about her. It was about Jesse, too, and their friendship, and his wanting to make her feel appreciated by people around town even if she wasn't exactly feeling the love in the newsroom.

Her "BGF," as Randy had dubbed him, looked divine in sleek black jeans, sharp-toed boots, bright orange T-shirt, and a chocolate brown jacket.

"C'mon, Mossy," he said, returning to her side to take her hand. "Let's head to the bar."

"So," she said, leaning toward his ear and talking above the noise, "are there enough med students and doctors from Barnes Jewish Hospital here tonight to satisfy you?"

"A few." He grinned impishly as they wove through the crowd.

"You're not going to dump me for a handsome urologist, are you?" she asked.

"I should get so lucky!" He tittered. "But I'm thinking more like a plastic surgeon, Mossy. Then it's free eye lifts for the rest of my life."

"Now that's a lovely thought."

He sat her down at a table and peeled her coat from her shoulders. "I'll get you a vodka martini, two olives," he shouted in her ear before heading toward the stretch of bar beneath a row of dangling pendant lights.

As she waited, Carla glanced around her.

Stairs went up to a second story that looked as packed with bodies as the ground floor. Nothing was plain vanilla. Yellow, purple, black, and green covered every wall, and displays of vibrant artwork added color atop color. Men—and a few women—wore everything from sedate shirts to silver lamé jackets and funky fuchsia hair. Above it all, a disco ball swirled, its tiny mirrors bouncing light in every direction. She would have thought nothing could faze this crowd. Then, slowly, heads began to swivel and people were pointing at her.

"Hey, it's Carla Moss," she heard someone say, and then noticed elbows nudge ribs and hands tap shoulders until she felt like all eyes were upon her.

Carla was used to being the center of attention, but usually when she was dressed in a pretty Chanel suit at a charity function, not when she was waiting for a martini at the local gay bar.

"Looking hot, Ms. Carla!" a ruddy-faced bald man called out, raising his glass to her, and a chorus of voices offered similar cheers.

"Thank you, darlings," she returned with a wave.

A Killers video flashed across the flat screens with Brandon Flowers jerkily dancing and singing achingly about love gone wrong, and suddenly no one seemed to notice her anymore.

Carla remembered when she'd come here for Jesse's birthday on Show Tunes Night, when patrons sang along to songs from the *The Wizard of Oz* and anything remotely Judy Garland, like grandiose video karaoke. He'd dressed her in her Diane von Furstenburg leopard-print wrap dress, which had the cutest dashes of hot pink mixed with whites, browns, and tans. But Jess had paired it with knee-high, hot pink, thigh-high Versace boots, a dozen skinny gold bracelets, chunky gold hoop earrings; and her hot pink Prada clutch, which seemed a little over-the-top even to her. She'd looked like an overzealous escapee from QVC, or a real-life Cougar Barbie.

She searched for Jesse, spotting his spiked-up hair and chocolate-hued jacket, standing shoulder-to-shoulder in the crowd at the bar. He kept laughing and tossing back his head like a girl.

Was he flirting with the bartender?

For God's sake, I'll die of thirst before he gets back at this rate.

Tired of waiting, she got up, grabbed her coat, and plowed her way toward the bar. She leaned over Jesse's shoulder, asking the bartender directly, "What do I have to do to get a drink around here?"

The blue-eyed bartender with the five o'clock stubble shot back at her, "Vodka martini, dry, two olives?"

"Yes." Carla blinked. "God, you're good."

"Oh, Mossy, I'm sorry," Jess babbled, his elfin face flushed, "but I got a wee bit distracted."

"I can see why," she murmured as the mixologist turned away from them and got busy fixing their drinks. "He looks like a young Mel Gibson."

"Doesn't he, though," Jesse agreed with a happy sigh.

Once Carla had her drink in hand, she plucked the olives out with the tiny red plastic sword, devouring them one by one. As she sipped, she put her back to the bar while Jesse resumed his tête-à-tête with the bartender. She watched two guys in bright crewneck sweaters who were shooting pool. Others congregated in groups at the round white tables and crowded the benches. A couple with their arms slung around each other's waists headed up the stairs, and another pair passed them on their way down.

Carla sighed and turned toward the bar, setting down her drink.

"Are you having fun yet?" Jesse asked, and she gave him her sweetest smile.

"Always when I'm with you," she said, touching his sleeve, and he took a sip of his Shiraz, peering at Mel Junior over the rim of his glass.

Carla stared down the bar, spotting a clean-cut man in a blue button-down and striped tie, with salt and pepper hair, standing shoulder-to-shoulder with a beaming bespectacled fellow. They kept grinning and leaning in toward each other, whispering and cracking each other up. As they interacted, one would pick lint off the other's sleeve, or brush the back of a hand gently against the other's cheek.

How good they looked together, Carla mused, like they were

in that honeymoon phase of the relationship where you want to keep touching.

Her heart tugged, and she thought of Randy. Would Jesse be pissed if she wanted to go home so soon? She'd take a cab so he wouldn't have to leave, too.

"Cute, aren't they?" Jesse said, having caught the direction of her gaze. "They're a couple of doctors in love." He nodded and set his glass down on the bar. "They're here all the time."

"Doctors, huh?"

"Plastic surgeons," he hissed into her ear, obviously down with the 4–1–1 on his homies. "But they're, like, attached at the hip, so I haven't got a shot."

"How awful for you," Carla murmured, trying to get a clear view of the man in blue. Something about him seemed very familiar.

The bespectacled doctor glanced her way and then said something to the guy in blue. Then both of them stared at her. She gave a little wave, figuring they'd pegged her as "Carla Moss, Anchorwoman," but neither man cracked a smile. In fact, Blue Button-Down looked freaked out at the sight of her.

Ding ding ding!

Bells as loud as cannonballs went off in her head.

"Oh, my God."

"Do you know him?" Jesse leaned in to ask.

Aw, hell, she didn't just *know* him. Not only had he fondled her breasts—well, it was more like he'd drawn on them with a Sharpie before he surgically enhanced them by a cup size—but he was married to one of her oldest friends.

Right now, he's been spending more time with his surgical partner than he spends with me.

Oh, boy, Elise was right about that, Carla realized. Her husband's heart—and his joystick—had obviously drifted.

"What's going on with you, Mossy?" Jesse tried again, nudging her this time. "Who is he to you?"

"He's Dr. Michael Randolph," she said under her breath. "He did my boobs a couple years back—"

"Ooh." Jesse's thin eyebrows peaked.

"—and he's married to a very dear girlfriend of mine."

"Ooooh!" Jesse squeaked as a No Doubt video started up and Gwen Stefani danced around in a white spacesuit and red lips. "So the doctor's been double-dipping, has he?"

"Looks that way, doesn't it?" Carla frowned. No wonder Lisie complained about Michael being MIA. Her dear hubby had a boyfriend.

"You okay?" Jesse inquired, sticking his face right in hers.

"No." She felt sick.

"Do you want to leave?"

"Hardly." What she wanted to do was walk over there and punch Michael in the nose. "I'm going over," she said, and set down her martini.

"Oh, Mossy, no!" Jesse called from behind her, but she was already on her way, not that she would have stopped.

Carla shouldered her way around the lip of the bar, keeping her gaze homed in on Michael, like that alone could pin him into place so he couldn't duck out the other way before she'd reached him. When she finally got to the spot, she was gratified to see that Michael and his boyfriend hadn't budged an inch. Maybe her superpowers actually worked.

"Carla." Michael said her name like a sigh, and his even features settled into lines of resignation. "I'm surprised to see you

here," he said, and she thought, I'll bet you are. "This is my partner, Phil Bernstein," he added, introducing the younger man.
"We're in practice together," he clarified.

Oh, yeah, she had a good idea what they'd been practicing all
right.

"You're Carla Moss from Channel 3." Phil's eyes went wide
behind the glasses of his trendy specs. "I've watched you on the
news since high school."

"Fabulous." She gave him a tight little nod so as not to be
completely impolite.

Jesse emerged from the crowd, his cheeks flushed, hanging
onto both their drinks. Carla angled him toward Michael's partner, introducing them briskly, "Dr. Phil, this is Jesse. Jesse, Dr.
Phil, the plastic surgeon. Now would you excuse me for a moment
while I have a chat with Michael?"

Jesse hardly needed prodding. Carla heard him asking, "So,
I was thinking of having my ears pinned back to make my head
look slimmer," when she turned and faced Michael.

She didn't waste another minute. "Do you realize you're par-
tying at a gay bar with your 'partner' while your wife sits home
alone, twiddling her thumbs and wondering where you are?"

"Elise isn't twiddling her thumbs," Michael calmly replied.
"She went with Kat to a hockey game."

Like that was any kind of excuse for what he was doing?

"Hello? Don't you get it? She should've been at that Blues game
with you!" She dug in her heels, because she had no patience for
men who made excuses for wandering penises. "You have to tell her
about *this*." She flicked her fingers toward apple-cheeked Phil, who
had to be at least ten years Michael's junior. "You have to explain to
Elise that you're in love with someone else. She deserves to know."

Michael blew out a breath. "Look, I've been meaning to, really I have, but there hasn't been a good time—"

"A good time? For Christ's sake!" Carla cut him off mid-excuse and chastised, "There's never a good time for a husband to confess to his wife that he's gay and break up their twenty-three-year marriage." She crossed her arms snugly and gave him the evil eye. "So do it fast and do it tonight."

"Tonight? Are you crazy?" Michael balked, glancing over her shoulder at Phil.

"You heard me. Go home right now and talk to her." Carla leaned toward him and poked him right in the middle of the chest. "And if you don't do it, I will."

He ran a finger beneath his button-down collar, and perspiration glistened on his upper lip. "I don't want to hurt Elise. She's a good woman."

"You're right," Carla agreed. "She's a good woman who deserves to be with a man who loves her. And I don't mean loves her like a sister."

"What if she cries?"

"Of course she'll cry!" Carla wanted to choke him.

What the hell was wrong with men—even the gay ones who should have more sense—that made them deathly afraid of confrontation? It was like their chromosomes were wired for avoidance, unless it meant sending an army in their stead to do the battling for them.

"News flash, Doc"—she poked his shoulder, punctuating each word—"you're hurting her now by leaving her hanging. I saw Lisie last night, and she's already acting like an old shoe that's lost its mate. So put an end to her misery, would you? Give her the chance to move on, because you've obviously got a head start in that department."

"I'll certainly take all that into consideration," Michael said, pretty much dismissing her. "It's been, um, interesting talking to you, Carla, but I think it's time we ran along." He tugged at the cuffs of his monogrammed shirt and glanced over her shoulder, trying to catch Phil's eye.

Oh, no, Carla thought, you're not getting off that easy.

"Hold on there, Mikey," she replied as she flipped open her bag and pulled out her iPhone. She touched on her app for stored numbers, found what she was looking for, and dialed.

Michael's face screwed up, watching her. "Who're you calling?"

Carla held up a finger as a voice on the other end answered. "Lisie? Thank God, you're there. Yes, it's Car," she said. "You won't believe who I've run into at the Loading Zone. What? No, it's not a shipyard, sweets, it's a gay bar. Do you have a minute?"

Before she could say another word, Michael had snatched the phone from her hand, setting it on the bar and pinning it down with his palm.

"Okay, you win," he said, all the blood drained from his face. "I'll go home now and talk to Elise. But I want to be the one to tell her, do you hear me?"

"Loud and clear," she assured him. Then she winced, eyeing her cell on the damp-looking bar counter. "Can I have that back now?"

He shoved it into her hands before reaching past her to grab Phil by the arm. "C'mon," he said, "we're leaving."

They disappeared into the crowd, and Carla picked up her

phone, put it to her ear for a second, and still heard the awful hold music-slash-advertising spiel from her local U. City Domino's Pizza. She hung up and slid the phone back in her bag.

"Did you set him straight, Mossy?" Jesse asked, sidling up beside her.

"Set him straight?" She wrinkled her nose. "Is that a joke?" She picked up her martini, finished it off, and ran a tongue over her lips. "Would you take me home, please," she asked, not in any mood to party. All she could think about was poor Lisie, who was about to get the shock of her sheltered suburban life.

Carla paid for their drinks, pulled on her coat, and waited for Jesse near the door so he could say good-bye to the bartender.

Her hand itched to dig into her bag and yank out her iPhone to warn Elise of what was coming; but she knew she had to give Michael first dibs on spilling all to his wife. *It'll be all right, Lisie,* she wanted to tell her friend. *Whatever happens, you'll survive and you'll move on. I should know.*

But nothing prevented her from calling Kat, right?

Only when Carla hit speed-dial for Kitty-Kat, she ended up in her voice mail. *Damn.* Instead of leaving a convoluted message, she hung up. How did one go about telling one friend that another friend's philandering husband was gay, anyway? She sighed. Ah, well, it would be out in the open soon enough. Thank God, Elise wouldn't have to go through any of it alone. She would be here for her, and she knew Kat would as well.

What the dickens is taking Jesse so long?

Carla peered toward the bar and tapped her foot impatiently. She was pulling on her gloves when Jesse finally approached. "There you are," she muttered. "For a moment, I thought you'd run away with the Mel Gibson clone."

"Not quite." He beamed, waving a folded napkin in the air.

"You got his number?" she asked, arching her eyebrows.

"And he's got mine." Jesse smiled gleefully as he tucked it away in his coat pocket.

"Tramp," she joked, and laced her fingers with his. "Now, let's go," she urged, and tugged him toward the door, dying to get home.

Carla told Jess not to take her back to her car in the lot at KMOK. She could have Randy drive her into work in the morning, and her Lexus would be fine sitting in her reserved spot in the underground lot overnight.

When they arrived at her pretty 1920s pillared brick home in University City, she gave him a peck on the cheek and scrambled out of the Mini-Cooper. Spotting Randy's Range Rover in the rear drive, she scurried quickly toward the door and let herself inside.

"Randy?" she called out upon entering the foyer.

"Up here!" he replied.

Carla raced up the stairs, tugging off scarves and gloves and leaving a trail in her wake. She had her coat off by the time she'd reached her bedroom, and it was a good thing.

Randy reclined in her queen bed, his adorable black-framed reading glasses propped on his nose, looking a lot like Clark Kent. Her copy of *The Secret* was propped open on his bare chest. "I think it works," he said, and closed the book, tapping its cover. "I envisioned you coming home and getting naked with me, and, well, here you are." He gestured at her and grinned.

Something inside her twanged. Maybe she pulled a heart muscle. Whatever it was, it propelled her forward faster than a booster rocket.

She dropped her coat on the floor and walked straight toward him. Without a word, she snatched the book from his hands and tossed it aside. Then she plucked his specs from his nose and folded them up, setting them on the table.

"Sure, that's a start," he said, "but I'm still waiting for the naked part."

Impatient, she peeled off her dress and tugged down her panty hose, kicking the wadded nylons away as she crawled onto the bed and straddled him in bra and panties. She slid her hands up his chest to his shoulders, and she leaned over so their lips were but a breath away.

"Promise me you're not gay," she whispered, as earnest as she'd ever been, and he snorted loudly.

"What the hell is that about?"

"Swear you won't ditch me for a pretty surgeon named Phil," she repeated, and gazed at him with furrowed brow. "Because I couldn't bear it if you did."

"You're insane, you know—"

Carla gave him a look, and he forced a stern expression on his face.

"I swear on my Hula Bowl Championship ring that I am not gay and will never leave you for anyone named Phil," he pledged, playing along, but eyed her curiously. "Babe, I'm not going anywhere, okay? I like things just the way they are." He snaked his arms around her, fingers toying with the clasp on the back of her brassiere. "Feel better now?"

"Much," she replied, and kissed him hard, and he kissed her right back.

ELISE

Dr. Elise Randolph
on a skin-care segment for "Great Day St. Louis":

Moving on can be scary. We all get so deep into our routines that it's like the world has ended when we can't find our usual products. But with new and better skin care solutions coming on the market all the time, it pays to step outside our comfort zone and give something new a try.

Chapter Nineteen

ELISE caught the faint strains of Rush on the radio and turned the volume up to hear Geddy Lee singing, "Fly by night away from here, change my life again."

Change my life, indeed, she thought, and sighed as a host of conflicting emotions pressed against her chest, making it hurt even to breathe.

I will talk to Michael, and we will clear the air, no matter how it ends.

As she flew west on the interstate, the speedometer nestled right around seventy, few other cars in sight, she held tight to the steering wheel and kept her eyes on the gray of highway unfurling before her headlights, trying her best to think of nothing. Whatever was coming, she couldn't stop it, and her ability to dissect and overanalyze wouldn't matter a whit.

In another fifteen minutes she took the exit ramp and eased off a bit on the accelerator, slowing down as she drove past lit-up shopping centers and grocery stores. She started chewing on the inside of her cheek as she left the malls behind, the night darker suddenly as she wound along Wild Horse Creek. Snow-covered branches and brush lined the road, the stark winter landscape interrupted by occasional yellow warning signs to watch for leaping deer.

Elise hit the blinker just before she turned into her subdivision, going up about a block and then rolling into her driveway, tires crackling on the thin crust of snow left behind by the shovels of their year-round lawn service.

As the garage door rolled up, she found herself praying that Michael's bright yellow Saab would be MIA, and she swallowed a thick knot of anxiety when she saw it there, covering the messy oil spot.

Maybe he's asleep already, she told herself. And what if he was? Would she have the nerve to wake him up, or would she put the unavoidable conversation off for another day and then another day after that?

Crap, why did this have to be so hard?

As quietly as she could, she let herself into the house, hanging up her coat and setting aside her gloves and bag. She slipped off her shoes and carried them in her hand as she tiptoed from the kitchen into the dark living room. She was halfway through when a lamp was switched on near the fireplace.

"Hello, Elise."

She stopped abruptly, dropping her shoes, and flung a hand to her heart; like if she held it there, it would keep it from beating right out of her chest. When her eyes stopped seeing spots, there was Michael sitting in one of the wing-back chairs that flanked the hearth. He leaned back, his legs crossed. Why the hell had he been sitting there in the dark?

"I didn't mean to scare you," he said, and she realized his eyes were bloodshot.

Has he been crying, she wondered, or drinking?

"Hey, nothing like a near heart attack to end the evening on a high note," she remarked, her pulse still racing as she dared to say, "I'm glad you're here, actually. I was hoping we could talk."

"Great minds think alike," he said, and gestured toward the companion chair on the other side of the fireplace. "Please, sit."

She did as he requested, walking across the large room and settling into the upholstered chair nearby him. Clutching at the wide arms, she fought to play it cool.

"I've been putting this off for too long," Michael started slowly, wringing his hands, hardly able to look at her. "I'm sorry I've put you through this."

Elise sat ramrod straight, her spine hardly touching the back of the chair. Now that the moment of truth had come, she wasn't all-fired certain she wanted to hear it. It took everything within her not to jump up and run from the room.

"Go on," she forced herself to say instead.

His eyes filled with sadness as they met hers. "I fooled myself into thinking you wouldn't notice what's been going on for months. I pretended that you couldn't see."

She squinted at him, waiting for him to speak the truth and not in riddles. "See what exactly?"

"The elephant in the room," he said as if it were obvious. "I can't imagine you don't know exactly what I'm talking about."

She curled her toes into the carpet, bracing herself for what was surely to come: his confession of unfaithfulness.

"I'm listening," she said.

"There's no easy way to say this except outright. So here goes."

He sucked in a deep breath, and Elise held hers. "I've been involved with someone for a while now, and I didn't know how to tell you."

"How serious is this 'involvement'?" Much as she thought she'd steeled herself for this, her right eye began a nervous twitch.

He shifted in his seat, not directly answering the question. "Please, understand that I never meant to hurt you, Elise. It's just that I realized a while ago that I'd changed, and that's when I started lying."

"I knew it," she murmured. "I knew it, I knew it."

All those after-hours consultations and late business meetings, all his excuses for staying away from home so many nights: lies upon lies upon lies. The barbecued wings she'd eaten half an hour earlier curdled in her stomach, and she hoped she didn't vomit all over the Berber carpet.

"I'm not who you think I am," Michael went on, and wouldn't meet her eyes. He kept staring down at his hands, rubbing one over the other. "I'm not the man you married, El. Maybe I never was."

She had to refrain from shouting out, *That's for damned sure!*

"No," she said quietly, and tasted bile in her mouth. "You're not. And I don't understand this new Michael at all. How could you break your vows? How could you cheat on me?" She hung onto the chair, fingers curled over the arms to keep her from shaking. "You should have brought it up as soon as it started so I wasn't always wondering and worrying, blaming myself for things that weren't my fault."

He leveled his gaze on her, and his eyes welled with tears. "I'm so sorry, Elise, so very sorry."

"Yes," she told him, nodding, "you are."

No matter that she'd figured it out in her heart already, it hurt worse than she had imagined it would, having her husband sit across from her and confess that he'd been cheating.

"So," she asked, hating how her voice quivered, "who is she?"

"Who is she?" His eyes widened suddenly and then a narrow smile settled on his lips, like what was going on between them was more comedy than tragedy. "Oh, God, you thought I've been seeing another woman?"

"You're not?"

He shook his head.

Elise wiped her nose with her sleeve and stared at him. She'd assumed the little slut who lured him away was a patient half his age with taut skin and tummy, whose breasts he'd rebuilt and butt he'd resculpted. So if he wasn't screwing around with a woman, it could only mean he was seeing—

"It's Phil," he said soberly, any trace of a smile vanished. "He's hated that I've lied to you, El. He wanted to tell you from the start, but I wouldn't let him."

Holy crap.

Her mind took a jolt, like the noise of an old stereo needle scratching across an LP. "Phil Bernstein?" She said the name, sure she'd gotten something wrong. "Dr. Phil, your surgical partner?"

"Yes." He nodded as tears dripped off his lashes and slithered down his cheeks, "It's been going on for months."

"But that means you're—" She struggled to get out the rest of it. "—gay?"

"I guess I am." He shrugged. "It feels right," he said, as if that made it all clear.

Elise sat there, dumbfounded. How was she supposed to react

to the news that her spouse of two decades had been playing hide the pickle with another man? Wasn't sexual orientation something he should've figured out in his teens? Why had he dated her for so long, proposed to her, married her, if he wanted to be with a man?

"You and Phil, Phil and you," she repeated until it sank in. She thought of all the nights he'd been gone when she imagined him in the arms of another woman. Did it make it any less hurtful to know that he'd been with a guy? That no matter how thin her thighs, how pert her breasts or flat her tummy, she could never compete?

Elise pressed her hands against her head, like the confusion inside her brain might split her skull in two.

"I still love you, El, and I always will. Just as I'll always love Joey," Michael said, brushing tears from his cheeks, "but I'm *in* love with him."

She lowered her hands to her lap, her lips tightly pursed, wanting to be rational; trying to understand.

"Did I turn you somehow?" she asked bluntly, wondering what had caused this to happen. How could someone be straight for years and years and then change his mind? "Was I not good enough at sex?"

"No, sweetheart, no," he replied, looking horrified that she had even asked. "It was nothing you did or didn't do. It was something inside me all along, feelings I ignored because I was too scared to acknowledge them. But Phil and I spent so much time together"—he shrugged again—"I fell for my best friend."

She had once believed that *she* was Michael's best friend, not to mention his lover and the mother of his only child. At least the mother part still held true.

Elise sat there, not knowing what to do, and her gaze wandered the room, looking everywhere but at him. She ended up staring at the family portrait hung over the mantel: the three of them, smiling, Michael's arm binding her so closely to him; and both of them with a hand on Joey's shoulder. They looked like the perfect family.

She sniffled, wiping the back of her hand across her cheeks to stop the tears, unable to fathom how they'd break this to Joey.

Sorry, son, but we're splitting up because your dad's partner, Dr. Phil, is now really and truly his partner, if you get my drift.

"How did we get here from there?" she asked, still looking at the portrait. "How could this happen to us?"

"Life doesn't come with an instruction manual. It's unpredictable," Michael said, and at least that much was true.

There was definitely nothing logical about what was happening to them, Elise silently agreed, afraid of what lay ahead for her. How would she cope as a single woman? She was so used to being part of a pair, even in name only. What would they do with the house and all their intermingled assets? And, even scarier still, would she die alone?

She thought of Carla and Kat suddenly, of how different she'd always believed her life was from their lives. She had considered herself the one who'd done everything right, or at least in the right order: man, marriage, career, and child. Now she'd be in their shoes, living alone and dating again. Could she handle it as well as they did? Or would she fall apart?

"Elise?" Michael asked, peering at her with a weird expression on his face. "Are you okay? You're awfully flushed."

"I'm flushed, did you say?" She put her hands to her cheeks, and, by God, they were burning up. "Flushed, as in down the toilet like our marriage, how apropos," she remarked, and began to laugh bitterly. "Right . . . down . . . the . . . crapper," she gasped between loud hyenalike wheezes.

She doubled over, tears streaming from her eyes for several endless minutes before her momentary hysteria wound down and she was quiet again. But the tears still fell, sliding down her cheeks as quickly as she brushed them off.

"Oh, please, sweetheart, don't do this." Michael leapt up from his chair and came to her side, putting a hand on her back and rubbing, as if that would solve anything.

For a doctor, he seemed awfully uncertain of how to take care of his own wife. Or perhaps that was his problem. He didn't know, had never known.

"If you thought I'd be big about this, you're wrong," she said, sniffling, and picked up the skirt of her dress to blot her face. "You're pulling the rug out from under me, Michael, and I don't know what you expect me to feel."

"I know, I know," he murmured.

"No," she told him, barely holding herself together, "you can't even begin to fathom what's going on inside me right now."

"Will you ever forgive me?" He knelt in front of her and tried to put his arms around her, hugging her awkwardly around the hips, and set his head in her lap.

"Please, don't ask me that so soon." Elise sat stiffly, unwilling to touch him.

"I wish I could change things, I do!" Michael moaned. "I wish I could've been the person you thought I was, and I tried to be. I really tried. But sometimes things happen, and you can't seem to stop them. Sometimes there's nothing you can do but follow your heart."

But it wasn't *her* heart he was talking about. It was his. He'd done exactly what he wanted, only where did that leave her? Elise wondered again, What do I want? Or did that not matter?

"Do you hate me?" he sobbed.

She wished she could. She really did. But she couldn't, not after all they'd been through together.

"I don't hate you, Michael," she replied with a sigh. "I just wish things had been different."

She wondered how she'd missed the signs for so long. She'd known Michael since high school, and still hadn't known him at all. Had he fooled her, or was she just that blind? How could she not have realized the man she married had started batting for the other side?

"Elise, talk to me," he whispered, lifting his head to look at her with soggy eyes.

"Can you leave me alone for a while, Michael," she finally said, setting her hand on his shoulder. She couldn't sort anything out with him there, crying and begging for her forgiveness.

He practically slobbered all over her. "Anything you want, El. I can stay in the guest room—"

"You can't stay here," she told him, a vague sort of numbness setting in. "I'd rather you go."

His brow wrinkled. "Are you sure?"

"Yes." All the times she'd wished he would come home to her and come to bed with her, talk to her again like they used to, and now she was asking him to leave.

"Okay, but I'll call you first thing in the morning," he said as he rose to his feet. "I don't want you to go through this alone."

"I won't be alone," she told him, thinking of Kat and Carla; of how much she needed them now, more than ever. "Good-bye, Michael."

"Good-bye," he said, and kissed her on the brow.

Elise closed her eyes and didn't open them again until she heard the door to the garage shut. Slowly, she rose from the chair and went toward the bay window. There, she pulled back the drapes and watched his yellow Saab drive off into the night.

She had thought nothing could feel worse than when her parents passed so close together, but having Michael leave her was like cutting off her left arm after she'd already lost her right.

I am stronger than I know, she told herself. *I made it through med school, internships, a residency, and giving birth, so I will get through this, too. I will.*

The grandfather clock ticked loudly in the quiet as she walked upstairs and went straight to Joey's room. She picked up her son's battered baseball glove and curled up on his bed with it pressed against her cheek like a pillow, breathing in its old leather scent; needing its comfort as she grieved for the only life she'd ever known; because it was over.

KAT

Kat Maguire on the Origin of Men:

I wouldn't say all men are from Mars, at least not the ones I've dated. More likely they came from Uranus, which would go a long way in explaining why they were such giant pains in the ass.

Chapter Twenty

NICE place you've got here," Roger said after Kat had unlocked the door to let him in and switched on some lights. "You must've been holding out on me, babe." He dropped his coat on the sofa and went to stand in front of the glass doors to the terrace. Even with the glow of lamps in the living room, the lights of downtown and the Arch flickered in the distance. He let out a whistle. "That's some view, although it's a far cry from Manhattan."

"It's only temporary," she told him, although she didn't owe him any explanation. She shrugged off her coat and draped it neatly over the arm of a chair. "You never answered my question. What're you doing here?"

He turned away from the sliding doors and faced her. The cocky smile was gone, and he wiped at his brow. Was he sweating? Roger rarely showed his nerves, so something big was going on. Had he joined AA and needed to repent?

"We need to talk," he said simply.

"Do we?" She crossed her arms, remembering his text telling her that if she ran away, to stay gone. So what was he doing in St. Louis? "What more is there to say?"

"You never gave me a chance to say anything at all," he reminded her. "Just let me have a few minutes. Is that too much to ask?"

His puppy dog eyes tugged at her heartstrings, as they always had. But Kat reminded herself that she'd only just gotten past him and everything she'd left behind. If he'd come to tell her how much he'd changed, she wasn't about to buy it. So maybe he looked a little different. His dark hair wasn't perfectly positioned with pomade, there were shadows beneath his eyes, and he had several days of stubble on his face. He wore jeans and a forest green polo-collared sweater instead of his usual trademark tailored shirt and slacks.

But it would take more than clothes to convince her that the old Roger was gone. And even if it was true, she didn't want him back. So if he'd come for her, he'd made the trip for nothing. Her mind had been made up the day she left.

"How did you find me?" she asked, because she hadn't told him where she was, and she was dead sure that Megan hadn't spilled. Her sister had never liked Roger, not even when Kat believed herself in love with him.

He gave a loose shrug. "I called your mom and pretended I was from D&M, said I had urgent paperwork I needed to FedEx ASAP for your signature so that your severance check could be cashed, and she coughed up this address right away."

Kat couldn't believe how proud he looked at deceiving Eileen. "You're a weasel, you know that."

"But a charming weasel," he replied, and actually had the nerve to smile.

How she ached to kick his toned gluts out of there and leave her boot imprint permanently on his ass.

But she remembered just how persistent he was when he wooed her, and she didn't want to drag this out. She needed to be rid of him once and for all.

"All right, all right, you've got five minutes," she told him, caving in as she always did, sure she would regret it in the morning. She flopped down angrily on the sleek modular sofa, and he walked toward her; but, to his credit, he didn't sit beside her.

"Thank you." Roger perched on the edge of the coffee table and leaned his forearms on his knees, bending forward. "I've missed you, Kat. More than I imagined. I really thought you'd come back."

She let out a noisy breath, deciding he was delusional. "You can't be serious?"

"Yes." He blinked, looking wounded. "I am."

"Look, it was never going to work between us," she assured him, shaking her head. "We were at such different places in our lives, and more importantly, I couldn't trust you, Rog. Not with the maid and not even with your computer."

"Jesus, you're still mad about that—"

"Think about it this way," she interrupted, deciding that giving him numbers was the only way to register the gulf between them in his financially attuned brain. "When I turn fifty, you'll be thirty-three. You won't be where I am now for seventeen years. I'll be sixty-two by then. I don't want to wait that long for you to catch up to me."

"What?" Now it was his turn to stare at her like she was deranged.

"Seventeen years, Rog," she reiterated. "That's what separates us. Do you realize that's 119 in dog years?"

Oh, God, now she was quoting Megan. That was how unhinged Roger made her.

When he merely squinted at her, appearing even more confused, she raised her hand, waving off the thought.

"Forget it," she said. "It's not worth explaining. "I've put it all behind me. I've put *us* behind me." She met his eyes. "And you should, too."

"I can't do that, Kat," he told her, his pretty-boy face settled into a frown. "I can't seem to move on."

Roger could walk into any bar in Manhattan and, within seconds, have ten women clinging to him like Velcro. The idea that he couldn't replace her with someone younger, bustier, and more pliable was laughable. She hardly knew how to respond.

"Keep trying. I'm sure you'll get the hang of it," she said, and patted her thighs, thinking she'd had enough. "I'd say we're done. So have a safe flight back." She stood and took a step around him, ready to open the door and usher him out.

"Hey!" He reached out and snagged her wrist. "You didn't let me finish. Damn it, Kat," he breathed, "just give me another minute."

At this rate he'd be here all night.

"Okay, one minute." She plunked down again and grabbed a throw pillow, holding it tight against her belly.

He leaned awkwardly to his left, sticking a hand in his right jeans pocket and removing something. Though whatever it was, he'd palmed it and held it in his lap.

"What I came to St. Louis to show you is how much I love you, Kat Maguire. I've figured out these past weeks that I don't want to live without you. You've won, all right? I see the error of my ways, and I want you back. For good," he declared without a breath in between.

Kat stared at him, wondering if he'd lost his mind, or if he was rehearsing lines for an off-Broadway production of "My Gullible Ex-Girlfriend: the Musical."

She opened her mouth to tell him to cut the crap, and he did the one thing she wouldn't have expected in a million years: he dropped down on bended knee and held his hand out to her. Pinched between his fingers was something that glinted mightily in the lamplight. Kat blinked a couple times, sure that she was seeing things.

"Marry me," he croaked, and stuck a ring in her face.

"What the—"

"Do you recognize it?" he cut her off, as though afraid to let her speak. "It's the one you looked at that time we stopped in Tiffany at Christmas. You said it reminded you of an antique."

Whoa, whoa, whoa.

Her eyes fixed on the Tiffany Legacy engagement ring that she'd once lusted after, when she was foolish enough to imagine herself in love with him; and even more foolish to envision them getting married one day. The cushion-cut center stone looked to be at least two carats, and then there were all those tiny bead-set diamonds surrounding it.

A pitiful sound squeezed from Kat's throat, kind of a strangled "Argh."

"Seriously, it's the real thing," Roger reassured her. "I've got the box back in the loft. I wore it here on my pinky finger. I didn't trust the TSA." When she didn't respond, he wet his lips and tried again. "Babe, say something, anything, please."

Kat didn't know what to do. She could hardly think straight much less speak, except to quietly murmur, "I can't do this . . . I can't."

"But this is what you wanted, isn't it?" he asked, and his tone turned petulant, as it was always wont to when he didn't get his way. "It's why you really left, because I wouldn't commit." He shook the ring at her. "How could I be more committed than this?"

That snapped Kat back to reality, and she remembered everything that was wrong with their relationship. The way it was always about what Roger wanted, and her needs got pushed to the wayside. Did he think a ring would change anything?

"Talk to me, babe," he begged. "Just say yes."

"No," she finally coughed up, and tossed the pillow from her lap, reaching out to him; but instead of taking the ring, she pushed it away, shaking her head. "This is not what I want from you, Roger."

Now it was his turn to stare at her with a what-the-fuck look on his face.

"I didn't leave you because you wouldn't marry me. I left you because I wasn't happy," she confessed. "I'd lost who I was, and I didn't even know it until everything I thought I had was gone."

"I don't understand." He tucked the ring away in his pocket. "You told me you loved me."

"And I did. I really did," she said with all honesty. "Only that was then and this is now. I've got a new life here, and I like it so far. I'm not going back to New York, not for you or for anything else."

He looked crushed by her words, but she was not about to give him any false impressions to cling to.

"Are you sure that's what you want?" he asked.

"Aw, Roger"—she touched his arm—"you're twenty-eight, for

God's sake. You're not ready for marriage. Hell, I'm forty-five, and I don't know if I'm ready. When you find your soul mate, it won't take her walking out for you to know you want to spend eternity with her. You'll feel it when it's right."

"What if it's right now?" he growled.

She laughed. "Take my word for it. It's not."

"Damn it, Kat, I don't get you." Red in the face, he glared at her. "I thought this would make up for everything."

"I know," she said, and smiled sadly. "And that's why we'd never work. We're not in the same place in our lives, and that's not a terrible thing. It just means we need to go our separate ways and find whatever it is we're looking for."

"Why are you doing this?" he groaned, dropping his head into his hands.

"Would you rather I lie to you?"

"I guess not." He pinched his nose, like he was warding off tears.

Oh, crap, don't let him cry, not for real.

"Come here," Kat said, and leaned forward, putting her arms around him. He stiffened at first but then hugged her back, burying his head in the crook of her neck. "I hope you find what you're looking for," she whispered before she let him go and stood up. "You will, I promise, someday, when you're truly ready."

He looked up at her. "So that's a no? You didn't change your mind?"

"I'm sorry," she said, and picked up his coat from the sofa.

"I'm sorry, too." He rose from the coffee table and took his lined cashmere bomber jacket. "For everything."

"Apology accepted."

Maybe she was wrong about him. Maybe he was trying to

change. Could be he'd learned a valuable lesson, and one of these days he would find a woman he loved and treat her right from the start. It was a pleasant thought anyway.

"You do have someplace to sleep tonight, don't you?" she asked, not that she'd let him stay with her. But she could point him across the way to the Ritz, and he could bunk down there until he caught a flight out in the morning.

"I've got it covered," he said as he zipped up his coat.

"Then it's good-bye, I guess." She hooked her thumbs in her belt loops and gazed at him. "Have a safe trip home."

"So long, Kat." He headed toward the foyer, and she followed. Before he opened the door, he paused and turned around. "Never settle, babe. You deserve the best."

"Don't worry," she promised, giving him a tired smile. "I won't."

He walked out of the condo and out of her life, and she had no regrets; although it might have been nice to try on that ring, just for sport.

God, but it's been a long day, she thought as she locked up tight and switched off lights en route to the bedroom.

All she wanted to do was undress and crawl into bed. She wasn't even sure if she had enough energy to wash her face and brush her teeth. She'd unzipped one boot and tugged it off when her BlackBerry buzzed from her back pocket.

Who'd call her at midnight? she wondered, until it hit her.

Lisie.

She answered instantly and heard Elise's soft voice on the other end, saying, "I know it's late, Kat, but can you come over?" She sounded like she'd been crying, and Kat couldn't imagine telling her no.

"Of course I can. I'll be right there."

She set her PDA down to pull her boot back on and then grabbed her coat on her way out the door.

When she arrived on Elise's doorstep twenty minutes later, Lisie let her in, still wearing the dress she'd had on at the hockey game. Her hair was a tangled mess and her eyes had turned a puffy pink. Kat's heart felt near to breaking at the sight. "It didn't go well with Michael, huh?"

Elise shook her head slowly. "It's over," she said in a ragged voice. "I told him to leave."

"Oh, God, I'm so sorry, sweetie." She hugged Lisie tight, rocking her gently before she pulled away, catching her friend's face between her hands. "Are you okay?"

"Honestly, Kat, I don't know."

Elise looked defeated and lost, like a frightened child with her arms wrapped around her middle, standing there in her stocking feet.

"C'mon"—Kat's mother hen instincts kicked in—"let's get you changed and in bed. I'll make hot cocoa, and we'll talk for as long as you want."

Lisie didn't even protest.

Kat led her upstairs and dug into several drawers before she found a soft old pair of flannel PJs. She left Lisie to undress and put them on while she went downstairs and banged around in the kitchen.

She found a quart-sized saucepan and turned on a burner to heat up milk while she melted chocolate chips in a bowl in the microwave. When she had two mugs of steaming hot chocolate, she carried them up.

Lisie had crawled into bed and had the covers tucked around her, several pillows behind her head. Kat set both mugs on the end table and crawled into the bed beside her.

"Do you want to talk first or drink the chocolate?" she asked.

"Talk, please," Lisie murmured, and laid her head on Kat's shoulder.

After a weighty sigh, the words began tumbling out of her, and Kat stroked her hair, saying little, mostly listening. Until hours had passed and the hot chocolate had gone cold, and Lisie wiped her nose on her pajama sleeve and declared, "I'm hungry. You want to split a pint of Chubby Hubby?"

Kat knew then for sure she'd be all right. They both would.

CARLA

Carla Moss on Manners

My mother started schooling me in manners before I could talk. Only I'm not sure how well they stuck. Sure, I know where to put my napkin and which fork to use with what; but if you push my back to the wall, any rules of etiquette get shucked.

Chapter Twenty-one

CARLA popped *The Best of Diana Krall* into the CD player and cranked it up as she pulled out of her driveway and headed to work. "Nothing's impossible I have found, for when my chin is on the ground, I pick myself up, dust myself off, and start all over again," sang Diana in her smooth silky tones as Carla smiled and tapped her fingers on the steering wheel.

Though winter was days from being officially over, it felt like spring had sprung. The sun warmed the air, puffy clouds filled blue skies, and snow-covered limbs and lawns had been replaced by budding green everywhere she looked.

She could practically smell new beginnings in the air, too, with Elise picking up the pieces and moving forward in dealing with Michael and their legal separation. In fact, Joey was in town on spring break this week, giving Lisie and Mikey both a chance to talk to him about what was happening. Even Kat had taken a further step toward her own Act Two, finally finding new digs, although Carla wouldn't get a peek until later. Kat was having her and Elise over for a late night unveiling of her "big surprise," as she put it. Kit-Kat had been so hush-hush these past few weeks, in fact, that she wouldn't even text Carla and Lisie the address until a few minutes before they were set to arrive, after her stint on the air this evening.

That left her as the only one of their tight little trio still stuck in the intermission between Act One and what was next. Only maybe that would all change within the next hour, if fate was on her side. Even Randy had detected her change in attitude.

"What're you so happy about, Car? You're strutting like a QB who's stumbled across the other team's playbook," he remarked when she'd come out of the shower humming.

"I've got a meeting with Burton this morning about my contract," she told him honestly, "and I've got a feeling things are about to break my way."

"That's the spirit!" he'd said, and gave her butt a pat, like she was one of his linemen.

He had a good reason to be suspicious of her perky mood. Ostensibly, she had little to be happy about. In another week her current contract with KMOK would expire, and she had yet to sign the only offer Burton sent her way, the one with just one year guaranteed and her work week and her pay cut by one-fifth. Twenty-four hours ago she had been gnashing her teeth, terrified about what the future held for her; but not anymore.

Thank heavens for small favors, she mused, or at the very least for stupid young girls who let people take naked pictures of them.

Her hand left the steering wheel to settle on the manila envelope tucked beside her. Her lawyers had delivered it yesterday when she was home alone. It was the report from the private investigator they'd had rifling through Amber Sue Evans's past, dipping into her Internet presence and even going back to her hometown in Indiana to talk to her old friends and acquaintances.

Carla had been on edge for weeks, waiting to hear something—anything—and the wait was worth it.

Poor Amber Sue, she mused, eyes on the road and a Cheshire cat grin on her lips, you won't even know what hit you, sweetie.

The private eye employed by the law firm of Snodgrass, McNally, et al., managed to unearth a tidbit about Amber Sue that was juicier than anything Carla had imagined. Apparently, the girl was quite the partyer during her college years, particularly when she was a freshman. Her high school sweetheart, who was still her boyfriend at the time, had snapped half a dozen digital images of sweet innocent Amber doing naughty things with her sorority roommate. He'd used them for his private enjoyment and forgot about them once they broke up and went their separate ways. Thankfully, he was a greedy SOB who was more than happy to put them on a DVD and sell them once he'd learned a dude with money in his pocket was poking around town, asking questions about Amber. He'd wanted $10,000 to hand them over, which sounded like a bargain to Carla. She'd told Snodgrass and McNally to pay the ransom and get the goods.

Carla exhaled slowly. She found it amazing how relaxed she suddenly felt, knowing the hard copies of Amber's naked girl-on-girl photos sat enclosed in the envelope beside her. She had a signed and notarized letter from the photographer, too (aka Amber's greedy ex-beau), giving her the right to reprint the images or otherwise display them. How delicious was that?

She wondered how anxious Burton would be to keep these

from the local press and from anyone at KMOK, most notably Graham Howell.

I'll bet he'll do anything short of groveling, she mused, already envisioning a second contract offer with terms much more to her liking coming very, very soon.

As she turned from Chestnut to Memorial Drive and headed to the underground parking ramp, she hit the brakes, abruptly stopping short of rear-ending one of the station's vans. Ahead of it sat a single police car with blue and red bubble lights rolling. Carla craned her neck out to spot an ambulance in front of that.

She could also see some Channel 3 staffers gathered in front of the building, arms crossed, frowns on their faces, the mild breeze flapping at skirts and tousling hair.

Maybe Graham Howell's pacemaker got zapped by the microwave, she thought with a snicker, knowing the old coot was too stubborn to go so easily. She only hoped it wasn't anyone she liked or anything too serious.

The last time she'd seen an ambulance in front of Channel 3, a yoga instructor who showed up to give a demonstration on the early show had pulled a muscle after twisting herself into the most painful-looking pose. They had to carry her out with her legs stuck behind her head like a human pretzel. Of course, Burton made sure a camera caught everything for the noon report.

Tweet, tweet!

She jumped at the noise of a whistle as a lone officer in blue uniform wove between the traffic, futilely tweeting and gesticulating. Carla couldn't tell if he wanted them all to stay put or drive around the mess. She was so close to the mouth of the parking entrance. If the van would pull up a smidge, she could just make it.

What the hell. She might as well try.

Carla held her breath and squeezed her Lexus through without a scratch. The car gently bumped down the incline and into the concrete cave. Once she slid her car into her spot, she popped two Tums to quell her queasy stomach. Five minutes later she emerged from the elevator and stepped into the lobby, the manila envelope clutched in her hand. Only something was missing: the ever-present LaTonya wasn't behind the front desk. Instead, the receptionist—like half a dozen others—had her nose pressed to the window, staring outside at the scene.

"What's going on?" she asked, and walked over to LaTonya's side. She squinted past the K in KMOK's call letters painted on the plate glass, just in time to witness the medics pushing a loaded stretcher toward the open doors at the rear of the ambulance. Then she turned her back to the window and mentioned, "I've got a meeting with Mr. Echols in ten minutes. Is he around?"

"Oh, Ms. Moss!" LaTonya turned to her with brown eyes wide. Her hand clutched the gold cross that dangled from her neck. "*That's* Mr. Echols," she said, and pointed outside. "He's had a heart attack!"

"You're joking," Carla said, making a noise of disbelief. If it were April Fool's Day, she would have figured it was some kind of trick. "That can't be," she murmured, because the Burton Echols she knew—and currently despised—didn't have a heart at all, kind of like the Tin Man.

"No, ma'am, it's true." LaTonya shook her head, still staring out the window. She didn't face Carla until the ambulance drove away in a wail of sirens. "He was in a meeting with Mr. Howell, and Wilfred said he went purple all of a sudden and clutched his chest. She shoved an aspirin in his mouth and called 911."

"Holy crap," Carla breathed, shifting the envelope from one hand to another. It seemed heavier than it had a few minutes ago. "So he won't be back today? I can't reschedule?"

"No, Ms. Moss, I'm sorry," the receptionist replied as she scurried back around her desk as the phone began to ring. She answered, "Channel 3, this is LaTonya, can you wait a moment, please?" And then she put the caller on hold. With a sniffle, she said, "I don't know when he'll be back, ma'am."

"Is he dying?" Carla asked, trying not to sound too hopeful.

"I don't think so." She cocked her head and squinted. "Wilfred said he was breathing and everything when they carted him off, though he might have to stay in the hospital for a while." The girl sniffled again.

Well, damn.

"Here you go, sweetie." Carla reached for the box of tissues on the desk and plucked one out, passing it to her.

"Thanks." LaTonya took it and wiped her nose. She dabbed her eyes, too, before she tossed the tissue and fumbled with her headset, hooking it around her ear.

With a shaky smile, she nodded at Carla before she pressed a button and said to no one in particular, "How can I help you?"

Good Lord, could the girl actually be upset?

Call her coldhearted, but she didn't feel much of anything. Was it possible that Burton wasn't a bastard to everyone? Was he merely that nasty to her because she'd divorced the louse? Their dismal marriage, his infidelity, her miscarriage: each had torn her up inside. It was a wonder he hadn't destroyed her. Nope, she wouldn't shed any tears for Burton or his faulty ticker, not at his hospital bedside and not even at his funeral.

Amber Sue can have him, she thought with a sniff. I just want to keep my job.

What was she supposed to do now? She hugged the envelope to her chest, knowing she couldn't wait even another week until Burton was back on his feet before she used the photos of Amber to finagle a new contract. She didn't have that kind of time to spare.

Damn him for ruining her plans! He couldn't even have the courtesy of dying and letting her legal reps negotiate with someone new; someone more sympathetic.

Then a thought struck her, one that actually prickled the hair on her arms. She swallowed down her hesitation, waiting for LaTonya to finish one call and put another on hold before she asked, "So Mr. Howell's still here?"

The girl nodded just as the phone started ringing off the hook again.

Time to take this to the top.

Carla headed toward the elevator and pressed 5 for the executive suites.

When the doors opened with a ping, she took a deep breath and stepped inside. She rode up in silence with several suits she didn't recognize; bean counters, she figured, if the number of pens tucked into their breast pockets was any indication.

When she reached the fifth floor, she got off and held her chin high as she strode toward Graham Howell's private office.

His secretary, Wilfred, stood as she approached. The woman was nearly as old as Graham himself. Every year that passed, she looked more and more like a bulldog. Maybe she didn't bite, but Carla wagered she drooled.

"I need to see Mr. Howell immediately," she said, feeling like a child in grade school who wanted an audience with the principal. "I have something important to discuss with him." She tapped the envelope with her fingertip.

Wilfred's jowly features scowled, a sight that doubtless sent plenty of folks scurrying. "Do you have an appointment, Miss Moss?"

"No, but—"

Wilfred cut her off. "Do you realize the station's general manager was just taken to the hospital by ambulance?"

"Yes, but—"

"Which means Mr. Howell is twice as busy trying to cover for Mr. Burton's absence, so I don't want anyone bothering him. If you'd like to make an appointment for Monday—"

"Oh, for God's sake," Carla huffed, unwilling to be put off by Howell's trained attack dog when her career was at stake. With a curt, "Excuse me," she walked right past Wilfred, pushing her way into the station owner's office.

Graham Howell glanced up as she strode in. "Well, if it isn't the Face of St. Louis come to see me," he said, frowning, and set aside the papers he'd been reading. His face wore a permanent golf tan, complete with brown spots like mini sand traps here and there across his pate. A white comb-over went almost from ear to ear, and his snowy eyebrows bristled in all directions, resembling a pair of woolly caterpillars butting heads.

"Hello, Mr. Howell," Carla said as Wilfred appeared on her footsteps.

"I'm sorry, sir, but I tried to stop her." His loyal secretary glared at Carla. "After what you've been through this morning already, I'm sure you don't need the distraction."

"Never mind, Willie," he said, dismissing her with a wave. "I've got a few things to discuss with Miss Moss anyhow. So leave us alone for a few minutes, please."

Though Wilfred appeared none too happy, she backed out and closed the door.

"May I sit?" Carla asked.

"That's what those are for." He gestured at a pair of barrel-backed chairs facing his desk.

Carla settled into one, putting the envelope in her lap. Heart pounding, she mustered her courage and looked him straight in the eye. "Mr. Howell, I have something I think you'll be quite interested in. I had intended to speak with Burton, but apparently he's indisposed."

"Indisposed?" Howell laughed. "What a genteel way to put it. Sounds a lot better than saying he nearly bit the dust! The son of a bitch needs to lay off cigars and steaks and broads half his age. I've been telling him that since I hired him some thirty years ago."

Carla blinked. That was hardly what she'd expected to hear. But then again, Graham Howell had been around the block enough times to wear out the treads on his orthopedic wingtips. "Sir, I've got information about Amber Sue Evans that could be detrimental to the station."

"Amber Sue who?" Howell squinted. "You mean the tall, big-breasted gal with big hair and Greta Garbo fuck-me voice? Kind of looks like that Angelina Jolie."

Good Lord, but the trolls from Human Resources must've flunked him soundly in sensitivity training. No wonder Wilfred played guardian of the gate so vigorously! Every time Graham Howell opened his mouth, potential lawsuits spewed forth.

Carla cleared her throat, attempting to regain her composure. "Yes, that's her," she said, and gripped the envelope so tightly it was starting to wrinkle. "And if you don't mind my saying so, Mr. Howell, she isn't fit for the anchor desk at Channel 3 now or ever."

"The anchor desk?" he repeated, and calmly folded his arms in front of him. Behind his wire-rimmed spectacles, his shrewd eyes sparked. "Ah, hell, has Burton been making moves to push the girl into your chair?"

Carla nodded, relief rushing through her. "I just want you to know I'm completely against the idea, for the good of the station, of course."

"Of course." He crossed his arms, and his gray suit puckered across his bony shoulders. "You know why I keep Burton on, Miss Moss?"

Did he expect her to say something nice? That would be tricky.

"Because you like him?" she offered.

"Like him?" His woolly eyebrows puckered. "Truth be told, I don't much like anyone, or trust anyone, either, except maybe Willie out there. But Burton's got an eye for on-air talent, so I let him run with it so long as he doesn't mess with what's working. That's not to say there aren't times when we butt heads. Like when he hired you." From behind his glasses, his rheumy eyes stared at her, and he rubbed his sagging chin. "I was dead-set against it, you know. I thought you were too young and too damned perky. But from the minute Burt put you in the hot seat, the city fell in love. Who am I to complain about that?"

If he'd leaned forward and said, "Boo!" Carla wouldn't have been more stunned. That sure sounded like praise to her, something she never thought she'd hear from a self-professed ornery cuss. "You think I'm doing a good job, then?"

"Our ratings say that you are." He nodded.

"But Sandy Chase was beloved, and you allowed Burton to push her out to make way for me," Carla said, not quite understanding this good ol' boys network that Graham Howell and Burton Echols had going on. Did they just operate on Burtie's whim? "Why'd you let him do that?"

He pursed his lips, seeming to think a bit more before he spoke this time. "Let's just say Sandy Chase was our test case, and she did all right. She got high scores with women but not with men. Lacked sex appeal, you know." He cleared his throat. "You, on the other hand, rank high with both. We've been the number one news station for a dozen years straight." He threw up his hands. "Wish I could take the credit for it, but I can't."

Was he acknowledging that the populace tuned in to see her? That maybe Burton was trying to "mess with what's working" and Graham Howell might be willing to butt heads with him over this?

"Thank you, sir," Carla said, hoping she wasn't walking into some kind of trap. Beneath her crisp white blouse, her armpits dampened. She swallowed hard and sat up straighter. "Excuse me for sounding dense, sir, but I'm very confused. If you think I'm so good for the station, how could you let Burton offer me such a lousy contract? One year only? Four days with less pay? It makes no sense, at least not to me. I haven't signed it, and I won't," she declared, her blood pumping hard and fast as she grasped the envelope in her lap and made to lift it. "I love what I do more than you can imagine, and I'd hate to have to leave Channel 3, which is why I feel compelled to bring to your attention—"

"Simmer down now, Miss Moss, simmer down," Howell said, and rubbed a knobby hand over his thinning hair. "Burton and I actually had words this morning over the way he was handling your negotiations. I wonder if that didn't get his blood pressure up, the damn fool. He should take better care of himself." His grumpy features softened suddenly. He looked far less menacing as he told her, "I had every intention of speaking with you myself about this. There's something we need to straighten out."

"Oh?" Carla settled back down in her seat. Her sweaty palms left damp smudges on the envelope, still pressed against her skirt.

"I made a mistake." Howell sighed and shook his head. "You and Burton have too much history, too much bad chemistry. But I try to stay out of things unless it's absolutely necessary to step in."

"So you *don't* want to let me go?"

"I don't," he said without preamble. "And believe me, missy, it's going to be a while before I let him plunk Miss Amber Sue behind that evening desk permanently. We've got to season her first."

Carla felt like her brain would explode. "So you're not going to let me go? You don't think I'm too old to anchor effectively?"

"Too old?" He laughed. "I may be an ornery cuss, but I'm not blind. You're still a gorgeous broad, and so long as you keep looking good and the numbers stay up, I've got no complaints. I told your lawyers that myself when they called for Burton not five minutes ago and got me instead. I was about to ask Wilfred to fax the papers to them when you showed up. Hold on, I've got a copy here somewhere." He fumbled through the slew of files on his desk, finally finding what he was looking for and holding it out to her. "This is the revised contract Burton was supposed to forward to your attorneys, only apparently it never made it there."

Revised contract?

Why that son of a bitch, she thought of her heartless ex. Her hand trembled as she stood and took the blue-backed pages from him.

"As you'll see, it's pretty much a carbon copy of the contract you're laboring under now." Howell removed his specs from his bulbous nose and wiped off the lenses with his handkerchief. "Sorry we can't offer you more than that this go-round. But with all those cable news stations and the economy in the crapper, our profits have flat-lined."

But Carla didn't care. She felt appreciated again, despite all Burton had done to make her feel like yesterday's news. She could work under the same conditions. What she'd been so firmly opposed to was settling for less.

"I understand," she said, and got up from the chair. "Thank you so much," she added, holding tight to the copy of her contract and to Amber's photos. Much as she was tempted to leave those behind as a little gift to the big boss, she couldn't do it. She looked into Howell's grumpy features and said, "You do realize, sir, that you're not the horrible monster you let everyone believe."

"Is that so?" His leathered cheeks flushed. "Come closer, Miss Moss, and listen to me," he instructed, and crooked a finger at her, urging her forward. When Carla got near enough, he whispered, "For the love of God, don't ever let it get around that I don't eat children and reporters for breakfast. I have a reputation to protect, you know."

"Mum's the word," she promised, and mimed zipping closed her lips and throwing away the key. She started to leave, and he called her back.

"Wait a minute now. What was it you wanted to show me about Amber Sue?"

"Oh, yes, that. It can wait," she told him with a smile. "I don't think it's quite so urgent anymore."

Blowing a kiss at Wilfred as she left Howell's domain, she flew down the stairs and dove past Deidre into her office, shutting herself inside.

For the next few minutes she sat at her desk with the paper shredder pulled up to her knees and, one by one, destroyed the photographs; although she kept the DVD with the digital images and the signed release, just in case. As each one turned to confetti, she realized how good it felt to keep her anchor seat without sinking to Burton's level.

Score one for the good guys, she thought, or at least for one middle-aged broad.

Jesse burst into her office just as the last naughty photo of Amber Sue went through the grinder.

"Oh, Mossy! I just got in and I heard about everything!" he blurted out, and flew toward her as if magnetized. He appeared beside her chair and threw his arms around her. "Talk about someone evil getting a karmic payback! I mean, I know it was completely deserved, but still! Are you okay?"

"So now I'm evil because Graham Howell himself renewed my contract?" she asked, puzzled.

"*What?* He did?" Jesse pulled away and ducked around her desk, staring at her with eyes wide as buttons. "When did this transpire? Before or after the Evil One had his heart attack?"

"Ah, so that's who you meant," she said, getting the picture. She hit her forehead lightly with the heel of her hand. "Silly me."

"I'm so happy for you, Mossy!" he squealed, beaming at her like a proud parent. "You got what you wanted in spite of Burton's tricks. Word is he'll be all right, the lucky bastard."

Carla stared at her dear friend and knew he truly meant it. Randy was wrong about the size of her circle of friends. Bigger wasn't always better, at least not in this case. So she didn't have a ton of women she lunched with? She had Jesse, Kat, and Lisie, and they were true blue.

She got sentimental all of a sudden and got up from her chair, going over to where he stood. "Thank you, Jesse, for everything." She hugged him properly and didn't let go. "You always seem to believe in me, even when I don't," she whispered, adding earnestly, "You're the best gay friend any girl could ever have."

"Good Lord, Mossy, where did that come from?" he asked, and stepped back to fan his misty eyes. "You're gonna make me cry and ruin my guy-liner."

Carla laughed. "I adore you, you know. I mean it."

"Ditto." He smiled his elfin smile. "Now stop with the mush, or I'll smack you."

CARLA PUT ON a smile as she heard the lock unlatch, and then the door opened inward to reveal Herbert Keegan's time-worn face. It lit up when he realized who was there. "Well, look who it is," he said as she leaned in to kiss his cheek. "We haven't seen you in weeks, doll-face. Busy as ever, I'll bet."

"That's no excuse, Professor," she said as she slipped past him into the small apartment. "I should've made a point to come by again before now."

"But at least you're here."

"That I am," she replied, and glanced around her at the tiny one-bedroom unit at the Gatesworth that Genevieve Moss shared with her third—and hopefully last—husband, a retired Wash U. physics professor who absolutely doted on her. It was furnished simply with antiques and shelves crammed with books. Carla knew Herbert read to Genevieve all the time, hoping it would keep her mind from getting worse. He also made sure she took her medications regularly, including the Aricept that was supposed to keep her synapses firing. "Is Mother here?"

Carla had come without calling, so she knew that Genevieve could very well be in some kind of therapy session or getting blood drawn. If that was the case, she would wait. This was something she had to do.

"Genny's on the patio," Herbert told her, indicating the sliding glass doors just past the round breakfast table. "It's so pretty outside, we thought we'd get a little fresh air."

"How's she doing?"

"Perfectly lucid today," he said. "So her tongue's sharp as ever."

"Ouch. Thanks for the warning." Ah, well, better to be criticized, she figured, than have her mother stare at her blankly and squawk, "Who *are* you?" That had freaked out Carla so badly, she'd avoided coming back for far too long.

"If you ever need anything—" she started to say, but Herbert stopped in his tracks, turned around and shook his head.

"We're doing fine, honey," he insisted, giving her a reassuring wink. "All we want from you is you, at least now and again. Got it?"

"Got it," she said, thinking Herbert was no Donald Moss; but he was exactly what Genevieve needed.

"You ready?"

"Yes." Carla steeled herself as the professor slid one of the doors wide-open. She followed him outside, spotting the tiny figure with snow-white hair and porcelain skin wrapped in a cardigan and seated in a wicker glider with sunny yellow cushions.

"We have a visitor, Genny," he said, and caught Carla's hand to tug her toward her mother. "It's your daughter, Carla Jean, in the flesh."

"Goodness, Herbert, I know who she is," Genevieve said crisply, and looked up at her with eyes the same shade of green as Carla's. She had the ever-present strand of pearls around her throat, lipstick on her mouth, but no smile for her daughter. "Although if she'd stayed away another month, I might not have recognized her."

"Cut her some slack." Herbert sighed as he sat down beside her and patted her hand. "She's a busy woman."

"Apparently one who's forgotten her manners," Genevieve murmured. "I don't see flowers or candy, do I?"

Oh, Lord, here we go again, Carla thought as she sidestepped a small table cluttered with newspapers and half-drunk mugs of coffee. She was in too good a mood. Even her mother couldn't ruin it.

"Hello, Mummy." She bent down to kiss her mother's powdered cheek and then began apologizing profusely. "Yes, yes, I'm horrible for not bearing gifts, but I came straight from the station to see you. And, yes, I'm sorry I missed seeing you the last few weeks, but work has been crazy, and did I mention Kat Maguire moved back to town? For good, she says, and I'm holding her to it. Oh, and, get this, Elise Randolph's divorcing her husband, Michael. You remember Michael, don't you? He's the brilliant surgeon who did my boob lift a while back, and he's only just recently realized that he's gay—"

"Good Lord, Carla!" her mother gasped, fanning her face, while Herbert chuckled.

"Is that a new lipstick color you're wearing?" Carla prattled on, while Genevieve blushed. "It really does suit you, you know, and you look lovely, by the way. Grandmother's pearls go with everything, don't they?"

So they were little white lies? Big whoop. The older she got, the more Carla realized that telling people what they wanted to hear wasn't such a horrible thing after all.

ELISE

Elise Randolph on her Mid-Life Crisis

I aced my SATs, was in the top ten percent of my high school class, graduated with honors from Washington University Med School, and yet I flunked Marriage 101. Is it too late to ask for a do-over?

Chapter Twenty-two

*H*ow cool is this, huh?" Joey said as he got out of the Audi and hooked laces over his shoulder so his old black hockey skates dangled. "We haven't been to the rink together forever."

"I think the last time we came out here, you were playing for Coach Evan's team," Elise said as she grabbed her own skates before she shut the car door, clicking on the remote to lock up.

"Those were good times, huh?"

"Yeah, good times," she agreed, leaning against the hood for a minute and looking around her, thinking the trees had been much smaller when she'd been here last. Now they stretched into the blue sky, budding branches waving in the breeze.

"Mom?"

"I'm coming," she said, and drew in a deep breath, still going nowhere as she watched Joey walk toward the building in his long-legged stride. Sometimes it was hard to imagine that her little boy was eighteen and taller than her by a head. In her mind's eye he was still three feet high, looking up at her with chubby cheeks and adoring eyes.

But he was very grown-up now and so poised, she realized. So much so that he seemed to be taking the news of her and Michael's separation in stride, as if it had come as no great shock. "Kids sense things," Kat had told her, and she was probably right.

She and Joey had spent his first few days home from spring break going through old photo albums, viewing videos of family trips, and talking about the past, alternately crying and laughing. They'd talked about the future as well and what it would mean. "I'm sorry for you and Dad, that's all," he had said, "because you'll lose each other, but I'll still have you both."

He was spending time with his father tonight, going out to dinner and staying over at the apartment Michael was leasing in Creve Coeur. It would be good for Joey and Michael both. They still had plenty of things to sort out. Besides, she'd promised Kat she'd share a late supper before Carla could meet them at Kat's new place. The only instruction Elise had gotten so far was to show up at Tiffany's Diner on Manchester in Maplewood at nine. Beyond that, she was clueless.

"Yo, Ma, stop dragging your feet," her son called across the parking lot, and Elise grinned, hearing her own words used against her.

How many times had she uttered that same phrase when he was a kid? Endlessly, she figured, wondering how he'd turned out so beautifully. Such a well-adjusted, level-headed boy who saw the bright side to everything? If she had failed at her relationship with Michael, at least she had succeeded at this. Joey was her gift.

"Mom!"

"I'm coming!" she called, sticking her remote in her pocket and hurrying after him. Carla's mother would even approve of his manners, which were good enough at least that he remembered to hold open the door.

"After you," Joey said when she reached the entrance and passed through.

"Thank you kindly." Elise felt the chill of the rinks as soon as she stepped indoors and memories instantly washed over her: of all the mornings she'd driven Joey here for stick and puck sessions, and all the evenings she'd spent sitting at rinkside with the other hockey moms and cheering on his team.

"This way," Joey said, coming up beside her. "He's rented out the NCAA rink."

The Hardee's Iceplex had three rinks, the biggest being the Olympic, which had more stands for viewing. They took a right, heading for one of the rinks with fewer bleachers. As Carla walked along behind him, she breathed in the strange mix of smells that had once been so familiar: the coffee and french fries from the grill, the lingering odor of testosterone and sweat, and the funky damp scent of melting ice and humidity leading directly to the third rink's double doors.

Elise hesitated before going in, peering through the scarred windows to see a lone figure on the ice. A man in dark blue hockey gear zipped around, smacking pucks into the net.

"Wait a minute, Joe, this doesn't look like it's open to the public," she told him, grabbing hold of his sweatshirt.

"It's okay, Mom. An old friend of mine has private ice time, and we were invited," he said with a sly smile.

"What old friend?"

"You'll see," he replied, and pushed his way inside, leaving Elise no choice but to go in after him.

Joey strode in like he owned the place. He waved his arms at the guy on the ice, and the blue-clad figure stopped shooting pucks and skated over.

Elise's eyes went wide as she recognized the face below the helmet, even with slightly longer hair and scruffy stubble on his jaw. "But that's—"

"Evan, dude!" Joe called out, and gave her a knowing look before he trotted rinkside.

"Joe, hey, man!" Evan Lawrence pushed through the door that swung outward from the ice. He set his stick aside, and he and Joey briefly hugged and slapped each other's backs. "Good to see you. You're looking fit."

"You kidding, right, Coach?" Joe patted his burnt orange Longhorns sweatshirt right above his belly. "I've got my freshman ten right here."

Oh, my God, Elise thought, watching as the two greeted one another, wondering if she could sneak out unnoticed. *Rats, too late.* Evan glanced at her over Joey's shoulder, and his brown eyes held hers long enough for Elise to know she'd been set up. Instinctively, one hand went to her mop of hair and then she glanced down at her blue jeans, torn at the knees, and her gray zip-up jacket with the ketchup smudge on the pocket. Could she have looked any sloppier if she'd tried?

"Let's get you suited up, and see if you can keep up with me out there," Evan told Joey, and patted his shoulder. "I've got extra gear for you over there"—he gestured at a large black canvas bag and stick sitting on the first bleacher. "Go on to the locker room across the way and change, okay?"

"Great." Joe turned around, looking as eager as a puppy. "Oh, hey, Mom, you remember Evan don't you?"

"Yes, I do," she uttered, feeling like she'd been played.

When he walked past her to pick up the bag, she managed to mouth, *I'm going to kill you for this.* He merely grinned wider.

"Be back in fifteen!" he called to Evan, and then he was gone.

Evan gazed over at her, lifting his eyebrows, and raised a gloved hand. "Hey, Doc," he said.

"So, you were in on this, huh?" she asked, and walked up to Evan, who towered above her in his skates. Elise felt tiny beside him, especially with all his pads on beneath his trunks and jersey. "How'd you connect with Joe again?"

"MySpace," he told her. "I looked him up after I saw you at your office, and we've been e-mailing for awhile. He didn't mention it?"

"No." But then again, she'd had so much on her mind these past three weeks that if Joe had said something, she didn't recall it.

Evan picked up his stick and leaned on it. "I tried to make another appointment with you, you know, but your office said you were taking some time off. Joe mentioned you were going through a rough patch."

"Yes," she said, giving him another monosyllabic response.

"I'm sorry to hear it."

"Thank you."

She hadn't even taken off her wedding band yet, couldn't even bear to think of selling the house. No matter that divorce was inevitable, she still felt uncomfortable telling people she was legally separated, although she was sure everyone in their subdivision would know Michael had left her for another man soon enough, if they didn't already. They'd be the talk of Wild Horse for a while, at least until a juicier scandal demoted them.

"It's my fault, getting you out here," he explained, not sounding at all like he regretted it. "Joe and I figured a little time on the ice might lift your spirits."

"I see," she murmured, wondering just how much Joey had told his old coach; although she honestly didn't care. So long as she didn't have to discuss any of the gory details with Evan. That, she couldn't handle yet.

"Are you doing okay?"

She took a deep breath, glancing down as she exhaled. Then she nodded, looking up at him. "I'm hanging in there."

"Sometimes that's enough," he said, probing no further. "Now how about we get you skating? I know a little ice time always cures what ails me."

"Is that so?"

"I won't work you out too hard," he said, and scratched his jaw. "We'll just do a few sets of sprints, some square passing, and side to side quickies. You'll do great."

Elise balked. "You're kidding, right?"

He flashed the boyish grin that had turned all the hockey moms to mush, and she spied the dimple in his chin, despite the shadow of his whiskers. There was something about him she flat-out liked—had always liked—and she felt oddly at ease with him. He made her feel like she had nothing to prove, except perhaps on the rink.

"Hey, you're smiling, Doc. My prescription must be working," he teased, and reached out to tap the white skates she hadn't put on in at least five years. "So, get laced up pronto and come show me your stuff."

"You don't seriously want me out there shooting pucks?" Elise headed toward the bench. "I might kill somebody."

"Naw, we'll skip the drills," he told her as she sat down and put her skates on the floor. "How about we just tool around the rink a little, see how fast you can go."

"Don't expect Michelle Kwan," Elise replied, but she was game to give it a try. She'd been ready to skate with Joey, right? How much more embarrassing would it be to fall on her ass in front of a pro hockey player?

Oh, boy.

She toed off her sneakers and shoved her right foot into a skate first and then her left. It only took a few minutes to hook the strings and tighten them. Then she slipped off her blade guards and set them on the bench.

When she stood, she wobbled slightly, but she didn't do a face-plant on the squishy floor as she hobbled over toward Evan. He'd ditched his stick and had the door open onto the rink.

"You ready?" he asked, and took her arm, drawing her onto the ice.

"As I'll ever be," she told him, feeling as if her feet would fly out from under her as her skate blades skidded across the frozen surface.

"That's it, you're doing great," Evan encouraged, propelling her forward and holding her steady. "Just take one step at a time."

Oh, my God, oh, my God, she thought as he swung around

and started skating backward in front of her so she could hold onto both his arms and gaze into his handsome face.

"Show-off!" she said with a laugh as he pulled her along a little faster until she felt like she was flying. "Evaaaaaan!" she squealed, giggling like a twelve-year-old and grabbing onto him like he was her lifeline. And maybe in some way he was.

KAT

Kat Maguire on Act Two

If you don't live each day like it's your last and wake up every morning excited about what you're doing, for God's sake, move on. It's never too late to find your passion.

Chapter Twenty-three

F LOORS are mopped, windows cleaned, and trash tossed,"
Megan said, and blew out a puff of air that lifted the long
strands of hair hanging down in her face. She tucked
them behind her ear before wiping her hands on her blue jeans.
The flannel shirt she'd layered on was now wrapped around her
waist by the sleeves. "You want me to stay and help you unpack
anything?"

"No, thanks, you've done enough." Kat stopped rubbing
Orange Glo on the built-in bookcase and turned around to face
her sister. "You're a doll to take off work today and help me move
in."

"Hey, I'm just glad you finally found a place to live before
the Neidermans move into the high rise," Megan replied, and sat
down on a pile of boxes marked BOOKS. She looked around at the
tiny five-hundred-square-foot studio apartment with its rough
hardwood floors, exposed brick walls, and stacks of Kat's books

and old furniture, shuttled over from the Maguires' basement, where they'd been stored for twenty years. "This is not what I would've picked for you, big sis. When you called and told me you'd seen the perfect spot to lease, I had no idea it would be a rental above a storefront."

"And the storefront, too, don't forget," Kat added with a grin.

"How could I forget that? My sister, the future art dealer," Meg teased, and nodded as rays of sunlight burst through the large front windows, filling the room. "I do like this area of Maplewood with all the shops and restaurants."

"But . . ." Kat said when her sister hesitated, because, with Megan, there was always a "but" involved.

Her sister opened her mouth.

Ah, ah, here it comes!

"But, the neighborhood's still in a pretty transitional state."

Was that it? Not *but you can't afford to live off your severance check and your savings forever, and what if your grand plans for a new career don't pan out*? This "but" was easy to defend.

Kat shrugged. "I don't mind," she said, and put down her rag, brushing off dirty hands. "I'm in a transitional state, too. And the space downstairs is just the right size for my gallery. I love it, so stop worrying."

"You didn't want something bigger and more, um, permanent?" Megan asked.

More *suburban* is what she meant. Kat wasn't surprised. Her sister and brother-in-law lived in a four-thousand-square-foot custom-built home in Town & Country. But then Megan drove a tank-sized Mercedes sedan, too. Bigger was always better, as far as Megan Maguire Barnes was concerned.

"No, it's perfect," Kat assured her. *Perfect for me.*

Besides, she'd done the rich-young-boyfriend-big-loft-fancy-dinners routine, and it hadn't made her happy. Rosalie Moore had told her to climb out on that mossy limb and pursue her passion, and that was precisely what she was doing. She had plans to put a gallery downstairs and fill it with lots of amazing work from emerging local artists. She'd e-mailed Rosalie with photos of her future showplace from her laptop, and her friend quickly replied with, "Good for you! You found your heart after all."

Kat knew she was right.

"Okay, then, if you don't need anything else, I think I'll take off," her sister said, getting up from the box of books. "Bill and I have a dinner party this evening, and I'd better hop in the shower unless I want to smell like Lysol, orange polish, and dust."

"He'll think you've bought a new perfume. Eau de housecleaning," Kat teased, and picked up her dust rag from the bottom shelf she'd been cleaning. She dropped it in a nearby bucket before rising from her bended knees. "I've got everything I need," she told her sister as she ushered Megan toward the rear door. "The electricity's working, the water runs, and the plumbing's not backing up."

She had a bed, some old chairs donated by Eileen Maguire to sit on, a clean bathroom with toilet paper and towels, and even new shelf paper in the few precious cabinets in her galley kitchen (which Megan had scrubbed until the stainless steel sink and flecked Formica countertops glowed). The rest, she'd piece together in due time. It was a far cry from Roger's high-end loft in Tribeca, but it was exactly what she needed at this point in her life.

"Later, big sis," Megan said, and gave her a hug, holding on for a few extra seconds. "If you want help unpacking this weekend, just holler."

"You bet I will," Kat replied, and followed her clip-clopping footsteps down the skinny back stairs and let her out the front door.

She stepped outside, standing on the sidewalk while Megan trotted toward her Merc and got in, waving as she drove off. The sun shone so brightly that it felt a lot warmer than seventy degrees, and Kat hung there for a moment, breathing in the fresh air and taking in her new surroundings.

There were shops on either side of her soon-to-be gallery: a tea and spice store on the left and a frame-it place on the right, which was very convenient, she thought. The buildings were all carved stone and brick, lovely old things that rehabbers had saved one by one as the enclave of Maplewood continued to grow and blossom.

Kat liked the feel of it, and she couldn't wait to show it off to Elise and Carla. She glanced at her wristwatch and grimaced when she saw it was four-thirty already. She had to straighten up her studio, shower, and get dressed before Lisie met her at Tiffany's Diner for dinner. Then she would share her big surprise with both her best friends at once, after Car got off work.

She hurried inside and upstairs, too much to do in the next few hours to dawdle outdoors, no matter how pretty the day.

It was ten minutes till eleven when Carla showed up outside the darkened storefront on Sutton. Kat and Lisie were turning the corner, coming from the diner, when they bumped into her. The evening was cool, the sky cloudless and dark. Even the moon cooperated, round as a wheel of Gouda, hanging yellow and bright in the sky.

"So what's the scoop, Mary Katherine?" Carla called from the curb as she remotely locked her Lexus. Her high heels tip-tapped on the sidewalk as she joined them, saying, "Hey, Lisie, you look good, sweetie," before she stopped moving and looked around them. "I thought we were getting a tour of your new apartment. I don't see anything but shops."

"Patience, Carla Jean." Kat smiled, taking Lisie's hand first and then reaching for Carla's. "Turn around," she said to both of them until they were facing the plate-glass windows. "Ta-da!" she trilled as her friends blinked, completely baffled.

"It's an empty store," Lisie said, wrinkling her nose.

"Um, Kat, if you live behind a giant window, you can't vacuum in the nude, my darling," Carla dryly remarked.

"Oh, no, I'm not living in there." She approached the façade and turned to face them, arms outspread. "This is the future home of Where the Art Is, my soon-to-be gallery. I'm going to fill it with carvings and sculptures and sketches and paintings by artists from the area," she explained breathlessly, and looked back at the glass, already envisioning the space filled with color and people and conversation. "It'll be amazing."

"Wow," Carla said, stepping up beside her and peering in. "You're really doing it, huh?"

"Yes." Kat nodded, beaming like a child on Christmas morning. Only this was even more exciting than running down the stairs to see if Santa had left her a talking Chrissy doll beneath the tree.

"It takes a lot of guts to change course like you have," Lisie quietly remarked, coming up on Kat's other side and linking arms so the reflection in the plate glass now showed the three of them side by side. "But then you never lacked for courage, Kat. You always did everything headfirst."

"Which explains her thick skull," Carla joked, nudging Kat in the side. "I'm proud of you, Kitty-Kat. I'm proud of all of us, not letting life stick it to us just because we're not spring chickens. We've done all right."

"We've only just started," Kat said, and glanced away from the glass, gazing warmly at Car and at Lisie. "Follow me," she said, "there's more!"

She dug in her pocket for the keys and unlocked the dead bolt to the front door. The streetlamp cast plenty of light on the stairs through the beveled glass. Their noisy footsteps in her ears, Kat hurried ahead of them, up the stairs and through the door to her apartment.

"Home, sweet home," she declared as she flipped on the overhead fixture, illuminating the open space with the galley kitchen; her mattress draped with a purple spread and covered in pillows, like a makeshift couch, and unpacked boxes set about like tables, each topped with a vase filled with flowers.

"Aw, Kat, it's great," Lisie gushed, and started walking around.

"Sweetie, it's you," Car agreed, and set her enormous handbag on the Formica counter, pulling out a bottle of champagne. "Now this truly calls for a toast."

"My God!" Kat laughed. "You're more prepared than the Boy Scouts," she said, following Car into the kitchen, where her friend started banging the doors to empty cabinets, searching for glasses. "Sorry, I don't even have plastic cups. We might have to use our shoes."

"Darling, I'm not getting these Louboutins wet, not even with Moët & Chandon," Carla replied, and tore off the foil seal. "We'll drink out of the bottle," she declared as she unwound the wire cage and let loose the cork with a *pop*. "It's not like we haven't done it before."

"On Kat's sixteenth birthday, to be precise," Lisie said, wandering over. "Car swiped a bottle from her parents' wine cellar and smuggled it over to the Maguires. We went up in the attic just to be sure no one heard us."

"And Lisie, the lightweight, thought it was so delicious, she drank half herself and ended up puking into a box of Christmas ornaments," Carla finished off the story.

"Thanks so much for that lovely memory," Lisie said, and swatted at her.

But Elise looked happy. In fact, Kat noticed a newfound spark in her eyes, like the light that had been turned off inside her all these weeks since Michael's confession was turned back on again.

"Okay," Carla said, holding the bottle before her, all uncorked and ready to go. "Should I do the honors? I know how you guys love my toasts."

"You do have the most practice," Lisie joked.

"Wait, wait, wait!" Kat interrupted. "I almost forgot!"

She scurried over to her makeshift bed and dug beneath the pillows, withdrawing two black boxes tied with pink ribbon.

"Sweetie, you didn't have to do this," Carla said, and Lisie echoed the sentiments; but it didn't stop Kat from handing one box to each.

"Open it," she directed, and they didn't waste any time.

"Oh, my God, it's gorgeous!" Carla plucked the bracelet from the box and held it up to the light. Delicate filigree curlicues bookended a thin oval of sterling silver inscribed, *Live Real*.

"I found an artist on the Loop who specially designed them,"

Kat eagerly explained. "I'm going to sell them at the store and others with simple messages. I've been wearing mine all day, but I hid it under my sleeve so Elise wouldn't see during dinner." She tugged up the cuff of her combed cotton shirt to reveal it.

"I'll never take it off," Lisie promised, tears flooding her eyes as she put hers on and then hugged Kat tightly.

"I won't either." Carla winked at Kat as she fastened hers on her slim wrist. Then she reached for the bubbly. "Okay, okay, toasting time! To us, of course, and to living real, because God knows that's the only way to do it. To the future and whatever it may bring, so long as it doesn't suck. And to Mary Katherine Maguire, who came back to town, picked up the pieces, and put the three of us back together for good. *Salud!*"

"Hear hear," Lisie said, sniffling as she smiled, not even bothering to brush the tears from her cheeks.

"To friendship," Kat chimed in, raising an invisible glass as Carla hoisted the Moët and took a sip.

They passed the bottle around once and then it came back to Carla.

Surprisingly, she waved it off. She looked a little green around the gills, and her hand went to her stomach. "Damn," she muttered. "I left my Tums in the car. I've been so freaking stressed out lately, I've had horrible indigestion, and my period's three weeks late. Hopefully once the contract stuff is ironed out, I'll feel like my old self again."

"Indigestion and a late period," Elise carefully repeated, and her mouth fell into a tiny O.

Kat looked at Lisie and blinked double time. "Are you thinking what I'm thinking?"

"I think I am." Elise nodded before she cleared her throat and started to sing, very softly and very off-key, "'Papa don't preach, I'm in trouble deep . . .'"

"' . . . but I've made up my mind,'" Kat quickly joined in, warbling the old Madonna tune, "'I'm keeping my baby . . .'"

"Stop that right this minute!" Carla glared at them, horrified. She set the champagne bottle on the counter with a *clunk* and snapped, "That's not funny in the least." Then she grabbed up her purse and began digging in it for keys. "Well, I hope you're both happy 'cause now I've got to leave."

"But, Car," Kat called out, "c'mon, we were just teasing—"

Before Kat could stop her, Carla bolted toward the door, only to abruptly stop with a crisp, "Aw, hell."

She glanced back at them, pink-cheeked and flustered. "Does either of you smartasses know where there's a twenty-four-hour Walgreens?"

Kat turned to Lisie, and they both burst out laughing.

Carla waved them off with a frenzied, "I'll be back!"

As Kat watched her go, she took Elise's hand and squeezed it hard. She had no idea what tomorrow—or the next day—would bring. But from where she was sitting right this moment, the second act of their lives looked to be shaping up into something pretty darned interesting. One thing she was sure of: there was nowhere else she'd rather be.

A+

AUTHOR
INSIGHTS,
EXTRAS &
MORE...

FROM
**SUSAN
McBRIDE**
AND
AVON A

The Accidental Cougar

When I think of the term "Cougar" to describe an older woman who dates younger men, it makes me chuckle. The word conjures up images of a very tanned and Botoxed blonde in a cheetah-print miniskirt, tight blouse, and sky-high stiletto heels—a modern-day Mrs. Robinson running a company with one hand and hoisting a vodka martini with the other. Well, that's how the media likes to play it, anyway. But it's a far cry from who I am, and I married a man nine years younger. So when I'm called a Cougar, I smile and take it in stride.

I guess that's because I kind of fell into my Cougardom, which makes me an Accidental Cougar. I never went out seeking a younger guy. In fact, the only man I ever dated who wasn't at least my age or older was a high school basketball player who was a year behind me in school: hardly an exemplary record of Cougar prowess.

But like so many other women, my life changed when I turned forty, and not in a good way at first. My cholesterol was high, my jeans were too tight, and I hadn't changed my hairstyle in two decades. My doctor wanted to place me on lipid-lowering medication, although I suggested changing my diet before resorting to a prescription. To be completely honest, I ate like a teenaged boy with a junk-food addiction, and I wasn't exercising the way I should. My doctor agreed to recheck my blood-work in six weeks, and I went cold turkey on the junk food and started piling on the veggies, soy, fish, and fruit. I got back on the treadmill, too, and the fat seemed to melt away along with the high cholesterol. I lost seven pounds and several dress sizes within a matter of weeks. Whew!

In dire need of new author photos, I went to see a top local photographer, Suzy Gorman, who actually told me I was "too skinny." She suggested I eat more protein and get a new hairdo. She didn't like my blunt cut, professing that I looked like an anchorwoman. "You're way cooler on the inside than you are on the outside," I remember her saying. She advised that I toss all my sweater sets and stop dressing like a soccer mom. She set me up with a stylist to find chic clothes that I could actually wear, and her makeup and hair expert, Suzy Bacino, gave my boring bob a bunch of spiky tweaks to freshen my look.

Wow! I absolutely loved it! I suddenly felt like the real me, or at least the woman I'd become at forty when my writing career was finally taking off after years and years of struggle, and my body was as healthy as it has ever been. My debut mystery with Avon, *Blue Blood*, kept going back to press, was nominated for several mystery awards (and won one), and I felt like the belle of the ball wherever I went. If this was a typical midlife crisis, I wanted more!

I was so happy and busy that I almost didn't notice that a part of my life was missing. I'd been so caught up in my writing career that I'd completely ignored my heart. But my mother noticed, big-time.

I know she worried about me, wondering if she'd ever get to plan my wedding or if I'd turn into one of those nutty cat ladies, writing books in my bathrobe and cleaning litter boxes for four hundred cats in my spare time.

She submitted my name to the folks at *St. Louis Magazine* when they were looking for their crop of 2005 "Top Singles." Lo and behold, I was one of ten women and ten men selected! I went to the photo shoot for the November feature in early September, and I realized I was only one of three Top Singles over forty. The rest of the group was in their twenties or early thirties.

Hey, no problem. I figured I'd be a living example of how fabulous forty could be.

I made friends with several others at the shoot, including a software applications engineer named Jeremy Nolle, who ended up on the cover of the magazine. Turns out Jeremy worked with a guy named Ed Spitznagel at Exegy, Inc., and Jeremy encouraged Ed to attend the very first Top Singles party held at the Contemporary Art Museum on November 3. I happened to be chatting with Jeremy when Ed showed up. We were introduced, tried to converse over the music, and he gave me his card (which I promptly lost). But Ed was no dummy. He e-mailed me through the magazine, and he asked me out to my first-ever hockey game. The next week he showed up at the bachelor/bachelorette auction that I participated in to raise money for charity. Armed with a wad of cash, Ed ended up "buying" me on the auction block, something he likes to tell people to this day.

One of the other Top Singles knew Ed's family, and she warned me, "He's, like, in his twenties, Susan!" On one of our early dates, I pointedly asked Ed how old he was. When I found out he was over thirty (barely!),

I was okay with it. I could handle a nine-year (and three months!) age difference, right? Besides, I wasn't sure just then if we'd just become friends or if it would amount to something more.

Until one hockey game snowballed into more hockey games and dinner and movies and just spending as much time together as we could. By Valentine's Day of 2006, I knew I was in love, and Ed was, too. By June of 2006, we were looking at houses and closed on one in late July.

He proposed to me on Christmas Eve of 2006. He actually got down on bended knee and said, "Susan McBride, will you marry me?" It was the stuff of dreams, and it all happened because of my mother writing a letter to *St. Louis Magazine* saying, "Please, help my daughter find a good guy." Ed's as good as they come, sticking by me like glue as I've gone through a breast cancer diagnosis and treatment. What a lucky girl I am.

We were married in Graham Chapel on the campus of Washington University in St. Louis and we held our reception in the Vault Room at the City Museum downtown. It was as magical a day as any I could imagine. By the time *The Cougar Club* is released in February of 2010, Ed and I will be approaching our second anniversary. So as you read this story about three forty-five-year-old friends coming back together and giving themselves a second chance at love with younger men, think of me and know I am one very happy Accidental Cougar!

Susan's Five Fabulous Rules for Forty-Somethings

1. Be your best self.

If you love who you are, inside and out, great! If you look hard in the mirror and see the possibility of change for the better, take a chance and do it. Whether that means eating healthier, trying out a Pilates or yoga class, or meeting with a clothing stylist to pinpoint a fashion sense for this new era in your life, go for it! To paraphrase Suzy Gorman, it's worth it to make your outer self as cool as your inner self.

2. Open your eyes to possibilities.

My mom likes to tease me about a really wonderful high school boyfriend I dumped because I didn't like his shoes. I had such a strict checklist for guys I dated, and those criteria didn't change much until I turned forty. Once I told myself to discard the list and open my eyes to all the possibilities, I met Ed. He's everything I ever wanted and more. I'm not telling you to settle. Far from it! I think that once successful, confident women reach a certain age, they deserve BETTER. But be willing to date outside your typical box and get to know men before you shoot them down.

3. Have fun all on your lonesome.

I know women who are terrified of being alone, even for a moment. Their worst fear is spending a Saturday night home with a good book. My grandmother used to say that "boring people get bored," and I think she has a point. If your life is full and happy while you're single, you'll attract men whose lives are also full and happy. The kind of relationship that comes of two fully-realized people uniting is like the tastiest cream-cheese icing on the cake! If you feel like your life has holes that need to be filled, figure out ways YOU can fill them instead of expecting someone else to do it for you.

4. Stop being a people pleaser.

Okay, this is actually a rule I'm stealing from my mother. When I turned forty, she specifically advised that I quit trying to please the world because I'd never succeed. At book signings, if I made forty people in the room laugh and one scowled throughout my presentation, I'd fixate on that one person. What had I said wrong? What could I have done differently? I nearly drove myself crazy worrying about the handful of people whom I would never please instead of enjoying my time with all the wonderful folks who enjoyed being with me. It's easier said than done, I know; but start small. Begin to weed toxic friends and acquaintances from your life. Who is there for you when you're up *and* when you're down?

Those are the friends to keep. Avoid the ones who suck the life out of you. I learned the hard way when I was diagnosed with breast cancer who my true friends are (and even what family members I can count on), and I value that lesson. Although I hope no one else has to go through a health crisis to figure that out! In a nutshell: Do what gives you joy and hang around people who energize you. Period.

5. Never stop being curious.

I read a study that said remaining curious throughout our lives keeps our brains young, and I believe it! I think the moment we stop exploring the world around us, we turn into sticks-in-the-mud. Read books in genres you don't typically read, visit somewhere in your city you've never been, take a painting class, learn how to cook, see a foreign film, or learn to salsa. There are so many interesting people, places, and things out there that we do ourselves a disservice when we shut ourselves off from something new. If your life feels stuck at forty, decide to take a new path for Act Two. Now is the time to do all those things you always said you wanted to do.

As Kat Maguire puts it in *The Cougar Club*:

Aging gracefully isn't about aging gratefully. It's about living life with your engine on overdrive, making love with all the lights on, trashing your diet books, and diving into the chocolate cake.

Amen to that!

Suzy Gorman

Susan McBride

SUSAN McBRIDE is an official member of the Cougar Club and proud of it. Named one of *St. Louis Magazine's* "Top Singles" at age forty, she met and (happily) married a younger man. Susan debuted on the literary scene with her award-winning Debutante Dropout Mysteries, including *Blue Blood* and *Too Pretty to Die*, and she also pens the Debs young adult series. Visit her web site at *www. SusanMcBride.com*.